PRAISE FOR KIM LAW

"*Montana Cherries* is a heartwarming yet heart-wrenching story of the heroine's struggle to accept the truth about her mother's death—and life."

—RT Book Reviews, 4 stars

"An entertaining romance with a well-developed plot and believable characters. The chemistry between Vega and JP is explosive and will have you rooting for the couple's success. Readers will definitely look forward to more works by this author."

—RT Book Reviews, 4 stars on *Caught on Camera*

"Kim Law pens a sexy, fast-paced romance."

—*New York Times* bestselling author Lori Wilde
on *Caught on Camera*

"A solid combination of sexy fun."

—*New York Times* bestselling author Carly Phillips
on *Ex on the Beach*

"*Sugar Springs* is a deeply emotional story about family ties and second chances. If you love heartwarming small towns, this is one place you'll definitely want to visit."

—*USA Today* bestselling author Hope Ramsay

"Filled with engaging characters, *Sugar Springs* is the typical everyone-knows-everyone's-business small town. Law skillfully portrays heroine Lee Ann's doubts and fears, as well as hero Cody's struggle to be a better person than he believes he can be. And Lee Ann's young nieces are a delight."

—RT Book Reviews, 4 stars

Montana
RESCUE

Also by Kim Law

The Wildes of Birch Bay series

Montana Cherries

The Turtle Island series

Ex on the Beach
Hot Buttered Yum
Two Turtle Island Doves (novella)
On the Rocks

The Sugar Springs series

Sugar Springs
Sweet Nothings
Sprinkles on Top

The Davenports series

Caught on Camera
Caught in the Act

The Holly Hills series

Marry Me, Cowboy (novella), in *Cowboys for Christmas*

Montana
RESCUE

Kim Law

Montlake
Romance

Published by Montlake Romance, Seattle

www.apub.com

Amazon, the Amazon logo, and Montlake Romance are trademarks of Amazon.com, Inc., or its affiliates.

ISBN-13: 9781503938731
ISBN-10: 1503938735

Cover design by Shasti O'Leary Soudant

Printed in the United States of America

To my mother.
Thank you for bravely heading into the unknown with
me so I could research these books. That nine-day,
four-state, twenty-five-hundred-mile trip was one of the
best times in my life, and it gave me memories that I'll
cherish forever.

Chapter One

Nick Wilde was a man who liked to ride the edge. He knew when to play loose and free, when to yuk it up for the crowds, and when to turn on the charm for the cameras. But he was also a man who knew when to shut it down and be 100 percent focused. And when climbing atop an eighteen-hundred-pound beast named Death Comes to Your Door, it was time to focus.

He paused before swinging his leg over the gate and into the chute and, as he'd done before every ride for the last seven years, he sent up a silent prayer. Then he pulled in a deep breath, and with his thoughts focused solely on winning, he got down to business. Thirty seconds later, with his gripping hand firmly in place and Death's muscles rippling under his thighs, Nick gave his cue. It was time to ride.

The gate swung open, and the clock started. And Death intended to win.

The bull bucked, shook, and twisted, doing things a lesser man would have crumbled under. But using his legs, and the strength of his core, Nick rode the animal, his free hand whipping in the air with each motion and his teeth rattling hard against his mouth guard. When the bell sounded eight seconds later, he flung himself from the back of the animal in one fluid move.

On his feet in a matter of seconds, he watched the bullfighters run Death from the ring, and Nick's smile fell easily into place. He was the last ride of the evening, and given how those eight seconds had played out, he'd be walking away with the pot tonight. His heart pumped. What a ride! He pulled the cowboy hat from his head and waved to the cheering crowd, most of whom were already on their feet. He was the reigning champ, two years running—a god to these people. And he loved that.

After tossing out one last wave, he dusted himself off and climbed onto the bottom rung of the exit gate to await his score. His agent patted his arm and gave a knowing nod.

"Going to take another season," Charlie Scott said.

"Why do anything else?" Nick agreed. He played to win, after all.

"Got a call today. Cuts for the new commercial are looking great. Ratings on the last one are still high, so they want to push to get this on the air ASAP." Charlie tilted his head and shot Nick a look. "And the minute you sign on for the PBR, they triple the payout for the endorsement deal."

Everybody wanted him to go national. "I like Montana Pro just fine."

Truth be told, he could have joined the Professional Bull Riders years ago. And won. And, at twenty-five, if he wanted to go that route, he should get to it. His time was limited. But he liked it here. He liked Montana. And he had yet to feel the need to change that.

"Nick Wilde takes an eighty-nine on Death Comes to Your Door."

The crowd went wild, knowing the score landed him easily in first, and Charlie gave a nod of approval as several of the other riders descended. Congrats were tossed out all around, and Nick noticed that a handful of the usual buckle bunnies waited not far from the clump of men. He recognized all the women. They were around after most rides.

He winked at Betsy, a strawberry-blonde he'd recently spent some time with, and then he felt himself being tugged toward the center of the arena where cameras and the rodeo director waited. As did a petite brunette—the owner of the beast who'd just manhandled him, and a longtime friend. Due to Death's own scores, the bull also took top billing this weekend. Nick gave Jewel a huge grin and took his place next to her, accepting the oversize winner's check and additional congratulations.

Within minutes, the place was emptying out and he found himself standing with Betsy, the buckle bunny he'd been eyeing earlier, but whom he had zero time for tonight—unfortunately. He was three hundred miles from his family home, and he needed to be in Birch Bay shortly after daybreak.

"I couldn't take my eyes off you tonight," Betsy purred.

Adrenaline continued to run high, so Nick took a moment and did what came naturally. He kissed Betsy, who was now curling into his side, and he lowered his palm to outline the curve of her very sweet hip. There was nothing quite like a warm body after a thrilling win. But . . . *sigh* . . . he and this particular body would have to wait.

"We could—" she started.

"I can't," Nick groaned. He gave her lips a final peck before pulling away. "I'm heading out of town as soon as I wrap up here." Assuming his truck was running. It had died earlier that day.

"I could go with you." There was a brazen naughtiness in both her words and her eyes that gave Nick pause. Because what went unspoken was her guarantee of making his drive far more entertaining than it could ever be alone.

But he and Betsy had never taken things beyond the rodeo, and he didn't think now was the time to change that. He was going *home*. To the house where he'd made it a point to visit just enough—but never too much—over the last seven years. His mind would be on things other than the hot woman at his side tonight.

When Betsy's bottom lip pouted at Nick's silence, his gaze fastened on that slip of pink, and he had the fleeting thought that he could call his dad and tell him that he'd be late. Like, maybe by a day or two. It wasn't as if Nick had to be there before his dad left town, anyway.

But at the same time, it wasn't as if Betsy wouldn't be around next weekend, either.

He gave a growl of need when her hand slipped under his protective vest, but he caught it in his before she could burrow down to skin. "You're tempting, Bets. You know you are." He leaned in to whisper across her lips. "But I really do have to go."

She nipped his lip in response, and he kissed her once more. They weren't serious *or* exclusive, but she was a hell of a good time.

"I'll be in Great Falls next weekend," he said when they separated. The annual event in Great Falls was one of his favorites of the year. "Find me Friday night?"

"You can count on it." Her words lost some of their heat as her eyes caught on something behind him, and Nick glanced over his shoulder to find Jeb Mauley passing them by. Jeb was a rookie, and far less *experienced* than Betsy, but that wouldn't stop her. She turned back to Nick. "I . . ."

Nick chuckled. "Go. Have fun." He inclined his head to where the nineteen-year-old rookie had stopped and was now talking to a couple of lingering reporters. "But leave the kid in one piece, will you? He has a lot of potential."

Laughter floated out behind Betsy as she made her way toward Jeb, and Nick caught himself wishing it bothered him to know that she'd be sleeping with another man tonight. Yet, it didn't. It never had. And though he'd never been one to envision tying himself to one woman for any length of time, he did occasionally wonder if he was missing a key ingredient to make him "normal." Didn't most men want the woman they were hooking up with to sleep only with them?

Or maybe they didn't. He honestly didn't know.

But there was a persistent voice in his head these days telling him that something wasn't right. That *he* wasn't right. Which struck him as oddly funny because if anyone in his family stood a chance of being "right," or *"normal,"* he'd always thought it would be him. Not that they weren't all royally screwed up.

Turning away from Betsy and the now-grinning Jeb, Nick retrieved his phone and saw that he'd gotten a voice mail from the garage. He listened as the owner explained that it would be late next week before they could get the part in they needed to fix his truck. Which meant . . . how in the hell would he be getting home tonight?

The answer came in the form of a five-foot-two bubbly brunette barreling toward him.

"Nick!" Jewel Brandon threw her arms around Nick's neck when she reached his side, leaving her toes dangling above the ground. Her husband waited behind her with the patience of a man used to seeing his exuberant wife in the arms of other men. Nick and Jewel had been friends since being paired together in a fourth-grade science project and finding out neither was particularly fond of science. And though he'd moved out of town immediately after high school graduation, he'd seen her around the rodeos for years. As a stock contractor, she not only raised several of the bucking bulls utilized at regional rodeos, but it was her job to get them there.

"Such a great job tonight." Jewel grinned up at him once she dropped back to her feet. Her cheeks were rosy. "Eighty-nine points! I thought for sure big Death was going to toss you."

Nick chuckled. They'd been standing side by side in the winner's circle earlier, but with all the people and cameras crowding around, the two of them hadn't had a chance to talk. "You know better than that." He winked at Jewel, then reached for her husband's hand. "Good to see you again, Bobby."

5

"You, too. Great riding tonight."

"Thanks. Couldn't do it without good bulls." Nick spoke to Bobby, but his attention had shifted to the woman now heading their way. A woman he hadn't seen in years. And one that made him feel twelve again.

Same as thirteen years earlier, he couldn't take his eyes off Jewel's oldest sister. Harper had the same facial features and hazel irises as all three of her sisters, but that was where the similarities ended. She strode with the same badass purpose she'd had as a teen; her expression announced her approachableness, while also making it clear that if you got too close, you might get scorched; and her hair—an unruly bob no longer than the length of Nick's fingers—was a mixture of navy blue and jet black. It had been *pink* the first time he'd met her.

"Harper Jackson," he said as she reached their small circle, managing not to sound as awestruck as he felt. He offered his hand, telling himself the move wasn't because he wanted to touch her, but who was he kidding? He'd wanted to touch her every time he'd ever seen her.

"Stone," she corrected. Her palm slid across his. "I'm a Stone now."

That's right. She'd married a man she'd met in the army. Nick also remembered hearing about the accident that had taken her husband's life. A knot formed behind his sternum. That had to be tough.

"How are you?" he asked.

The corners of her mouth tightened a fraction, and her eyes shifted slightly away. "Couldn't be better," she murmured. She turned to her sister. "Congratulations, hon. Death came through for you again."

"That boy knows his job." Jewel slipped an arm through Bobby's.

Nick stood quietly as the sisters talked, registering the same thick throatiness in Harper's voice that he remembered as a kid, but he tuned out her actual words. Instead, he replayed the day he'd watched Harper dive off a cliff on the west shore of Flathead Lake. The day he'd fallen in love with her. Only, ideal woman aside, she'd been three years older

6

than him, and a lifetime more mature. While he'd been nothing more than a kid with his first bout of acne.

She turned back to him then, and her gaze locked onto his. He held his breath. "Congratulations to you, too," she said. "Good to see Montana's favorite cowboy is maintaining the status quo."

"Montana's favorite has an image to uphold."

He gave her the smile reserved for women he deemed to be wearing too many clothes, but she didn't appear impressed. She rolled her eyes at him. Embarrassment immediately flared, threatening to color his cheeks, and he suspected he'd forever make a fool of himself over Harper Stone.

"Harper came tonight to see what Bobby and I do during a rodeo," Jewel explained.

"That so?" Nick lifted a brow at Jewel's sister. "Planning to take up bull riding?"

She lifted a brow in return. "Been there, and done that."

She had a ballsy smugness about her that he could appreciate. And he remembered that same smugness directed his way any number of times when he was a kid. He'd been incapable of *not* looking away from her whenever she'd been around. And she'd seemingly been incapable of not showing off for him.

But did she really expect him to believe she rode bulls?

Not that he couldn't picture her on one. Her lean thighs would grip its flank, her body would be tight and—

"She's going to be helping me out for a few weeks." Jewel's words pulled Nick's attention away from the idea of her sister straddling a wild animal. She put a hand to her flat stomach, and her smile grew wide. "We haven't announced it yet, but we have exciting news."

Nick's eyes rounded when he realized what Jewel's gesture implied. His gaze dropped to her stomach. "Pregnant?"

"Yes!" she squealed.

"Congratulations, J." Nick closed the gap and gave his friend a hug—banishing Harper and her taut body to his later musings—then clapped Bobby on the back. "To both of you." He turned back to Jewel. "You think the world is ready for a mini you?"

She giggled. She was what his Aunt Sadie would call a "pistol." Full of energy, happiness, and always into the last possible thing someone would expect of her. Like raising bucking bulls. "It better be," she said. She propped both hands on her hips and gave him a cocky smirk. "And if it's not, it has a limited time to get that way."

"When are you due?" He looked her over. "You doing okay?"

"Couldn't be better. And not until the first of the year. I'm only six weeks, but I haven't even been sick one time."

"It's early to tell everyone"—Bobby joined the conversation—"but we're too excited to keep it a secret. Plus, I'm about to be out of town for the next six weeks. Finally taking the dream to the next level. Got a wood-carving apprenticeship just outside of Boston."

"Congrats, man." Bobby had been selling small handmade art in a local tourist store for the last few years. "I've seen some of your stuff. Impressive."

"Thank you. If I make it through this six weeks, it should only improve."

"Which is where Harper comes in," Jewel added.

Nick's focus returned to Harper, who was smiling politely at her sister.

"She promised to keep an eye on me," Jewel added. She curled under her husband's arm, practically cooing up at him. "Do the heavy lifting so Bobby doesn't have to worry about me while he's gone."

"I'll still worry," Bobby corrected. He kissed the top of Jewel's head, and she snuggled in tighter. Harper's smile seemed to stiffen.

"That's awfully sweet of you," Nick said. His words brought Harper's gaze back to his.

"I'm a sweet person." Her tone was right: teasing and cheerful. And she even tugged up the corners of her mouth another notch. Yet her eyes seemed suddenly flat.

And she looked a little green.

"Are you—"

"Thrilled for my sister?" she interjected before he could ask if she was okay. She nodded enthusiastically. "Absolutely." With a blink of her lashes, what Nick thought he'd seen disappeared. "I can't wait to help her out." Then she turned her back to Nick and addressed her sister and brother-in-law. "Anything else I can do before heading to the hotel?"

"You all aren't leaving tonight?" Nick asked before Jewel could respond.

Jewel peeked around her sister's side. "Bobby and I aren't going home for a couple of days," she explained. She sent a swooning look her husband's way. "We're boarding the bulls with a local rancher, then heading down to Big Sky for a romantic getaway before Bobby leaves town."

And there went Nick's hope of catching a ride.

"Did you need us to take something for you when we go?" Bobby asked.

"Yeah." Nick shot them both a wry look. *"Me."*

"Oh." Jewel blinked. "Wait . . . *you're* going home? I figured you'd go back to Butte."

He lived in a furnished one-bedroom apartment three hours from his hometown. "Dad and Gloria are heading out on a belated honeymoon tomorrow morning," he explained. His father had gotten married over the holidays the year before. "I promised to watch the farm while they're gone, but my truck broke down today."

Jewel's brow scrunched as if the problem was suddenly hers.

"Don't worry about it," he said. Along with a two-story, six-bedroom log home, his family owned one of the larger cherry orchards on the east shore of Flathead Lake. It was still early in the growing season, and though the crops would need regular maintenance during his father's month-long absence, Nick didn't actually need to see his dad beforehand to know what had to be done. Very little had changed since he'd performed the same chores as a kid. "I'll hang around here until a car-rental place opens in the morning. I'll still get home tomorrow, and I'll see Dad when he gets back."

"But I wish we could help out . . ." Jewel's words trailed off as she shifted her attention to Harper. Then a light began to take root in her eyes. Harper's shoulders stiffened slightly at the change, before she slowly turned to face Nick.

She gave him a small smile. "I'll be glad to take you."

"I wouldn't want to impose," he replied automatically. He and Harper hadn't exactly been close in the past—the extent of their relationship had been his lusting and her barely suppressed laughter. He wouldn't want to put her out for that long of a trip. "I'll have to drive back in a few days to pick up my truck, anyway," he added. "It would be best to rent a car."

"But that's the thing," Jewel said. "She could bring you back, too. She could *fly* you back."

The shock that sprang to Nick's eyes stirred a hot thrill inside Harper. She loved knocking people off balance. "Helicopter," she said in answer to his unspoken question.

"You have a helicopter?" The darker blue circling his pupils spread outward.

"My very own." She'd seen that kind of look from men before. Plenty of times. The idea of knowing someone who owned their own helicopter was exciting enough, but knowing a *woman* who owned one? And knew how to fly it? It was a turn-on—unless they assumed she was joking. "I flew in the army," she explained.

He stared at her, unspeaking, as if weighing his options. Catch a flight home with a woman he hadn't seen in years—or drive the four-plus hours in a rental? A woman, who may or may not be a good pilot. And possibly he tossed her widow status into the mix, too—not that the fact should matter in the decision to fly with her or not. But Thomas's death had made statewide news, so she didn't doubt that Nick was aware. Plus, Harper had seen the sympathy flash through his eyes after she'd corrected him on her name.

Finally, he spoke. "You're leaving tonight?"

"First thing in the morning." She *could* fly in the dark. The helicopter was equipped for it, but she preferred not to. "And Jewel is right. I'd be glad to bring you back, as well."

She remembered Nick with fondness, and would never refuse a favor she could easily provide. Plus, it wouldn't be a hardship to be around him. The man looked *fine* in a pair of leather-trimmed chaps.

She pulled her gaze back up to his, realizing with embarrassment that it'd momentarily drifted down to those particular chaps. While he'd been waiting for his score earlier, she'd noticed how well they fit. Her recognition of his physical attributes had caught her off guard, as well as the heat her thoughts had evoked.

She glanced at her sister, mostly to break the connection with Nick. He was far too attractive. And it had been a long time since her senses had done anything more than make a note of such.

"Call me when you get back," she said to Jewel. "Let me know what time you want to leave on Friday." They had to be in Great Falls for a two-day event the next weekend. She nodded at Bobby. "Have a good trip, Bob. I'll take good care of her."

Bobby reached out and gave Harper a tight hug. "Thank you," he whispered into her ear. And that simple, soft-spoken phrase—weighted heavily with his love and concern for his wife—nearly sucked Harper back into her own past. Her husband had loved *her* just as fiercely.

She shoved her feelings out of the way when her brother-in-law released her, and she once again faced Nick. "I leave at first light." She gave him the name of the hotel where she'd be spending the night. They had a small landing pad in the field out back. "Be there or I go without you."

Not waiting to see if he planned to show up, she did a one-eighty and walked away. As she left, she heard Nick's voice behind her. *"She has a helicopter?"*

She grinned at his incredulity.

Yes, she did. And she even knew how to fly it.

Chapter Two

They'd been in the air for an hour so far, and they'd chatted about the weather, a handful of the locations where Harper had been stationed during her deployments, and about the ranches spread out below them. And all the while, Nick had been slowly driving Harper insane.

It wasn't that he hadn't been a perfect gentleman. He had. He'd been polite, conversational, and he'd done nothing to get in her way.

But he was also far too easy on the eyes. And dang it, but he smelled *good*.

She wasn't used to having someone take up space in her aircraft who not only smelled like heaven in a tightly wrapped package but was also hot enough to touch. Nor was she used to *wanting* to touch. But she was a changed woman today, and she found herself wanting her hands on that man.

It had been eighteen months since Thomas had died, and in all that time she'd gone through a gamut of emotions. Most days, alone, she went through the entire gamut. But in all those months, she hadn't once been lit up inside over another man. In fact, since the day she'd met Thomas, no one had so much as turned her head. Or, at least, no one had turned it and made her pulse pound faster at the same time. Because with Thomas, it had been love at first sight. She'd lost her heart to that man the instant they'd met.

Yet Nick . . . scrawny Nick, who'd been her *little sister's best friend*—and who had remained a solid two inches shorter than Harper until *after* she'd gone away and joined the army—had sat in her passenger's seat for the last sixty minutes, his jaw scratchy with day-old whiskers and his eyes seeming to see everything they landed on far too well . . . while she'd sat over here silently wanting him to turn those eyes on *her*. What was wrong with her?

First, she had a helicopter to concentrate on flying. She had no time to get lost in a man's blue eyes. And second . . . she was still in mourning.

Last, she really didn't want Nick looking too closely at her, anyway. Because he'd done that very thing the night before, and she was aware that he'd already seen way too much.

While Jewel and Bobby had been telling Nick about their pregnancy, Harper had quietly slipped into her past. She hadn't meant to, but the past was a bitch, and it rarely cared about timing. Instead, it showed up, snatched her breath away when she least expected it, and tried to smother her with pain.

Her sister was pregnant. The first grandchild. Harper was thrilled for her.

But she'd once expected to be the one providing the first grandchild.

Deciding that additional conversation with Nick would be preferable to thinking about things that would never be, she turned her focus to something fun. Specifically, setting the precedent for her and Nick's *adult* relationship. Same as she'd set the tone over a decade ago, when he'd been nothing more than a boy with a crush.

As a teen, Nick Wilde had sported some serious puppy love for her. And, right or not, Harper had been ruthless in her taunting him about it.

Of course, he'd never actually admitted to the infatuation. But she'd known. Girls always knew these things. And she'd made sure *he'd* known that *she'd* known. Which had made teasing him all the more fun. But it hadn't been cute clothes and saucy winks that had done it for this boy. At least not for the most part. It had been walking the line between safe and death defying. And simply daring him to watch.

"So," she began, and Nick finally swung his gaze her way. She smiled to cover the sudden flurry of her pulse. "Did you ever outgrow that crush you had on me?"

The corners of his eyes crinkled. "Who said I had a crush?"

"No one had to say it, little boy. You had a steady stream of drool lining a path to your chin."

At the term "little boy," Nick's brows shot up. He looked her over then, before bringing his gaze back to hers. Then he graced her with a smile. It was the same naughty curve of his lips he'd directed her way the night before. And like last night, she heated up from the suggestions implied within. The man was a hell of a charmer. With*out* having to utter a single word.

"Little boy?" His voice was like hot buttered rum, spreading slowly throughout her body.

"Not as little as you used to be, maybe." She shrugged, going for casual, but her gaze flickered over him. The fact was, the man wasn't little at all. She was above average herself, coming in at five eight, and Nick had a good four inches on her. Maybe more. He was lean, and had a powerful build. Taller than most bull riders, but it didn't seem to affect his abilities any. "The crush was cute." She had to keep this light. "That's all I'm saying."

"And you were a tease."

"I was the friend's big sister. It was my job to tease."

His laugh sounded through her headphones then, coming at her an octave deeper than his words, and it somehow managed to ping off of every single nerve ending in her body.

"Should I apologize?" She forced the words out. "I will if you're still crushed over it, but honestly, I don't remember doing anything worth apologizing for."

He shifted on his seat, bringing his body into better alignment with hers. "You kissed me on my thirteenth birthday."

"On the cheek!" She'd forgotten about that until now.

The corners of Nick's mouth twitched. "You kissed me," he repeated. "And I about peed in my pants."

"Or worse," she mumbled.

He chuckled again, and when his gaze darkened, she got the distinct impression that he might have truly gone home and given her a bit more thought alone in his room that night. And she really *should* feel bad about that. He'd practically been a baby!

"Can I make it up to you?" She heard the flirtation in her voice. She hadn't meant for it to come out that way.

"I suppose I could think of something."

He winked at her then, and went quiet, turning his gaze to the windshield and stroking the stubble covering his chin as if in serious contemplation of how she might possibly repay him for making his teen years more painful. Harper grew tight with anticipation. She returned to concentrating on flying, yet kept a watchful eye on the man at her side.

When he finally had his answer, he once again looked her way. "You can tell me about the bull you rode."

She kept the smile off her face. She'd known her claim had riled him the night before. "What about it?"

"How long did you last?"

"How long did *you* last on your first ride?" Not that she'd admit the length of time *or* the pain induced from her first ride. It had taken more than a few tries to even stay on for more than two seconds.

"My first ride was on a sheep," he told her wryly. His right thumb tapped softly against his jean-covered leg. "And I was seven."

She glanced at him. "Did you go eight seconds on the sheep?"

"Not even close."

"And your first time on a bull?" she asked again, but he slowly shook his head.

"I asked you first. And anyway, this is supposed to be your way of making up for your years of cruelty. Not me telling you my secrets."

"And your first attempt at a bull is a secret?"

He didn't answer. He merely eyed her steadily. She said nothing else immediately, her nerves itching under his scrutiny, and returned to focusing on flying. She'd gone bull riding with Thomas the summer they'd spent in San Antonio. It'd been one of the many adventures they'd taken together.

And probably one of the many things they *shouldn't* have done.

"Come on." Nick pleaded playfully. He leaned into her space then, his presence suddenly seeming to suck the air out of the cockpit. "Tell me what happened?" he taunted. "Did he toss you and hurt your precious ego?"

She snorted, but kept her eyes straight ahead. "My ego is just fine, *thankyouverymuch.*"

"You lasted only a second, then?" He tsked, as if understanding that she couldn't possibly have stayed on for eight seconds, and she couldn't help the ghost of a smile that touched her mouth. He was seriously cute.

"Less than one second?" This time he added horror to his voice. Then he held one finger up and announced, "I've got it."

She finally looked at him, anxious to hear his next guess. And found him way too close. Her pulse pounded in her throat.

He nodded, as if having complete confidence in his final answer. But she didn't trust the twinkle in his eyes. "It scared away that big set of balls you once had," he announced. "The ones that used to impress me so much."

At his insulting suggestion, Harper immediately tilted the helicopter on its side. She fully enjoyed the sight of Nick's jaw dropping open and him clutching at the ceiling with both hands, and she was pretty sure he bit back more than one expletive as he fumbled to make purchase with *anything*. Meanwhile, she easily kept them tilted at such a pitch that she hoped the urge to pee himself resurrected.

About the time Nick seemed to come to grips with the new norm, she righted them, and before giving him time to catch his breath, she dipped them to the other side. Which left him hanging toward her by his seat belt. She was smiling now. She was having a fantastic time.

Nick's fingers landed on her shoulder, and she turned her head and met his gaze. But that was no longer fear she saw in his eyes. It was heat. As well as . . . understanding?

She blinked, clearing the notion from her head. What would he be understanding?

What she'd seen was appreciation for her skills as a pilot, plain and simple. Which he *should* be feeling. In fact, the man ought to be grateful that he hadn't been stupid enough to ask if she was sure she could fly this thing. If he'd made that statement, she would have turned him green the moment they'd gotten in the air.

She finally righted the helicopter, and when he muttered, "So your balls are intact, then?" she burst out laughing.

The laughter eventually faded, but her smile remained. This had turned out to be a very nice morning. She didn't normally fly anyone except family or paid fares, and had wondered if bringing Nick along would be awkward. They'd never had an actual relationship of any sort, so she'd had no real idea what he was like. But she'd found the time with him to be comfortable.

She peered down at the ground below them as she flew, taking in the green lands and the protruding buttes. It was late May and they were just coming out of their wet season. Everything was lush with growth. The thought made her wonder when—or if—she'd ever come out of her *hibernative* season. She'd felt as if she'd been walking around in a coma for most of the last year and a half. And though she had no idea how to shake it, she was quickly growing weary of it.

"I'm sorry about your husband," Nick said softly at her side.

What was left of her smile disappeared. "Thank you." She didn't look at him.

"I heard about the accident when it first happened. I wondered how you were hanging in."

"I'm hanging in fine." *Just fine.* It's what she'd said to her family for over a year now.

"And *you* were okay? You didn't get hurt?"

She swallowed around the lump in her throat. "Nothing that wouldn't heal."

There was a beat of silence before Nick continued. "It's good to see you're doing well. I'm sure it's been rough."

She wouldn't acknowledge details, but she did appreciate the sentiment. She glanced at him, the opening of her windpipe having grown tight. "Thank you. I know you understand the pain of loss."

He'd lost his mother as a kid. She couldn't remember how old he'd been, but it had been sometime before he'd hit the age of crushes and noticing girls. Since Jewel and Nick had been friends, and since Harper had gone to school with one of the older Wilde siblings, the Jacksons had attended the funeral.

Nick went quiet for several seconds, and when he spoke again, his tone was casual. "I'm sure we all handle loss differently. And because of that, I won't venture to guess how well you're really holding up—even though you say you're fine."

She shot him a quick look.

"But I will say that I'll be around here for a while if you ever want to talk." He gave her a closed-mouth smile. "I have broad shoulders."

Why would he think she might want to talk? And why would she talk to him?

His offer set her on edge. She didn't need to talk to anyone. Thomas was dead. She'd moved on. She was over it. She didn't know why no one wanted to believe that.

Without responding, she refocused all her attention on her duties as pilot. Grateful silence fell over them, and before too long, she bypassed the Wilde Cherry Farm and circled out over Flathead Lake. Nick didn't question the delay, he simply sat up straighter and leaned forward so he could have a less obstructed view. The lake was huge below them, resting with quiet beauty in the middle of the valley. It always brought a calm peace to her soul. She'd spent countless hours flying solo above the clear waters over the last few months. And she'd probably spend countless more in the months to come.

The whip of the blades continued overhead, the sound the only noise in the cockpit, as they spent twenty more minutes taking in the islands dotting the lake and the stillness of the water. There was a single sailboat in their line of sight. With it being a Sunday in late May and the forecast calling for seventy degrees for that day, there would be additional locals making their way onto the water soon. In a couple of months it would be busier, but this time of year, being out on the water was like having the lake all to yourself.

Harper circled back toward Nick's family property, finally putting the helicopter down in one of the few places that wasn't covered with cherry trees. She didn't kill the engine.

"Thanks for the ride," he said. He removed his headset after her murmured acknowledgment, and turned to go, but she put a hand to his arm before he could get out.

"That bull," she said, when he looked back. "The one I rode." She raised her voice to be heard over the whip of the blades, and at the same time asked herself why she'd delayed him. And why she was telling him *anything* about herself. When he leaned in closer, she turned her mouth to his ear. "I stayed on him for the full eight seconds."

He stared at her, seemingly impressed—if a little unbelieving. But whether he wanted to believe her or not, she'd done it. Eight seconds. She was proud of that.

Even if that had sealed the coffin on her relationship with her in-laws.

Without another word, Nick reached over and plucked her cell phone from the pocket of her desert-fatigue overshirt, and motioned for her to unlock it. He entered a number and handed it back. "Call me," he mouthed.

Then he jumped from the helicopter and hurried from under the blades.

Chapter Three

W hat the . . ."
Nick flipped back and forth between computer files once again, looking at the totals for the two columns, and trying to figure out why they didn't match. And by not match, he meant by a lot. Which made no sense.

With a grunt of frustration, he pushed away from the oversize desk and spun the office chair so he faced the windows overlooking the front porch. And he scowled. The discrepancies bothered him. He knew he'd never had proper training in accounting, but when it came down to it, it was just numbers. And he *had* taken accounting before he'd dropped out of college.

Granted, the class had been basic, but still.

He spun back to the desk and stared at the computer in frustration, then reached for his phone. But he changed his mind and pulled his hand back. Just because his sister, Dani, had done the books for the orchard up until she'd moved out of the house last year, that didn't mean she needed Nick calling and bugging her about it now. Plus, she was busy with her own work.

Not that the finances were Nick's job either—his dad had been handling things since coming out of retirement after last year's harvest. But Nick had thought he'd pitch in and help out while at home. But what he was seeing simply didn't add up.

Had Dani left things in this big a mess or had his dad done this? The worry had Nick questioning his father's ability. Or maybe his senility. Of course, his dad *had* been out of the business for several years . . . but he hadn't been that old when he'd turned the farm over to Dani and their oldest brother. Keeping the books straight should be a nonissue for him.

With a shake of his head, Nick shut down the program and stood. He had better things to do than to try to figure out this mess. Like . . .

He walked out into the hall and looked first one way and then the other, and finished his own thought. Like . . . *nothing*. He had nothing to do. The house was eerily silent, and the rooms seemed to echo mockingly around him. It was only day two of being there, and he was ready to climb the exposed-log walls. He'd spent all of yesterday weeding the orchard and this morning double-checking the irrigation system and taking a look at the old coolant system. The coolant system was on the blink, and though a new one was scheduled to arrive before this year's harvest, he'd thought maybe he could fix it. He couldn't. So instead he'd walked the full fifteen acres to check that no animals had done damage to any of the trees . . . and then he'd swept out the barn.

Yes, being there alone bored him enough to sweep out the barn. Two days in, and he felt as if he'd been dropped into solitary confinement for a decade. It made him wonder if Dani and Gabe had been this stir crazy during their tenure here. Other than during harvest and pruning season, the farm was mostly family run. But then, his siblings had each other to talk to while they'd lived here. As well as Gabe's evil wife, Michelle. And eventually, Gabe and Michelle's daughter.

That was the problem, Nick decided. He needed someone here, too. Which made him think of Harper.

She hadn't called. Not that he'd really expected her to.

But he'd hoped she would.

When she'd told him about staying on that bull for eight seconds, he'd sworn he'd seen something more than pride in her eyes. Something haunting and sad. And angry. It was the same flicker of emotions he'd caught when he'd brought up her husband. Therefore, he'd convinced himself she could use a friend. That she *needed* someone to talk to.

And what? He thought *he* could be that friend? That he could help her move beyond fine?

He laughed at the absurdity. As a person who'd kept his own issues tucked tightly away over the years, he knew the implausibility of simply opening up. Wasn't likely to happen. And especially not with a near stranger. Even if they *had* had a moment.

He thought about that second of time in the helicopter when he'd reached out and touched her shoulder. It had been brief, but as he'd hung suspended toward her and their gazes had connected, he'd felt as if he got her. As if he were more than a stranger.

Her younger self had flashed through his head, and he'd known that, though she'd changed over the years, though she'd suffered loss, the same person still lived inside her.

She'd been fearless and tough back then, willing to do anything or go anywhere. The word "independent" hadn't come close to describing her. Yet as tough as she'd been, as much as she'd had no fear at facing down any perceived threat to her family or friends, she'd also had a gooey-soft center. She'd wanted to save the world.

And Nick remembered how he'd wanted that heart of gold of hers, and all the feelings it was capable of having, to be directed at him. Even though he'd have had *no* idea what to do with them if they had been.

His body grew tight from thinking about her now. He still wanted her attentions directed at him. He still wanted *her*.

Only, today he knew completely what to do with her.

His phone rang, and his pulse spiked with the thought that it could be Harper, but it was only Nate. His twin lived in Alaska these days, a crab fisherman in the Bering Sea in the wintertime, and a man of many other traits in the summer. He'd come home the least over the years, but he *had* come in for harvest the year before. At least for part of it. He'd also returned for Thanksgiving. It'd been the first time the entire family had been under one roof for a holiday since they'd all scattered to different parts of the country.

Nate hadn't made it back for their dad's Christmas wedding, but he'd promised to try being here for harvest again this year. It was a standing rule that if family members *could* be home during late July to help, then they *would* be home. It was the family business—whether they appreciated being saddled with it or not—and they should treat it as such.

"Well, if it isn't the prodigal son." Nick smiled as he answered the phone.

"And if it isn't the sucker who got his arm twisted into going home," Nate replied.

Nick finally moved from the hallway, heading toward the back of the house. He made his way through the connected kitchen and great room, and as he'd done when he'd first arrived home, he took in the many changes that had happened since his dad and Gloria had moved in. The house had once been the family home, housing his dad and mom, as well as all six kids. It was a huge two-story log home that his parents had built to fill with their many kids. From the outside looking in, they'd seemed like the perfect family. Which had been his mother's plan. Show the world how great they were . . . then make everyone's lives miserable at home.

She'd died when Nick and Nate had been ten, and though everyone had felt huge relief at no longer having to walk on eggshells around their narcissistic mother, nothing had ever really been the same.

"I don't actually feel suckered," Nick admitted now. He picked up a crocheted doily, which he knew to be something his new stepmother had made, and thought of how happy his dad had sounded as he and Gloria had headed out for their cruise. "I'm glad to do it," Nick confessed. And it was the truth. He was glad to help out. He was also glad to be home.

Nate chuckled in his ear. "Sure you are. Because it's such a happening place around there. So tell me about all the exciting things you've done today. Ride any bulls? Rope any ladies?"

Nick pictured Harper and her blue hair. "I don't have to ride a bull to be satisfied."

He continued moving through the room until he reached the wall of windows lining the back of the house. The scene outside included their orchard, as well as Flathead Lake, and Nick pulled in a deep breath as he took it in. It was a million-dollar view, and one he'd often forgotten to appreciate.

"My only issue is the silence," he admitted. "I'm not used to being so alone."

"It is a solitary job."

"Kind of like yours?" Months at sea couldn't be easy.

"I'm not the only man on the boat."

"Not a lot of women with you, though, huh?"

They'd had this conversation before. It wasn't as if Nate had any trouble getting a woman, but his schedule often made that difficult. Which probably suited his brother fine. Nate was in no more of a hurry to look for more than the occasional hookup than Nick. In fact, Nick wasn't sure either of them would ever be ready for more. Their mother had done a number on all of them, and then their oldest brother had gone and married someone just like her. It was enough to scare the idea of commitment right out of a person.

Again, Nick thought about Harper. She'd been married for several years, and he found himself wondering if it had been a happy marriage.

Had she discovered so-called love? He hoped so. She was a good person, and she deserved happiness. And yes, though he didn't seek love out, he did believe in it. Sort of. But that had only begun recently, and only because he'd watched his sister fall hard herself.

Thankfully, her husband, Ben, was a good guy, and nothing like their mom. Otherwise, Nick and every one of his brothers would have run the man out of town the minute he'd looked Dani's way.

"So what's going on other than your miserable loneliness?" Nate asked.

"Pretty much nothing. I'm here without my truck—it broke down over the weekend. I can't even get into town to go to the gym."

"Use Dad's truck. He and Gloria got a ride to the airport, didn't they?"

"Dani and Ben took them."

"So his truck is there. Use it."

"But I want *my* truck." Actually, he wanted to know for certain that Harper truly did plan to take him back to get it. He wanted to be up in the air with her again.

"Then sit there and be bored to death," Nate muttered.

Nick grunted. "Why are you calling, exactly?"

"Can I not just want to talk?"

"Sure you can, but didn't we just talk a couple of days ago? What's up?" he asked again. "Going off the grid again, or heading out on a salmon boat?"

"Actually"—Nate paused—"I'm thinking of getting out of here for a while."

"Getting out to where?" Nick couldn't help but wonder if his brother's sudden urge to mix up his norm was similar to what was going on in Nick's head.

Last summer the entire family had finally cleared the air about their mother. She'd been manipulative, she'd tried to turn family members against one another, and she'd royally screwed with everyone's heads.

Even their dad's. And they'd not talked about it as a family for fourteen long years. That had been another by-product of the way they'd been raised. Show the world they were perfect. Don't talk about issues. No need to face reality.

So they'd not faced reality. And as such, they'd allowed their sister to effectively repaint their earlier years into something they'd all wanted to believe it had been.

Their head-in-the-sand mentality had done more harm than good, though, and reality had finally blown up in their faces as Dani made plans to move to New York City—with Gabe also declaring his intentions to move away. No one wanted to be *here*, and that had become painfully obvious. So they'd talked—*argued*—and everyone had finally begun to move forward. Then Dani had up and done a one-eighty. Her lifelong dream—having a big-time career in New York—turned out to *not* be her dream after all. After only three months away, she'd broken her lease and come home.

Her actions had affected Nick personally, causing him to take a hard look at his own life. Dani had wanted New York for as long as Nick could remember. Yet, she'd been wrong. And her ability to finally see her life clearly had been due to dealing with their family dysfunction.

Therefore, he'd had to ask himself: Was she the only one who'd gotten it wrong?

Was going national truly his next step, as everyone believed? Or could it be something else? This question had nagged at him for months, yet he was no closer to an answer now than he'd been when it had first slithered through his mind.

"Still trying to decide what I want to do," Nate finally answered, pulling Nick back out of his own thoughts. "I've put in for leave but given no definite start or end dates yet."

"Then come home," Nick said. "Help me out here."

"There's not enough to do there right now. I spent too much time doing the same as a kid not to know that. Mowing and weeding mostly.

Around-the-clock watering should start soon. But you don't need me to turn the sprinklers on."

"But if you're here doing half the job, I'd have more time to chase those women you think I need to chase." The reality was, he was tired of the women he chased.

"Yeah. Not gonna happen. I have about a million better options." A couple of noises sounded through the phone. "I need to go," Nate said. "I'll let you know what I decide."

"There's always a bed for you here."

Nate laughed. "You're so lonely that you want me to come home and bunk in the same room with you like we did when we were kids?"

"Too good to sleep with me these days?"

"I can find better people to sleep with."

Nick smiled, feeling less lonely just talking to his brother. He hoped Nate *would* come home. Forward steps and all that. They could all use some. But he also wouldn't bet on it. Nate had even more issues than their mom when it came to being here. And Nick couldn't blame him.

They signed off, and Nick made a quick decision and left through the back door. They had a small section of lake access on their property, as well as a boat dock. Their sister had spent many evenings there over the years. *Searching for herself.* So he decided that he could use a little searching himself.

And just maybe while he was at it, he'd see a certain red-and-white helicopter fly over.

Chapter Four

Harper switched the aircraft's radio over to the station monitoring search and rescue missions as she flew, and blew out a soft breath at the lack of emergencies being reported. Not that she would have done anything if she'd heard a distress call. She no longer volunteered for the valley's SAR program. But that didn't mean she didn't continue to listen in on a regular basis. With the mountains around them, and the entire area a prime spot for outdoor activities, too many people routinely got lost or hurt. And occasionally, someone didn't make it out alive.

Every time that happened, it stole another piece of her heart. Not because she knew the casualties personally, but because she felt a deep-seated need to take care of the area and all the people in it. She'd always been that way. Or she had until . . .

Since Thomas's death . . .

She gritted her teeth and pushed the 212 harder. Thomas *shouldn't* have died. They'd been a team. They'd been the best thing she could ever imagine.

Hurt and anger mixed as she swept out over Flathead Lake, but she ignored all of it. She was returning from dropping off a team

Montana Rescue

of corporate executives at a guest ranch not far from here—with a pickup scheduled for Sunday afternoon to take them back to Missoula International—and she had her aircraft pointed toward home. Only, there was nothing waiting for her at her house except another long evening alone, and she suddenly couldn't do it. She didn't want to be home. In the house that Thomas had built for them.

And she most definitely didn't want to be alone.

She peered at the ground as she passed over the area, knowing her parents would love to see her. They hadn't been shy recently in pointing out that she didn't visit enough. And she didn't. But her parents' house wasn't where she wanted to be, either. So she headed north along the eastern shoreline. Toward Wilde Cherry Farm. And she called herself a fool as she did it.

But she rationalized her move with facts. She hadn't talked to Nick since dropping him off Sunday morning, and she *had* promised to give him a ride back to his truck. Therefore, she should check on the state of his truck repairs.

Of course, she could call. Or text. She had his number.

But she didn't want to call or text.

Only, as she neared the orchard, her inner voice spoke up once again, having one single word to say to her. *Fool.* Because she could see Nick from her altitude, and she recognized the quick zing of attraction for what it was. He was behind a push mower in one of the fields, working between two rows of trees, and she would almost swear that she could make out each and every muscle group bunching under his T-shirt as he moved.

She knew better, of course. She was too far up to really be able to see the sculpted dips and valleys of his upper torso. But that didn't keep her from imagining what it would look like. Same as she'd done all week. The man turned her on in a way that she should definitely avoid.

She hovered above him, lowering only until he stopped what he was doing and peered up. He tugged earbuds from his ears and shaded his eyes with one hand—and Harper bit her lip at the sight. Sweaty, a little rumpled, and a whole lot hot. The man was definitely too good-looking.

Either that, or she'd hit middle age early and was having her first hot flash.

She tilted the helo a couple of times, "waving" the blades at him, and smiled when he lifted a hand in return. Then she headed for the open field where she'd put down the last time she'd been there. She saw Nick move in the same direction, and danged if her fingers didn't begin to twitch with excitement. She was happy to see him. And that feeling was as foreign to her as the fact that she'd intentionally sought him out.

As she lowered to the ground, she silently instructed herself to get a grip. He was simply a hot guy. There were plenty of hot guys in the world. Hotness didn't mean anything.

Unless she decided to do something about it.

After letting the machine cool off, she shut it down, but she continued sitting in the pilot's seat as Nick neared. She thought about the fact that he was younger than her. Then she pictured the more-than-willing, much-younger woman she'd seen wrapped around him after his win Saturday night. He'd seemed quite content with someone like that. And chances were he'd gotten over his crush on *her* years ago, anyway.

Except, she'd seen the heat in his eyes Sunday morning.

She might have tried to convince herself that's not what it had been, but she hadn't believed it, even then. He was attracted to her.

And *she* was attracted to *him*.

She jumped to the ground before he could make it all the way across the field, and headed through the grass to meet him. His smile was broad by the time she reached his side, and she couldn't help but smile in return. And subtly check him out. His T-shirt clung to his body—she could definitely make out the outlines of his muscles now—and his dark hair was damp and mussed.

Nick motioned behind her. "You do know that isn't a helicopter parking lot, right?"

She glanced over her shoulder, taking the moment to pull in a deep breath. He even smelled good. Manly good. "Wouldn't take much to make it one." She turned back. "A small concrete pad. A couple of tie-downs." She gave a lazy one-shoulder shrug. "It's totally doable."

His blue eyes sparkled. "Yet you don't seem to have a problem landing it on the grass, either. In fact, I'd be willing to bet you wouldn't have a problem putting it down most anywhere. Not if your flying abilities the other day are anything to go by."

Her smile widened at his reminder of their prior conversation. "Not *most* anywhere," she corrected. "*Any*where. But that's because my balls are bigger than yours."

Nick looked her over then. Slowly. And his scrutiny lit goose bumps along her skin. This was why she'd come here instead of to her parents' house. Because Nick Wilde made her feel. And whether that dredged up guilt or not, she wanted to feel.

When his gaze returned to hers, his direct stare sent a shiver down her spine. "You might have balls," he started, his voice dropping lower, "but I could take you on size."

She gulped. Things had suddenly turned intense.

Panic snatched at her, and she glanced away. She had to change the subject. She wasn't ready for this. Turning her body so she was at a right angle to him, she slowed her breathing and took in the lake. It glistened in the afternoon sunlight. Staring at it, Nick's hotness temporarily evaporated, and she was suddenly overwhelmed with love for this area. Not that she'd ever not loved her hometown, but her gratitude seemed to be larger today. Her senses sharper.

When she turned back, once again having herself under control and pretending they hadn't just been flirting, she silently begged him to do the same. "Heard when your truck will be ready yet?"

"Tomorrow afternoon."

"Did you still want me to take you?" Her heart beat faster as she asked the question.

"If you don't mind." He'd clearly picked up on her need to back off, and he put an additional foot of space between them. Then he motioned with his head toward the path leading out of the field. "I need a break. Want to take a walk since you're here?"

It was her turn to nod.

She hadn't meant to get flirty with him, and now she didn't mean for them to be so serious. There had to be a balance. But she didn't know how to get to that point yet. So she walked. And she enjoyed the scenery as they went.

They moved through the fields side by side, skirting around cherry trees—whose branches were filled with tiny green cherries—until they came out on a ridge providing an even better view of the lake. They stopped at the edge, and she took in the clear water and the mountains on the far side. There was still snow on the peaks, and the sky behind them was the kind of vivid blue that had always made her know she'd return to Montana after leaving the army.

Without warning, her shoulders relaxed. She'd been carrying too much tension since the accident, she knew that, but she'd been unable to shed any of it. Today, though, a bit of it seeped from her body.

"I forget how much I miss home until every time I visit," Nick said.

She looked at him. His words made him sound lonely. "Do you come home often?"

"Often enough. A few times a year. But . . ." He shook his head. "I come home and I look at this view and I suck in the smell of the air, and . . . I know I'm not that far away, but the air here is different. I used to be here during visits, and do nothing but think of how soon I could leave again. But now, I'm already concerned that my father will return before I'm ready to go."

"Then don't go."

He chuckled drily. "But I don't live here." He blew out a breath, his cheeks puffing with the motion, then shook his head once again as if flinging his thoughts from his mind. "How about you?" He turned to her. "How long have you been home?"

"Four years." Sort of. The west shore wasn't really *home*, even though Lakeside was where she lived now. She intended to end her words there, but found herself continuing. "Thomas and I spent a couple of years traveling after we both got out of the army. We wanted to experience more, you know? Live in different parts of the world on our own terms. We got out at twenty-two, then came home at twenty-four. Or, we came *here*. Thomas wasn't originally from the valley, but he'd visited as a kid. His parents had a summer home on the lake at one point, and they used to ski up in Whitefish . . ." She trailed off as she thought about why they'd stopped coming to Montana. Why they'd never been willing to accept her as part of Thomas's life.

"Did you know him then?"

She shook her head. "We were only kids. I never met him until after we both enlisted, and that was on the other side of the world." She glanced at Nick. "Strange how things happen, huh?"

"Sounds like fate to me."

"Fate?" She shot him a disbelieving look. "You a romantic, Wilde? A big-time charmer like you?"

He chuckled. "Hardly. Okay, then, a happy coincidence? I mean, his parents had to like that, right? If they'd vacationed here in the past. Him meeting a girl from the same area must have been ideal. Nice reason to visit again."

She fought to hide her true feelings. "They would have preferred he meet someone from California."

"Why is that?"

She shrugged and went back to staring out at the lake. "That's where they live. They didn't like it when he signed up for the army and appreciated it even less when he never returned home."

"He didn't get along with them?"

"They just saw the world through different lenses." She slid a sideways glance toward Nick, wondering if she was sharing too much, but he seemed genuinely interested. That's when she realized that she *wanted* to talk about Thomas. It'd been too long since she'd done anything but think of her husband in anything other than a bad light.

Yet, Thomas had been an honorable man. He'd entered the military for a noble cause.

"They came from money," she told Nick. "So much that Thomas wouldn't have had to work if he hadn't wanted to. But Thomas was their only child, so his dad expected him to follow in his footsteps. Work in the family business. Only, Thomas was dead set on enlisting."

"What kind of business?"

"Vacation resorts. They have them all over the world. Third-generation business that his great-grandfather started with a small inheritance and a dream." She repeated the words as she'd heard them said so many times.

"And Thomas wasn't interested?"

"It's not that he wasn't interested in the business, he was just *more* interested in other things. He'd grown up listening to his maternal grandfather tell stories of his time in the service. And that's what Thomas wanted to do." She couldn't bring herself to share the additional reasoning behind Thomas's mind-set.

"You two had a lot in common . . . didn't your grandfather serve, too?"

"Good memory. And yes, a lot in common." They'd often seemed like one person.

They'd had similar outlooks in life—to live for the moment. They'd both been vigilant about maintaining right from wrong. About seeing that no one was left behind—in any fashion, whether that meant vacationers on a mountaintop or comrades in the desert. And they'd both wanted to pass their love of living for the moment on to their kids.

But at the same time, she'd often wondered if Thomas's life motto hadn't been kept alive more by her than by him. She'd certainly heard that accusation enough.

"You loved him a lot." Nick said, not making it a question, and she nodded mutely.

"I loved him a lot," she whispered. "From the very first moment that we met."

She really hadn't intended to talk about her husband when she'd set out to come here today. Or had she? Wasn't that why Nick had given her his phone number?

But how had he known that she needed to talk about Thomas?

They stood in silence for several more minutes, and she thought about her marriage. Losing Thomas had never once crossed her mind when they were married. They were supposed to grow old together.

They were supposed to have kids.

The thought of all she'd lost had her turning away and heading back toward her helicopter. She'd talked enough for one day. Nick let her lead for several minutes before catching up, but he didn't immediately speak. When they came out of the trees, though, and the helo sat across the field in front of them, he finally broke the silence. And she appreciated his levity.

"So is that thing your only means of transportation?"

She smiled halfheartedly. "I also own a four-wheel-drive truck, as well as a jeep."

"No car for you?"

"Cars don't always go where I want to take them." They reached the perimeter of the helicopter, and she turned to him. "But I'd just finished up a job today. Hadn't made it back home yet."

"What do you do?"

"Whatever someone will pay me for." She spent a couple of minutes filling him in on the types of fares she contracted for. Tours over Glacier

National Park, a pickup or drop-off from airports, showing realtors and potential buyers around the area.

"You stay busy?"

"I do okay." Only, she didn't do what they'd purchased the helicopter for. She glanced toward the lake once again. "So . . . tomorrow?"

"You're not going to try to make me puke again, are you?"

She deadpanned. "Only if you get on my nerves again."

"Well, I'm not sure I can promise not to do that." He smiled at her then. It wasn't the panty-dropping, making-women-beg-at-his-feet smile that he seemed to enjoy bandying about so much . . . but it was potent enough. In fact, she had the same reaction to this one as she'd had when he *had* turned the super-sexy smile on her. She got hot all over.

But the thing was, she'd thought her response was about attraction. A simple reawakening of her libido. Only, at the moment, it wasn't merely parts of her coming back to life. It was desire. It was *hunger*.

She wanted sex, and she wanted it with Nick.

The realization floored her.

"Let me pay you for the ride tomorrow."

She looked down her nose at him. "As if."

Then he shifted and leaned in. It was a subtle move, but she couldn't miss it. He was crowding her. Testing her boundaries. And her internal panic button blazed to life.

And what she realized was that just because she had a reawakened urge to do more than lie alone in her own bed at night, it *didn't* necessarily mean she was actually ready to do more. She took a step back. "We'll call it a favor for my little sister's friend," she suggested.

"How about a favor for *your* friend?"

Her pulse thumped harder. Did friendship come with responsibilities she wasn't ready for?

Nick studied her as she battled with her internal dialogue, and she sensed that he wouldn't let her tease the moment away. He was pushing her, seeing where she'd let him in. But she couldn't bring herself to answer. Because she didn't know the answer. Friendship somehow seemed scarier than the idea of sex.

"Could you use a friend, Harper?"

"I—"

"Because *I* could use one."

The moment had grown heavy once again. "I somehow suspect that you have all the friends you need, Mr. Montana's Favorite Cowboy. You certainly didn't seem to be lacking for any Saturday night."

Interest flared in his eyes at her words, and she realized he could take them to mean that she'd been watching him at the rodeo last weekend. As she had been. But he politely didn't point that out.

Instead, his voice lowered, and he said, "But I don't have any who know my secrets."

Shock froze her. Nick Wilde had secrets? He seemed so carefree.

"I'll pick you up here after lunch." She backed toward the cockpit door. She didn't want to talk about secrets, his *or* hers. "I have an early charter in the morning, but I'll be here by one."

"I'll be waiting."

Forcing herself to break eye contact, she turned and climbed into the cockpit. Her hands were shaking as she powered up, but she ignored them. She didn't know *what* she wanted from Nick. Someone to talk to? Sex? A friend?

And what were his secrets?

Dang. He had her all kinds of confused.

But more than that, he had her all kinds of interested.

Chapter Five

That's eight seconds for Jeb Mauley, folks!"

Nick kept his face impassive as he stood, arms slung over the top rung of the gate, and waited for his competitor's score to be announced. It was night one in Great Falls, and it seemed everyone had upped their game. Especially the rookie out of Fort Benton. Nick's agent had already pointed the same fact out several times that evening, until Nick had barked at him to find someone else to annoy. It wasn't that Nick was overly concerned with one event. He never won every competition. Nobody did. It was that Charlie had also been badgering him about the PBR all night.

Jeb's score flashed on the scoreboard hanging above the crowd, and Nick pressed his lips together. That was a good score.

"That kid might just beat you this weekend."

He glanced over to find Harper standing next to him, her arms slung over the gate like his.

She nodded toward Jeb. "He seems to be on a streak. Nipping at your heels last weekend, and that score right there just overtook yours."

"It's only day one of the competition."

"I'm just saying . . ."

Nick frowned at her. "It's not a crime not to win every weekend."

"No," she mused. Her head tilted slightly. "But if you're 'the man' . . ."

Which was the exact problem he was having tonight. Everyone expected him to be "the man." "Jeb's good," he pointed out. "He's going to win a few."

"True. But he's going at it like maybe *he* wants to be the man," Harper teased. Mischief danced in her eyes "I mean . . . watch him. He's not giving you an inch."

Nick didn't reply. He merely squinted at her in frustration. Because he very much suspected that Jeb not only could be the man—with a bit more time—but that he someday would be.

They both turned their attention to the next rider readying in the chute. The guy's spotter was a friend of Nick's. They'd met his first year out on his own, and Nick had pulled him into the sport. The bull dropped his front legs and twisted before the rider could get properly seated, nearly pinning his leg between the bull and the back gate, and Nick and Harper both sucked in a sharp breath. The spotter jabbed at the bull just in time.

"It's a dangerous sport," Harper murmured.

"Definitely not for the faint of heart." A leg could easily be crushed by that move.

The rider repositioned himself, gave his okay, and the gate opened. And within three seconds the bull was riderless. The crowd groaned, and Nick looked back over at Harper. Their flight to get his truck the day before had been uneventful. They'd surpassed the weather and mundane topics they'd stuck to the first time, but he wouldn't say they'd breached the line of personal either—other than that brief moment on the farm earlier in the week.

But personal or not, they *had* talked for the full length of the ride. And whether she recognized it or not, they *were* becoming friends.

They'd had a good time the day before. Her showing up at his side tonight only reiterated the budding friendship.

"Jewel turned you loose for a while?" Friends or not, though, what he couldn't figure out was why he'd tossed out the idea that *he* could use someone to share secrets with.

"She's got it under control."

"She doing okay?"

"Puking her guts up every few minutes." Harper shot him an annoyed look. "I swear she purposely waited until Bobby was out of town to start that."

He chuckled. "Probably not exactly her plan."

"I know." She turned her gaze back to the arena, but Nick kept an eye on her for a moment longer. A tiny flicker of sadness had flashed across her face right before she'd looked away. She was good at hiding it, but it was there. All the time.

And *that* was why he wanted to be her friend.

They both continued watching the action in the arena, their eyes on the bullfighter now entertaining the crowd, but Nick spent the time thinking about Harper. He liked her. A lot. He would give his left nut to sleep with her. But she wasn't like the women he usually went for.

Instead of curvy and soft, she was tough and strong—which blew the top off of hot. She marched entirely to her own drum. But he also suspected that sleeping with *him* wasn't what she needed at the moment. Him poking at her, trying to have a few nights of fun, might only soothe *his* needs. And he wasn't into that.

It wasn't that she wasn't attracted to him. He'd seen her attraction at his place. Where she'd also given him a peek at how much she'd loved her husband.

An arm circled him from behind, and he looked down, taking in the pink nails and long, narrow fingers now laying flat against his chest, and he knew in an instant who it was. Betsy breathed out a flirty laugh behind him as her body pressed into his back, her softness and heat grazing him to midthigh. He smiled in welcome, turning so she could slip in between Harper and him, and Harper glanced their way. Her brows inched up when Betsy snuggled in tight, but she didn't say anything.

"I missed you this week," Betsy singsonged. She lifted to her toes. "And Jeb wasn't half the man you are," she whispered hotly in his ear. "Please tell me I'll be in your bed tonight."

Harper's brows rose even more with that, and she very carefully didn't look at them.

"I . . ." Nick started. He swallowed. He hadn't given Betsy the first thought, neither during the week nor tonight. And honestly, if he weren't at least thinking about a woman once in a while, should he be sleeping with her? "Bets." He untwined her body from his, and nodded toward Harper. "I'd like you to meet a friend of mine. Harper Stone."

Harper shifted on her feet, looking as uncomfortable as *he* felt, and said hello to Betsy. Then her hazel gaze flicked quickly to his before once again shifting away, and that brief glance left him furrowing his brow. What had that look been about? He'd swear it was determination.

But determination to do what?

Betsy turned back to him, and Nick took her hands in his before she could reattach herself. "I'll holler at you later, okay?"

A bad-girl smile immediately covered her face. "I'm going to hold you to that, champ." She lifted to her toes again, this time whispering details far more comprehensive as to her wishes for that evening, and he almost blushed.

His gaze shot to Harper, and by the stiffness of her posture, he knew she'd overheard.

Betsy walked away then, and he took the moment to track her movements. Her skirt, barely covering her round bottom, was ultra-short, leaving her legs bare and mouthwatering, and her top left a two-inch gap of skin showing at her trim waist. She was looking seriously banging tonight. And he found that it did nothing for him.

Damn.

When he finally turned back to Harper, intending to shrug an apology her way for Betsy's blatant proposition, he was caught off guard by her proximity. He had only a second to register details. She was within inches of him, *her* body heat now tickled at his, and the soft scent of baby powder drifted up to his nose.

Then she burrowed one hand under the back of his hat . . . and pulled his mouth down to hers.

He stood rooted in shock before groaning when Harper's tongue slipped between his lips.

The lady knew how to kiss. Her lips were soft and warm. Plush. And she attacked the act as if there would be only one chance to get it right. She lifted her other hand to hold his head in place, knocking his hat to the ground as she deepened her exploration, and he finally registered that he was standing there letting her lead. Letting her do everything!

His hands sought out her hips, intending to take control, and he tugged her closer. And damned if her tight body didn't immediately mold to his. He grew rock hard in an instant. She tasted like funnel cake, and he decided it was his favorite treat in the world. But then she pulled back as abruptly as she'd started the kiss. She blinked, looked at his mouth. And then took a step back.

After she walked away—without saying another word—Nick spent a full fifteen seconds simply focusing on breathing. What in the hell had that been about?

Because damn, he had not seen it coming. But his next question was the more important one. When would he get to experience it again?

Later that evening, the sounds of retching hit Harper's ears for the sixth time in as many hours, and she grimaced in commiseration with her sister. The poor thing. Harper rose from where she'd been watching the local news in her hotel room, and passed through the open connecting doors. She reached Jewel's bathroom and put a hand to the door.

"Can I do anything to help?" She'd asked this same lame question the five previous times she'd been in this situation today, but she didn't know what else she could do.

"No." Jewel's voice barely whispered out. "I'm sorry it's happening again."

Harper dropped her forehead to the door. "It's not your fault, hon." Harper had not been the most sympathetic sister when it came to this part of Jewel's pregnancy—she could freely admit that. But she just didn't have it in her.

"Can you get me a soda?" Jewel's weak voice croaked out. "Caffeine free."

"Sure thing."

Harper hurried back to her own room and grabbed the room key and a handful of change, then zipped a hoodie on over her T-shirt and slipped out into the night. They were staying in an old-but-charming two-story motel with a basket of flowers and a single rocking chair gracing each room's porch, and earlier, Harper had spotted vending machines tucked beneath the set of whitewashed concrete stairs. As she headed in that direction, she thought back over the day. For her first weekend helping her sister, it had gone well. There had been the vomiting, yes. And Harper's guilty desire to be anywhere but here. But she'd also easily gotten a handle on the tasks at hand and had been an asset to Jewel. Plus, she'd enjoyed the atmosphere.

It wasn't as if she'd never been to a rodeo before. One couldn't very well call themselves a Montanan and not have attended rodeos over the years. She'd just never been a part of the back end of things.

And though her favorite event in past years had been barrel racing—her best friend in high school had been captain of the girls' barrel racing team—these days, she found her preference leaning more toward bull riding. And it had absolutely everything to do with one tall, sexy cowboy. Whom she'd had her lips on earlier that day.

She pulled Jewel's soda from the dispenser and fed in enough money for a second, then paused long enough to press the tips of her fingers to her lips. Christ Almighty, Nick Wilde was hot.

But seriously, what in the world had gotten into her?

She somehow doubted he'd let her pretend the kiss hadn't happened. And really, she wasn't sure she wanted to pretend it away. Because she might want to do it again.

She hadn't seen him since she'd walked away. Between helping with the stock and providing needed sympathy to her sister, she'd been too busy. But now that the evening was over and she could let herself think, she couldn't help but scold herself for allowing jealousy to rear its head.

One minute she'd been standing there trying to avoid watching "Bets" wiggling herself all over Nick, and the next minute she'd wanted to be the one Nick wiggled with.

She pressed the button for a drink for herself and scanned the parking lot as the bottle tumbled to the dispenser. The small, paved area was loaded with pickups of all sizes, but it was the brown metallic four-door parked ten spots away that held her interest. Nick was staying in the same hotel as them.

Was Betsy in his room tonight?

The question made her want to bang her head against the machine.

Only, her next question was even more embarrassing than the first. Was he thinking about *her* while sleeping with Betsy? It was a humiliating thought, but she owned it. She wanted Nick thinking of her—picturing her—whether he hooked up with the cute strawberry-blonde tonight or not. Which was why she'd kissed him. And wrong on so many levels.

She wasn't the jealous type. Never had been. And even if she were, there was no reason to be jealous of Betsy. Nick and Harper were nothing to each other. They wouldn't *be* anything.

Yet . . .

Was Betsy in his room tonight?

The stupid question wouldn't stop running through her head.

She checked the money left in her hand and made a last-minute decision to buy a bag of popcorn from the adjacent machine. There was a microwave in her room, and something told her this would be a long night with little sleep. Might as well be prepared.

After returning to her sister's room, she discovered Jewel tucked under the covers in bed, a cool cloth on her forehead, and no color in her face. Harper opened the drink and handed it over before digging out a sleeve of saltines from a plastic grocery bag. She'd made a dash to a local convenience store earlier in the evening for the crackers, and had logged a mental note not to travel with Jewel again without them.

"How are you feeling?" she asked softly. She sat on the edge of the bed, and handed over a cracker when a feeble hand reached out for one.

"Awful."

Harper didn't point out that Jewel probably looked even worse than she felt. "You think it's over this time?"

Tears suddenly streamed from the corners of Jewel's eyes.

"Oh, honey," Harper cooed. She scooted down on the bed and hugged her sister tight. "What can I do?"

"Nothing." Jewel sniffed. "I want Bobby."

"Of course you do."

Harper stroked her hand up and down Jewel's back, her fingers sliding over the cool nylon of the nightgown, and considered calling her brother-in-law. He'd come home if she asked him to. The man would do anything for his wife. But Harper just as quickly vetoed the idea. The notion of calling him was driven more from her own mental self-preservation than true need. Jewel might miss her husband and prefer him by her side at the moment, but she'd also be fine without him. Bobby was pursuing a dream that both he and Jewel were fully behind, and now was the time to do it. *Before* the baby arrived.

Therefore, Harper would stay put, she'd take care of her sister, and she'd do as she had for months. Ignore her own thoughts of grief.

Cracker crumbs scattered on the sheets, but instead of sweeping them off the bed, Harper lifted the covers and slid in underneath, where she held her sister even tighter. "You talked to him tonight, right? Did you tell him how bad your morning sickness is?"

Jewel snorted into Harper's chest. "You mean my all-day sickness?" She shook her head. "No." The barely whispered word made her sound so pitiful.

"Why not?"

"What good would it do? He'd want to be here for me."

"I know, but talking about it with him might help. That way it might *feel* like he's here."

"So you now think that talking helps?" Jewel looked up from her position tucked in tight against Harper, a knowing look in her eye, and unease swept through Harper. She'd declared for months that talking didn't help anything. Jewel had offered that very opportunity on numerous occasions. Their mother, too. Even their other two sisters and father had been willing to jump in with both feet.

Harper had turned each of them away.

She'd talked to no one. Because what could she possibly say?

"It's not the same," she mumbled. She tucked Jewel's face back to her chest.

"No, it isn't. I'm simply puking my guts up. And you—"

"Don't want to talk about it."

They both grew quiet, the only sounds in the room Jewel's soft breathing. Harper kept her gaze focused on the far wall, hot anger beginning to swirl in her belly. She not only didn't want to talk about it, she didn't want to think about it. Therefore, she allowed the only topic she'd found capable of taking her mind off of all things Thomas. *Nick Wilde.*

She replayed the moment her lips had connected with his. How soft his hair had been under her fingers. And the utter shock that had flashed through his eyes as he'd recognized what was about to happen.

She'd caught him off guard, and she'd liked that. It had given her a chance to feel less out of control than she'd been while standing there with inane jealousy rushing through her. She didn't like being out of control. But good Lord, that kiss. His mouth could be as addictive as his smile. As could his body—if the brief encounter she'd had with it was anything to go by.

One touch, and she could pinpoint its main attributes. Enticing. Habit-forming. And *hard*.

It had taken Nick several seconds to jump into the action himself, giving her a brief taste of all he might have to offer once he had, but uncertainty had eventually stopped her. One week ago she couldn't have imagined sleeping with a man other than her husband. As much as she hated the situation she now found herself in, she still loved Thomas. She always would. And though she didn't intend to go through the rest of her life in a nunlike state, it hadn't even been two years yet.

However, when she was around Nick . . .

She closed her eyes tight. She didn't just *want* to sleep with Nick. She'd developed a visceral desperation to do so. She'd thought about him for the remainder of the afternoon. Imagining his hands on her body. Her hands on his.

She'd sculpted every inch of him in her mind, and she would place bets as to what he'd feel like pushing inside her, his body swollen and hard with desire. He would make her forget. At least for a moment. And she would thoroughly enjoy the reprieve.

"I'm fine now."

Harper opened her eyes at her sister's words. "You're sure?"

"Positive." Jewel pushed at her. "And anyway, you're making me hot. I swear your body temperature just rose ten degrees. Go back to your own room."

Jewel flung the covers off and scooted to the middle of her bed, leaving Harper alone and suddenly lighthearted. Jewel was hot? Because *she'd* been thinking about Nick? Harper almost laughed.

That was likely exactly what had caused her external body temperature to rise. Because she'd definitely heated up on the inside from thinking about him.

After climbing from the bed, she tucked the top down on the pack of crackers and screwed the lid back onto Jewel's drink. She then turned out the lights and whispered good night. They'd considered staying in the same room, but Harper preferred her privacy. There were still too many nights when she didn't sleep well, and the last thing she wanted was to keep Jewel awake. Or have Jewel badgering her to *talk*. And now with Nick playing havoc with her mind, Harper was even more grateful for her own space.

She closed both doors between the two rooms, then leaned back against them and shut her eyes. And again pictured Nick naked. What was it with that man? What was it with *her*?

Grabbing her own soda, she rubbed the cool condensation against her neck and turned on the TV. If only it would be so simple to sleep with him. She could bask in an overload of feelings and wear herself out enough to sleep like the dead. And orgasms. Oh geez . . . orgasms. It had been so long, she'd almost forgotten what one felt like.

She'd bet Nick was the type to see that she got off before him, though. Maybe more than once.

Her pulse pounded in her neck. She freaking missed orgasms.

But the problem with all those feelings, and all that sleeping like the dead was . . . what feelings would she experience afterward?

Satisfaction? Guilt?

Disgust?

She shook her head and unscrewed the cap on her drink. It would be best to keep Nick at a distance until she had some answers. Until she could ensure she'd wake up the next morning with no regrets.

Taking a long gulp, and with a firm decision made, she kicked off her boots and shrugged out of her hoodie. Then she flipped through the channels and set her mind to *not* giving a certain cowboy any additional thought. Instead, she'd find a gory, hopefully B-rated movie to watch, and indulge in some buttery goodness.

With her plan in mind, she put the popcorn in the microwave, and located a bad but exactly-what-she-wanted '80s horror flick. When the popping stopped, she turned out all the lights and settled in against the headboard to watch. And just as a skewer was jabbed through the eye of the movie's first victim, a knock sounded softly at her door.

Chapter Six

T he door cracked opened three narrow inches in front of him, and the first thing to register was the scream in the background. Nick's eyes widened in question.

"Horror movie," Harper said. She licked her lips before doing the same to her fingers, and Nick picked up on the smell of butter.

"With popcorn?"

"Of course."

The door remained open only a sliver of space, telling him he should turn and walk away. She didn't want him here. Instead, he held up two beers. "Need something to drink with the popcorn?"

She eyed the offering, and he would have bet money she'd pass on the opportunity, but one arm snaked out of the darkness, and, after twisting off the cap, she drank half the bottle.

Another scream sounded as light flickered in the room behind her, and she peeked back. He could tell by her total absorption in staring across the room that she'd immediately gotten sucked in to whatever was happening on the television screen. And he had a sudden urge to see the movie himself.

"Want company?" he asked.

Harper turned back to him. The look on her face said that she could see through him as easily as a sheet of glass. "What are you doing here, Nick?"

I was hoping you might want to finish that kiss.

Instead of answering, he gulped.

Harper turned up her beer again, eyeing him from beneath lowered lids as she drained the bottle. He couldn't have spoken at that moment if he'd wanted to. He was too transfixed by watching her drink. The woman could make any action sexy.

When the bottle was empty, she wiped her mouth, narrowed her eyes on him, then gave a single nod and stepped back. She pushed the door open and motioned with her head for him to come inside. "I suppose you're here to ask what that kiss was about?"

The lady got right to the point. "I"—he shrugged, trying to look casual—"actually just thought you might want some company. And beer."

She guffawed at his attempted diversion, and moved away. She muted the television and turned on a lamp, then swiped at a spray of popcorn on the bed, raking it into a pile in the middle of the bedspread before scooping it up with both hands.

"Messy eater," Nick observed from behind her.

"Your knock came at an inopportune time," she replied. She dumped the popcorn into a wastebasket and dusted off her hands. "Scared the shit out of me, actually." When she faced him again, she crossed her arms just beneath her breasts and jutted one hip out to the side. She gave him a pointed look, as if to say, *Get on with it, little boy. Let's talk about that kiss and be done with it.*

But again, no words would come. Instead, his gaze went into motion, traveling over her shoulders and biceps. He'd known she was toned before. That was obvious in her moves as well as the fit of her clothes. But until this moment, he hadn't seen her in anything that *fit* quite the way her T-shirt did. It was thin, its sleeves a couple of inches shorter than the standard "short sleeve," and it seemed to be made up of at least a small percentage of spandex. The pale-pink shirt wasn't so tight that it couldn't be worn in public, but it *was* tight enough that he noticed she wasn't only trim and in great shape. She was ripped.

"What do you do for a workout?" he asked.

Her chin angled down, even as her eyes looked up at him. "Really? You're here in my room at close to midnight. Uninvited, I might add. *After* I knocked your socks off with a kiss. And you want to talk about my exercise regime?"

"Okay." He dared her with his return look. If she wanted to get right to the point, he'd go there. "Then let's talk about the kiss." And while he was at it, he'd back her against the wall and *show* her what it meant to knock someone's socks off. He took another step toward her.

But instead of replying, Harper disappeared into the bathroom.

The door closed behind her, and the space went deathly silent, and in the next instant Nick let out a ragged breath and asked himself what kind of fool he was. He could be hooking up with Betsy or any number of other women there tonight. Women who would *love* to spend time with him.

Or he could be asleep. A good night's rest certainly wouldn't hurt since he'd had a poor showing that evening. He had a lot of ground to make up tomorrow.

Yet what he was doing instead was standing in the middle of his pubescent crush's motel room, letting her taunt him as she'd always done—while ridiculously hoping that she might kiss him just one more time.

He laughed at himself. Would he never quit crushing on this woman?

He should have stuck with the original plan of being her friend only. He turned his back to the still-closed bathroom door and moved to the window. The curtains were pulled tight, so he opened them before removing the cap to his beer. The light outside the motel's office showed an empty parking lot and highlighted the closed and dark café across the street. Everyone was tucked away in their rooms for the night. Which was where he should be.

The water came on in the bathroom behind him, and he tilted up his beer, trying *not* to imagine what Harper might be doing inside that room. He was an idiot. Because the one thing he should not have done tonight was let his dick lead him straight to Harper.

Harper stood in front of the mirror, water running into the sink, and stared at her overheated face. Her breaths had grown shallow as her thoughts fought to be heard. The minute she'd opened the door to Nick, her innermost secrets had demanded to be the center of attention. At first there'd been only whispers of things she could do to Nick. That Nick could do to her. But then naughty visions of those exact scenarios began playing out for her to see. Her naked. Nick naked.

And neither of them remaining separate from the other.

She gulped as she once again imagined the man in her bedroom with no clothes on, and she splashed water on her cheeks. Its startling coolness seemed to sizzle on contact.

Then she asked herself if she could really do it? If she *should* do it? Because, oh, she so wanted to.

She pulled her shirt over her head and took off her bra, and simply stared at her reflection. She'd been so alone since Thomas had left. So sad and angry. And damn, but she'd hurt. She dropped the clothing at her feet and studied her body. She was fit, with few extra curves, but that lack had never bothered Thomas. In fact, he'd liked it.

She lifted her hands, bringing her palms to her breasts, and sucking in a sharp breath at the contact. It had been far too long since she'd been touched.

Her nipples pebbled, scratching at her skin, and she gently squeezed herself. And with the pressure, she closed her eyes at the immediate flood of sensations. She may have just been thinking of her husband, but the only thing in the world she could focus on in that moment was Nick. And how she wanted nothing more than his hands replacing hers.

She needed to feel again. Something more than hurt. And she needed to do that tonight.

With no additional thought, she added her jeans and panties to the pile at her feet and she exited the small bathroom. It didn't take but a second for Nick to turn from the window, and when he did, Harper took note of the quick change from normal, casual movement to every single muscle inside him tensing up. His beer hovered halfway to his mouth, and his eyes didn't blink.

"Is this why you showed up at my door?" she asked.

Finally, something about him moved—he gulped. She saw the movement in his throat from across the room, and that simple token of nervousness managed to evaporate her tension over what she was about to do.

"Close the curtains, Nick." She began to move toward him. "We don't need anyone watching us tonight."

"This isn't why I came over here."

Her feet stalled at his choked-out words, and her nerves flared. Had she been wrong? "You want me to put my clothes back on?"

"No." The answer came fast and strained. Then he fumbled to set his beer on the bedside table, sloshing out several drops before righting it, while never once taking his eyes off her. When he subsequently reached blindly behind him, tugging at the curtains one-handed, her nerves subsided. He looked ridiculous. Like the kid who'd once wanted her but had been too young to know how to handle it. His Adam's apple rose and fell once again.

"Then what do you want?" she asked softly. She forced her fear back behind her boldness.

"I . . ." His words trailed off as she again began moving. This time she didn't stop until she stood directly in front of him.

"Turn off the light," she commanded.

One hand reached out and flipped off the lamp, and the room went dark except for the flash of the muted horror movie continuing to play out behind her.

"Now put your hands on me."

When he didn't immediately move, she ignored the voice telling her this was her out. That she could change her mind and walk away, no harm done. Because she didn't want to change her mind and walk away. She might regret it in the morning, but at that moment, regret was the last word on her mind. So she reached for Nick.

She covered her body with his hands, his palms fully encasing both her breasts, and the skin-on-skin contact shut down her ability to breathe. When she realized she'd also closed her eyes, she forced them open. She didn't want to miss a moment of this. And what she found when she once again looked at Nick was his dark, unwavering gaze.

He shifted slightly, lowering his hands just enough so that his palms cupped the undersides of each breast a bit more fully. More possessively. And when he squeezed, his eyes still glued to hers, she felt the imprint of ten long strokes of heat where his fingers imprisoned her.

She bit back a groan as her entire body began to shimmer with need.

"You're sure about this?" he asked.

"Positive." *Almost.*

His head nodded almost imperceptibly, and his eyes dipped, taking in her naked body. His fingers kneaded her as he drank his fill, and when he dragged his gaze back up the length of her, she watched his chest rise and fall with each of his breaths. "I did come over with the intention of kissing you," he confessed. "Or, at least trying to." His eyes flitted over her again, as if they had a mind of their own. "I will admit that much. But I swear I didn't plan to push for anything more."

She smiled softly and lifted her fingers to his plaid shirt. "Then it's a good thing I made that push for you." But when his thumbs began to flick over her turgid nipples, she expelled a burst of air from between her lips. "But you better tell me you have a condom somewhere on your body."

"I have a condom somewhere on my body."

And with those eight words, Nick lost both hesitancy and shock. His mouth came down hard, his tongue parting her lips with the assurance of a man who knew how to move this evening toward a grand finale, and his hands sought out the contours of her butt. He tested the lower curve of her cheeks in his palms, a groan ripping from the back of his throat, then jerked her forward, bringing her into full contact with his body. Her own moan joined his.

"You're wearing too many clothes," she whispered.

"Then take them off me."

She didn't have to be told twice. She ripped open the buttons of his shirt, her fingers flying over the material, while he continued a more leisurely tour of her backside. Once his skin was exposed, she thrust her hands inside the shirt and flattened her chest to his. A shiver wracked her body. His mouth latched onto the curve of her neck, nibbling, and he began inching her backward.

She allowed him do whatever he wanted, barely conscious of his movements, while she focused solely on one thing. Touch. He was a symphony of textures. Hot, tight skin beneath the pads of her fingers, scratchy hair teasing at her nipples. The cool metal of his belt buckle pressing into her belly, and the soft rub of worn denim sliding along her thighs.

When he palmed her butt and urged her upward, she lifted both legs and let him fit her to the hardness behind the zipper of his jeans. Her fingers shook as she shifted her hands to his belt buckle, ready to uncover all the treasures he held dear. She tugged, trying to free his belt, but progress quickly slowed. Because while she tried to remain on task, he'd started something new. His hands gripped her with clear determination, the fullest part of her rear filling his palms and his fingertips meeting in the middle. They dug deep into her soft flesh.

Then with a fast squeeze, he angled her slightly down and away.

"Oh, sheesh." She sucked in a breath. His move had dragged her swollen, sensitive flesh over the denim. Her body throbbed.

When he loosened his grip, she immediately thrust forward, grinding onto the ridge of his jeans. Her breath hitched. Then his knees bumped into the side of the bed, and the thought that he would put her down—disconnect her body from his—pulled a strangled whimper from her lips.

"Please," she begged. She was panting now.

He didn't lay her down, though. Instead he gripped and tipped her away from him once again, then reconnected her to his front. Each of her bumps against his body was accompanied by a small thrust of his own.

The movements were subtle, but they were enough to drive her mad. Back and forth. Over and over.

He kept it up, and her whimpers increased. He wouldn't let her stay connected to him long enough to send her over the edge, but taunted her with all the different sensations instead. With each tiny thrust.

"Please," she begged again. Her body was tight now. Ready to fly.

"Come for me." His words were a whisper against her shoulder as he continued pumping her. His lips grazed over her skin.

"I can't . . ." She twitched in his hands.

"You can." He angled her away again. "You *will*."

She grabbed frantically at his shoulders, hoping to still his motions and control the game. But when his mouth shifted and his teeth bit into the flesh just above one breast, her entire body arched. She began to shake.

He ducked his head and caught a nipple between his lips, and the shock of the touch had her shouting out. Her head dropped back. And she handed over complete surrender to Nick. His move had been the final push she'd needed. She was connected solidly with the denim now, and she ground herself tight.

"Come," his demanded hoarsely. Then his lips sucked her hard, pulling urgently at her breast, and she had no choice. She did exactly as he'd asked.

The orgasm didn't start slow. It immediately engulfed her, licking at her entire body with flames. Her thighs clenched, and her eyes rolled back in her head. Control was a thing of the past as spasms vibrated through her, almost to the point of pain.

Only, it wasn't pain she felt tonight. And she didn't want to ever stop feeling it.

After what seemed like forever, when her body finally calmed, her hands dropped to her sides, and her forehead landed on Nick's shoulder. She was drained. And only after her breaths began to slow did she once again become aware of her surroundings, realizing that she'd not even managed to get one piece of clothing off his body. But she wasn't about to apologize for her failure. She'd needed this. And danged, but he'd delivered.

"You okay?" he asked. His words whispered across her ear, and her body shivered.

"Maybe," she murmured.

He chuckled. "Ready for me to put you on the bed?"

Honestly, she wanted to stay right where she was for a while longer. She liked the feel of his arms holding her. They were really strong. But she didn't say any of that. Instead, she nodded, and only after he'd tugged the covers back and gently settled her head on her pillow, did she finally lift her gaze.

His brows inched up. He was asking if he could join her. Or if she'd had enough.

She hadn't had nearly enough. "Take off your clothes."

Her throaty words were all he needed. The heat in his eyes turned to cinders, and in thirty seconds he was naked from head to toe. But when he put one knee on the bed at her side, she stopped him with a lifted palm. He groaned, but he didn't finish climbing in with her. He stayed right where he was, his body inches away. So she took a really long, fascinated stare.

He was hard all over, his muscles well defined, with little body fat anywhere. Clearly he worked out. Often. And the highlight of his body—the really amazing area that she'd just rubbed herself all over—was thick. And not shy. It jutted right at her. So she slid a hand over him.

"Harper," Nick warned. His hips clenched, thrusting him farther into her grip.

"You're big," she noted.

Masculine pride flashed in his eyes.

"And I'll bet you're good at this," she went on. The line of his mouth remained flat as she spoke, his eyes carefully watching her again. She was stalling, but only for a minute. Only long enough to let her mind catch up with her body.

It had been a really long time since she'd done this. Understandably, she was a little nervous. As well as fascinated.

And also angry.

She'd never wanted to sleep with anyone but Thomas.

She stroked her hand to the base of Nick and back up, shoving her husband from her mind. Then she repeated her action a second time. The third sweep of her grip up to the head of Nick's penis had her fingers squeezing harder, and a tiny bead of moisture appeared on the tip. So she leaned in.

He remained in her hand, so she felt him tense. At the same time, his breaths shortened. Peering up from her intimate position, she thrilled at the look of pleading on his face. And finally, she felt back in control.

She stuck her tongue out and touched him, and his body jerked. Then without further hesitation, she fit her lips around his head and his hands came down on her shoulders. His fingers dug in hard, and a heavy grunt hit her ears. And after a few seconds of simply absorbing—the way her mouth stretched around him, the feel of his blood pumping so close to the skin—Harper finally began to move. She took him deeper into her mouth, sliding her lips and hands up and down the length of him together, while her tongue played its own game over the heated flesh.

She worked him for several minutes, finding her own thrill as long-ago techniques came back. Then she slid both palms to his butt and gripped, and pulled him tight to her. He was large in her mouth, but she didn't shy away. It was too damned exhilarating just to be doing this.

When she finally broke for a breath, easing her mouth slowly off him, she intended to mutter something clever and teasing, but was caught by surprise instead. Nick's face was suddenly in front of hers, his thumb and forefinger gripping her chin. Then he was punishing her mouth with his.

There was no playing in him now. He demanded her obedience, and in one smooth move, his body covered hers.

Within seconds, Nick had the promised condom on and had lifted slightly off her. He stared down, his eyes blazing, but seeming to ask for permission one last time. She gave it with a nod, and his thighs wasted no time nudging hers apart. He positioned himself at her opening, and though she had one tiny second of panic at the thought of what she was about to do, she didn't change course. She merely closed her eyes so Nick wouldn't see, and pulled his mouth back down to hers. He pushed inside her.

The feel of him was intense and heady, and a darned-near out-of-body experience. Their breaths mingled, and their bodies fit together with not a single breath of air between them. And Nick felt right inside of her.

Chapter Seven

It took more than a few minutes before Nick's breathing allowed speech again. While he waited, he kept his eyes closed and noted several key facts.

First, the television was still on. The movie had flashed in silence as they'd come together. It had been fascinating to watch her reach orgasm in the strobe-light effect.

Additionally, since they'd finished, Harper hadn't uttered a sound.

Nick swallowed a bout of nerves as the final observation hit his consciousness. She remained beside him, but she lay completely still. No part of her touched any part of him.

Had they just made a mistake?

And if so, what was he supposed to say to make it better now?

This wasn't how his "after" usually played out, so he decided that until proven otherwise, he'd go with the theory that Harper was simply not a cuddler. Hopefully her stillness was par for the course.

"Did you have sex with Betsy before coming over here?"

His eyes popped open. "What?" he snapped. He gaped at her. "Of course not."

"Okay." She looked neither upset nor relieved. "I was just checking."

And he was just pissed.

He rolled to his elbow and frowned when she closed her eyes. "Harper," he said.

She didn't reply. Nor did she open her eyes. So he brought her face around to his. When she still didn't look at him, he continued to glare at her, hoping the look would somehow burn its way through her eyelids. It took a moment, but his determination paid off. She finally peeked at him, and he could tell by her now-smug expression that she was going for a superior look, trying to play off the moment with humor. But he wasn't laughing.

"Why would you think that?"

Her smugness faltered, uncertainty replacing the self-assured, bold woman he knew her to be. "She was just . . . And you were . . ." She shrugged. "Not that it would matter either way. You can do whatever you want."

"Of course I can. But do you really think *that's* what I would do?"

"I don't really know you, Nick." Her words were soft spoken, and the honesty in them immediately drained him of anger. She was right. Neither of them knew much about the other.

"Well, that's one thing you now know." He gentled his words. "I wouldn't do that. To anyone."

She licked her lips, relief flashing through her eyes.

And he suddenly wondered who she really was if that kind of vulnerability lived inside her. He told himself to return to his side of the bed. To resume their post-sex non-cuddling. To not make more of the moment than it was. But he didn't want to roll away from her. Especially not with that slight look of uncertainty still lingering on her face. So he kissed her again.

He could still taste the mix of beer and popcorn on her lips, and when he pulled back, she was looking at him. The vulnerability had disappeared, but the moment remained heavy.

At a loss for what to do next, he fell back on his old standby. Charm.

He gave her a knowing smile, and he picked up her hand and turned it over. He pressed his mouth to the inside of her wrist and inhaled. As she had earlier in the day, she smelled like baby powder. "I had an amazing time," he murmured. He watched her as he began to nip along her forearm, noting that she wasn't immune to his touch. A renewed flare of heat began to burn behind her eyes. He liked that.

He worked his way toward her inner elbow, enjoying the slide of smooth skin beneath his lips. He hadn't brought it up, but he also had a second condom tucked away in his wallet.

"I hope it was fun for you, too," he said. He tugged at the sheet she'd pulled up over her, inching it down just enough to expose the top curves of her breasts. He hadn't had nearly enough time exploring those.

He gave one more tug, and one dusty-rose nipple popped free. His mouth watered.

"I definitely had fun," she agreed. Her gaze swept down to his mouth. "But . . ."

He froze. He hated that word. "But what?"

She paused for a second, her eyes steady on his, as if trying to decide whether to say what was on her mind or not. Then she glanced toward the door, and he got it.

"But you want me to go?" He sighed.

She offered a tight smile. "Will you hate me if I say yes?"

"Of course not."

He didn't waste any time rising and reaching for his jeans. He'd been right before. He shouldn't have shown up there tonight. Sex hadn't been what she'd needed. He'd known that. Hadn't he told himself that very thing with every step he'd made from his room to hers?

He could kick himself for forgetting. However, no judge, whether moral or judicial, would find him guilty for sticking around after she'd come out of her bathroom the way she had.

He fastened his jeans and took a moment longer than necessary to shrug into his shirt. He didn't look at her as he dressed; he needed to get his thoughts together first. He wasn't mad—he'd never be mad because a woman asked him to leave. But he was disappointed. Mostly in himself. He shouldn't have let this go so far.

But he was also asking himself: *What the hell?*

As the last whirl of the helicopter blades came to a stop, Harper found herself going as motionless as everything around her. She'd just arrived home after dropping the corporate execs back at the Missoula airport. And though there were still several hours of daylight ahead of her, she had no additional flights scheduled, nor did she want any.

What she wanted was to crawl into her own bed and forget. Or maybe relive.

Sex with Nick had been off the charts.

Only . . . she'd had *sex* with *Nick.*

The thoughts were conflicting, and each had been battling to be heard since she'd kicked him out of her motel room Friday night. She'd managed to make it all the way through Saturday without getting caught alone with him, then she and Jewel had driven back immediately after the last bull-riding event. Harper had stayed over at Jewel's last night, both because they'd gotten in so late and because Jewel had once again been sick. Yet through every minute that had passed the remainder of the weekend, even with everything she'd had going on, her head had continuously carried out the fight.

Sex with Nick had been off the charts.

She'd had *sex* with *Nick.*

Was she supposed to be thrilled or feel guilty? And if guilty . . . should it be directed toward Thomas? Or Nick? Or herself?

She suddenly felt antsy and forced herself to exit the aircraft and head toward her house. She was on the back side of her property, land spread out in every direction, with her enormous two-story home sitting directly in front of her. Thomas had not only taken a chunk of his trust the minute he'd gained full access to it and bought them a souped-up helicopter, but he'd also had a huge house built for them. He'd even poured a helicopter pad in their backyard. They'd had everything they would ever need here.

She focused straight ahead as she kept her feet moving. She lived on the west side of the lake, and the property sat high enough that even though she was several miles from the shoreline, she had a view all the way across the water. And as she'd done at the end of every flight since Thomas had died, she looked beyond the lake, across to where Birch Bay was nestled snugly among the pines and birches . . . and felt even more alone than she was.

Entering the house through the back door, she pulled out her cell and checked for messages. There were three. She didn't advertise regular business hours and rarely bothered answering her phone when working.

"Hello," a male voice said after she hit the button to play the messages. "I was told that you don't have a problem taking people to the top of Mount Cleveland."

Nope. She didn't have a problem doing anything.

"If that's the case. My girlfriend and I"—the owner of the voice cleared his throat and then lowered his voice—"I want to propose to my girlfriend. She loves to hike Glacier, so I want to take her to the top."

Harper's heart squeezed. Proposals were both her favorite and the most bittersweet.

The caller left his number, and Harper listened to the remaining two messages, both of them inquiring about chartering a personalized tour of the area. She wrote down all the numbers and decided to fix herself a late lunch. She'd taken a snack with her when she'd headed out to pick up her passengers that morning but hadn't been in the mood to eat when lunchtime had rolled around. How could she eat when her insides were in turmoil?

But the funny thing was, the turmoil hadn't shown up in the form she'd expected.

Immediately after sleeping with Nick, she'd been overwhelmed by what she'd done. She'd expected that. It was her first and only time with another man, after all. But she'd also been bowled over by how much she'd enjoyed it. And she had *not* expected that. Not because she'd doubted Nick's skill, but for the pure fact that he wasn't Thomas. It had never once crossed her mind that another man's touch could make her feel anything similar to Thomas's.

Therefore, she'd kicked Nick out. And had felt a little bad about it ever since.

She smiled at the memory as she stood at the sink and rinsed off lettuce and spinach to go on a sandwich. She'd caught him off guard again. That time, not in a good way. She'd instigated the entire thing, had been a full participant, and she'd gotten way more than she'd ever hoped for. Yet the minute it had been over, the thought of touching him—of snuggling up to him—had terrified her.

Her sending him away had hurt his feelings, she knew. Though he'd assured her that leaving was perfectly fine. *He slept better alone, after all.*

But she hadn't bought it. It had bothered him how she'd changed course so quickly. And the truth was, it bothered her, too. But she'd needed to be alone in that moment. It had all been too much. He'd made her feel and need and want *so* much. Way more than one night in bed with him could ever provide. But the worst part had been that she'd wanted to curl into him in the aftermath. Just let him hold her. Only, if he'd held her . . .

She blew out a harsh breath. If Nick had held her after showing such tenderness and concern before he'd even touched her, she feared she would've fallen apart.

Ditching the idea of food, she moved to the living room and turned on the TV. There was little she ever watched with interest—mostly it was about having noise in the house—so she dropped to the couch and started flipping through channels. She stopped when she got to a commercial that caught her attention. It was the one featuring Nick.

She sat up straighter as his face filled the seventy-inch screen. He was wearing that smile he was so good at. Then the camera panned back, and she trailed down over the rest of him. His thumbs were tucked securely behind a championship belt buckle, dark-washed jeans hugged every inch of his lower body, and his cowboy hat was pushed slightly off his forehead. Not the tugged-low way he wore it when standing off to the side watching his competitors.

The entire package had her drooling.

And wasn't that something? She'd seen this commercial many times before, but she'd barely paid attention. She'd known who Nick was, of course—her younger sister's long-ago friend. Therefore, the extent of her thoughts before today had been happiness that he'd done well for himself.

The commercial ended and she hit rewind, backing it up so she could watch again. She'd slept with a man that wasn't her husband. And she'd really, really enjoyed it. And she should probably feel guilty about that.

Only, she didn't *want* to feel guilt. Not about any of it.

Was spending one evening having a good time such a bad thing? Because if she could have a redo . . . she would re*do*. Everything. Exactly as she had Friday night.

She shook her head as she sat there, making up her mind based on facts. *No.* She would not have guilt. Not over this. If Thomas had been here, she wouldn't even be in a position to do anything to feel guilty about. But even more telling—and this was where she kept landing—for the first time since waking up in the hospital and realizing that her world was no longer her world, she'd taken a step forward.

The commercial ended again, and she hit "Mute." She brought her cell phone up and scrolled through the contacts until she found the number Nick had entered the first day she'd given him a lift.

Nick.

He hadn't even bothered with his last name. She tapped the screen to bring up the number, thinking about why he'd given it to her. He'd offered to be someone she could talk to.

Of course, he'd been attracted to her, too. She'd known that. But she didn't think that had been the full impetus for the phone number. He'd genuinely come across as if he'd be an impartial ear if she ever needed one. And hadn't she already shared things with him? She'd talked about Thomas at his house the other day. A conversation that had felt right.

But did she want to share more? To try to get past this wall she was stuck behind?

Or did she just want more sex?

Her heart rate picked up at the thought of letting someone in, either physically or mentally. She liked to claim that she could handle everything on her own. That help was the last thing she needed. But eighteen months had passed, and until Friday night she'd been in the exact same spot she'd been since the accident. And even in her messed-up state, she could admit that *that* was not a good place to linger.

She studied the phone number for a minute longer before clearing the screen and setting her cell down. Then she opened the drawer of the end table. There was one picture of Thomas she hadn't packed away, and she kept it there. She hadn't looked at it since tucking it inside, but she took it out now, still in its black matte frame. Thomas stood beside her in the picture, his arm around her shoulders, both of them beaming with pride. Their helicopter sat immediately behind them. They'd just returned from their first search and rescue mission. They hadn't located the missing hikers themselves, but they'd played a part in the couple's lives being saved. And that had been the key. They'd been following their dreams. Together. They'd been unstoppable.

She glanced out the back door to where the aircraft sat waiting in the distance, its red-and-white colors a sharp contrast against the green of the emerging foliage. The sun glinted off the windshield, as if it were winking at her. Or maybe it was asking why she'd changed. She still took it up most days. That wouldn't alter; she loved to fly too much. No one would take that away from her.

But she *hadn't* participated in an SAR mission since losing Thomas. And the blame for that one was on him.

For the two days since returning from Great Falls, Nick had gotten up early to get in a ninety-minute workout at the local gym, had showered, eaten breakfast, and had taken care of whatever needed to be seen to on the farm that day. He'd then driven into town for a late lunch. Afterward, he'd returned home and either walked the empty halls of the house or found himself sitting on the boat dock "contemplating." And what he'd ended up contemplating, every single time, had been Harper.

He hadn't heard from her since he'd left her room Friday night.

He wasn't worried that something might be wrong with her, because honestly, she was the most self-sufficient woman he'd ever met. She could handle herself just fine. But he *was* still concerned, seeing as she'd run in the opposite direction any time she'd caught sight of him Saturday.

What did she think? That he'd rush over and demand a do-over?

Or was her avoidance more in line with what he kept telling himself? That she hadn't needed sex. That his sleeping with her had possibly hurt more than helped.

That she regretted the act.

Up until the moment, he'd been wondering if she'd been with anyone since losing her husband. Then she'd come out of her bathroom, and he'd convinced himself that she had. That sleeping with others wasn't an odd occurrence for her. However, her behavior afterward—her closing herself off and kicking him out—had told a different story. Yet, she'd slept with him.

Why?

And why did he keep replaying those few seconds before she'd taken him into her mouth, and asking himself if he'd really seen a flash of anger at that point?

He dragged a hand over his face and shut down the accounting files he was once again sorting through. He should have stopped it. Should have walked out. And he shouldn't have let her get away with ignoring him the next day.

It ripped him apart to think that she'd been sitting around all weekend regretting being with him.

With an irritated grunt, he pulled out his cell and found her number. He'd gotten it when she'd flown him back to get his truck. He pressed "Send" before he changed his mind, and after four rings, Harper's voice came on the line. It was a business greeting. With mounting frustration, he tossed the phone onto the desk and stood to pace the room. When the phone began to chirp two minutes later, he raced back to get it.

"Hello." He held his breath.

"I saw that you called." Harper's voice came out timid. Which kicked him in the back of the knees.

"Do you regret it?" he blurted out. Then he closed his eyes in disgust. He sounded so needy. "I just mean, we didn't do anything wrong. You know that, right? I know you—" He stopped the words, not wanting to presume he knew how she felt. "I'm pretty sure this was the first time for you," he said instead. "*Since.* And I—"

"I'm fine," she interrupted.

He waited. Her words had been too clipped.

When she didn't say anything else, he pressed on. "I think we should talk."

"We don't need to talk. And no, I don't regret it."

"Good. Because you shouldn't." He wanted to point out that the way she'd run him from her room implied otherwise. And the way she'd avoided him the following day had only backed it up. But he kept the words to himself. He paced to the far wall, stopping in front of the framed college degrees earned by each of his siblings. His sister had hung those in here. The study had always been the one room holding less of his mother's presence and more of the rest of them.

He eyed each document—six kids, five degrees—and at Harper's continued silence, kept his mouth firmly closed, determined for her to be the next one to speak.

Only, instead of words, a soft sigh finally sounded in his ear. That was close enough.

"Let me take you out," he suggested.

"I don't want to go on a date, Nick."

"I don't mean a date. Just out. Just fun." He waited two seconds before pushing ahead with the idea. "Come on. I'm stuck here on the farm by myself every day. Help a man out." He smiled, hoping she could feel it. "I know you're adventurous. How about bungee jumping?"

He hadn't bungee jumped in years, and wasn't sure there was even a place around that still did it.

"I don't—"

"Ice climbing?" he interrupted. "There's still enough ice on the higher peaks." Now that he'd had the idea, he wouldn't let it go. He wanted to spend time with her. "Name your poison. I know you want to. Bull riding? You really should prove to me that you can stay on for eight seconds, you know? I'm not saying you lied, but . . ."

"I didn't lie."

"Then prove it." He smiled again.

"No."

He didn't let her rejection deter him. "Sky diving?"

Dead silence hit the space between them, and he felt immediately ill. "Harper." The heat of horror filled him. That's how her husband had died. He thumped his head against the wall. "I'm so sorry. I didn't thi—"

"BASE jumping." All emotion disappeared from her voice. "I have a free day tomorrow."

"BASE jumping?" Crap. He wasn't actually sure *he* had the balls for that. He'd hang glided plenty of times, had even cliff dived. Once. But he'd yet to have the desire to jump off a tall structure with nothing but a wind suit to get him down.

"Unless you're too scared," she taunted. Her words landed hard. Not teasing like he was used to.

"I'm not too scared," he began slowly. Would he have to BASE jump to make up for reminding her of the accident with Thomas? "Harper, really. I'm sorry. I didn't mean to—"

"Lucky for you there're no legal places to jump nearby," she interrupted. "And I'm not in the mood to fly to Idaho and back tomorrow." She chuckled, but the sound fell flat. "Therefore, your little-boy fear can rest safely and comfortably for the time being. But if we're going to do something," she continued, and finally the hard edge to her voice broke, "then I want to break a sweat. How about rock climbing?"

"Deal," he agreed before she could change her mind.

"I have all the equipment we'll need."

"Even better. So tomorrow, then? You and me."

She went silent once more, and he held his breath. Waiting. He knew his faux pas had hurt her. He would do anything to take it back.

"Tomorrow," she agreed. "But it is *not* a date. It's two friends hanging out."

"Hey, wasn't friendship all I requested to begin with?"

"Not a date," she repeated.

"Agreed." Friendship was a better plan, anyway. "Can I pick you up?"

"I'll come to your house."

She named a time and he agreed. "I'll see you then."

After they hung up, he once again paced the length of the room. It wasn't a date—he was in complete agreement on that. But that didn't keep him from reliving his body stretched out alongside hers. His body entering hers.

Good Lord, she'd been magnificent.

It might have been a onetime thing, but it was one time he'd never forget.

A car pulled up outside, interrupting his visual of Harper's lean body striding across the room toward him, and when he glanced out the windows, he saw that it was his sister. He'd talked to Dani a couple of times since he'd been home, but she'd been heavily involved in a work project and hadn't had the time to meet up.

After she exited her car, she went around to the other side and opened the back door, and a thrill rushed through Nick. She'd brought her stepdaughter with her. Haley was great. Nick had met the five-year-old last summer when she'd stayed here at the house, then he'd spent additional time with her over the holidays after her father and Dani had gotten together. And he'd totally fallen in love with the little girl.

He headed out to greet them. With a non-date with Harper lined up for tomorrow, and hopefully a fun afternoon with Dani and Haley today, his boredom was suddenly taking a backseat.

Chapter Eight

It was late the following afternoon, and Nick found himself sweating, starving, and feeling more than a little worse for wear, yet Harper—who was about sixty-five feet up from him and currently swinging by one hand out over a steep drop—looked as if they'd only just started their day. The woman was a machine.

Her left hand made contact with the rock she'd been reaching for, which was immediately followed by her foot arching through the air and landing right beside her fingers. She scaled the side of the canyon like a freaking monkey, and Nick had to admit that he was impressed—though he'd also been stripped of air more than once during the day. She was too risky. Of course, when he'd mentioned that *maybe* she could plant an anchor a bit closer than every twenty feet, or that she could, just once, take the more traveled route instead of scaling the steepest part of the canyon face, she'd scoffed.

But he was right. She was pushing limits for no good reason.

He wiped sweat from his brow as he pulled his gaze back from her leggings-clad legs, and he once again set himself into motion. He'd stopped to catch his breath on a barely there ledge, but with the two of them attached, he knew she'd soon be tossing out taunts if his inaction held her up.

After progressing another twenty-five feet, he had the sudden sensation of being watched, and he looked up. Though he couldn't make out her features due to the brightness of the sky behind her, he *could* tell that she had her eyes on him.

"You tired yet?" she shouted down.

He'd gotten there two hours ago. "Not even close."

She laughed and turned one hand loose, letting her body hang in midair, and Nick refocused on the rock in front of him. He began to climb again, reminding himself that she was safe. Relatively. She was harnessed in, and he'd seen the protection point she'd planted right beside her hip. If her hand slipped off the rock at that very moment, she wouldn't go far. Pretty much the distance of the slack in the rope between them. And as the second climber, he'd seen to it that the slack remained short.

He gritted his teeth as he swung out himself, similarly to how she'd done earlier, then grunted as his body made contact with more of the rock than he'd intended. It had definitely been too long since he'd done this.

Again, a light trill of laughter rained down from above.

Hanging by his fingers and the toes of a pair of Nate's climbing shoes Nick had found at the house, he once again looked up. Harper had stopped just above where she'd been the last time he'd seen her, putting the two of them closer together than he'd expected. He squinted into the light. "You think you're tougher than me, do you?"

She gave him a sexy smirk. "I do think I'm pretty tough."

And she definitely was.

He continued his climb, encouraged to up the speed when he realized she'd found a decent resting spot and was waiting on him. When he finally crested the ridge, he was out of breath and he couldn't hide it, but there was no way he'd admit the level of pleading the muscles in his arms and shoulders were doing, begging for him to stop.

"You're definitely tough," he told her as he hoisted himself over the edge. She stood several feet back, one spandex-covered arm gripping the trunk of a small tree protruding from the rock above her head and her gear and dangling from her harness. She looked completely in her element. He dropped to the ground with an exhausted sigh and bumped his head against the rock behind him. "But I'm tougher," he finished on a whisper.

And as he'd hoped, her laughter filled the air. Today had been good for her. She'd smiled and laughed a lot, and he'd not once seen anything more focused than a look of determination pass through her eyes.

"I'll pretend you didn't just say that to me while you're sitting at my feet." Her statement was followed by the sound of a zipper, and Nick cracked open his now-closed eyes. A protein bar appeared in his face.

With a grunt of thanks, he took it.

She pulled out another and lowered to sit beside him, and as she leaned back, he heard a soft grunt of her own. And this time, it was him that chuckled.

"You hide it well, don't you?"

"Hide what?" She closed her eyes and lifted her face to the sun.

"The fact that you're probably as exhausted as I am. You'd rather pretend you could keep going without a break."

"I could keep going without a break."

He eyed her. "So this stop is all for me?"

She turned to him then, and her hazel gaze locked onto his. He had no clue what thoughts ran through her head. Finally, she looked away and broke off a chunk off her bar. "I could use something to eat," she explained. "And this is a good spot."

He didn't laugh at her refusal to admit she'd been caught. Instead, he veered to a new topic. "Do you come to this canyon often?"

He'd never been on this climb himself, though he'd participated in his own share of the sport over the years, usually over in Bozeman.

"A few times," she answered. "There's a group of people we've—I've—been climbing with for years. Not just on this mountain, but all around. I hook up with them enough to stay in shape for it."

At least she didn't routinely go on her own. Though if Nick were to bet, he'd say that wasn't unheard of, either. He'd gotten the sense, after watching her all morning, that if she could heighten the risk, she would do it. "When we start up again, do you think you could behave a little better?" he asked now.

She looked at him. "What do you mean?"

"Quit being such a daredevil. If you slip and fall between anchors, I won't be able to protect you."

Her gaze went cold. "I don't recall requesting your protection."

"You know what I mean. I'm too far away. Not to mention your falling will pull me off my feet. That'll make it even harder for me to get to you."

"I don't need taking care of, Nick. I never asked—"

"I'm not saying—"

"Then stop talking."

Her words were harsh, and they stung. So he tilted his head back to stare at the sky. Anger radiated off her, but he had plenty of his own to deal with, too. Granted, he probably shouldn't have brought it up. It was her business if she wanted to kill herself or not. But hell, he was just trying to help. He'd been thinking of *her*.

The day had been going well, though, and he really didn't want that to change. So he did what he'd grown up watching his father do, and what his oldest brother *still* did, and he buried his arguments.

"My apologies." He didn't look at her as he spoke—he felt like a sap. "I didn't mean to imply that you couldn't handle things on your own."

She didn't respond, and when she remained quiet for far too long, he finally peeked over at her. He really did hope he hadn't ruined her mood. She'd been having such a good time. But she didn't look angry now. Instead she was studying him with a critical eye. "You put up a good show of being the carefree rodeo star, wooing women and smiling for the cameras, but that's not the real you, is it?"

"Of course it's the real me."

She shook her head. "You're a worrier. Your heart is much softer than you let on."

He frowned. His heart was not soft. But she had him on the worrying part. And though few recognized that fact about him, he appreciated that she'd looked close enough to notice. Since he didn't want to be angry with her for the rest of the day, he pushed their previous spat from his mind and went with her change of subject. "I do worry," he admitted. "Too much sometimes."

"The other night, you kept asking . . ."

She quit talking, her gaze flicking away as embarrassment suddenly colored her cheeks.

But he knew exactly what she'd been about to say. He'd been worried about her Friday night. He had loved what they'd been doing, but at the same time he'd been cautious. Wanting to ensure it was what she'd *wanted* to be doing.

When she continued not looking at him, he let the subject drop, and they both spent the next several minutes in silence. He focused on the view. What lay before them was the beauty that was Montana. The Rockies required respect, and in return they provided surreal views and a calming effect on the soul. Mountain ranges as far as the eyes could see, snow-covered peaks touching the sky, emerging grass coming to life farther below. And hovering over all of it were soft clouds and the bluest blue he'd ever seen. He couldn't live without this.

"I love Montana," he stated. He rubbed his palms over his thighs, today's calluses scratching against his nylon pants. "*This* is why I don't want to join the PBR. I wouldn't get to breathe in Montana any time I wanted."

Harper looked at him, surprise on her face. "I'd wondered why you'd never joined."

"So you've thought about me over the years, then?" He wiggled his brows teasingly, his own embarrassment now climbing. He hadn't meant to speak his thoughts out loud.

"Don't let your head swell, big guy. A big-time champ from my hometown, a guy who used to *lust* after me with all the efforts a small boy could muster?" She gave him a smug smile. "Yeah, I've wondered about you. I'm sure everyone around here has."

"I wasn't *that* small," he complained. But his teenage heart skipped at the idea of her thinking about him.

"We're not getting into the size of your balls again, are we? Because I suspect that at that age . . ." She dipped her gaze to his crotch then, before seeming to struggle to bring it back up. Laughter remained in her eyes, but heat now sizzled there, as well. She didn't finish her sentence.

"It was dark the other night." His voice lowered, turning scratchy. "You might not have been able to see well enough to get a good look, but I'm no teenager these days." He locked his gaze on hers. "Want a better look?"

Her breathing quickened . . . but then she glanced away. He groaned.

"Not a date," he grumbled. "I know. And that was not an appropriate thing to say to a friend. I swear, I'm trying like hell not to flirt with you out here. It's just that you're so . . ."

Her eyes slid back to his, and he saw curiosity there. She wanted to hear what he had to say. Yet he struggled to put to words what it was about her that got him so fired up. She was fun, hot, needy—whether she wanted to admit her neediness or not—and he knew without a doubt that he could drown in her body for days and still want more.

The corners of her mouth finally softened. "No apology necessary. Really. I was the one to bring up your . . ." Her glance once again landed in his lap, and Nick went as hard as the rock they sat on. But hell, the woman had to quit looking at his junk.

They both ignored the addition of the third attendee begging to join their party on the ledge, and she pulled out her water bottle and passed it over to him—as if knowing he'd finished his a while back. It really chapped his ass that she was in better shape at this than he was.

"Thanks," he muttered, but he only took a sip.

"You can have more."

"I'll survive without it." They still had another pitch to climb, and though he'd probably regret not being more hydrated before they got to the top, he would *not* sit there and drink all of her water. He passed the bottle back and let his thoughts wander back to Harper. This might *not* be a date, but it had certainly felt like one since the minute he'd gotten out of bed that morning. Or since he'd put his head to his pillow the night before.

Of course, when she'd arrived and informed him that *she* would be the one driving today—because her jeep was already packed with the gear—that had stripped away some of his steam. He wasn't used to a woman taking charge quite the way she did. But he also found that he didn't hate it.

So he'd climbed in beside her, and he'd made sure to keep his thoughts platonic. Mostly. Yet the sexual tension had lurked under the surface all day. It wasn't easy to have sex with someone and then act as if it had never happened.

He turned to her. "Want to talk about it?"

She grimaced. "Friday night?"

He nodded but said nothing. This was up to her. She'd slept with someone other than her husband, and that had to weigh heavy on her. If she didn't want to talk about it, he'd let it drop.

When her lips parted as if to speak, he pressed his tightly shut. Her eyes flared for a second, before she shook her head and grim determination appeared on her face. "I am *not* going to feel guilty that we slept together," she said.

"Good."

"My husband is gone. It might not be the way things were supposed to be, but it's today's reality." She swallowed and then licked her lips. "And I'm not going to apologize for kicking you out, either."

"Even better." He bit back a smile.

"And I had a really good time," she finished with a whisper.

Relief hit him hard. "I did, too."

After a few moments of the suddenly easier silence, he gave her a crooked smile. "In fact, I'd be willing to have a really good time again if you ever wanted to."

She snorted. "I think once was enough. I got the chance to blow off some steam, you know?" She nodded with bolstered confidence. "So yeah. I'm good. Once was enough."

He couldn't say the same. "So your steam is gone, then?"

He knew he shouldn't push, but man, he wanted to sleep with her again. And he wanted the chance to do it several times in one night. And then the next night. Because he, personally, had a lot of steam built up when it came to Harper.

She didn't immediately respond, so without letting himself think about the consequences, he leaned over and put his mouth to hers. When no protest came, he kissed her gently, nibbling at the corner of her mouth, taking tiny sips and enjoying her taste and the slight movements her lips made under his. And when he finally pulled back, his breathing heavy, he forced his eyes open and found her staring at the ground. He dipped his head, and when he saw his own heavy desire reflected back at him, he nodded. Good enough. He sat back against the rock.

After several seconds, she said, "This really wasn't supposed to be a date."

"It's not a date."

She raised her brows.

"It's not," he protested. "Just two friends hanging out. And this"—he motioned with one hand between them—"what we just did? It was just two friends kissing. No big deal."

"Sort of like friends with benefits?"

He couldn't hold back the hopeful look, and she let out a sad chuckle.

"You tempt me, Nick Wilde." She bumped her shoulder against his. "I'll give you that much. No wonder you have buckle bunnies chasing you every weekend."

He winked at her, not giving away anything on his buckle bunny situation. He liked the fact that she was clearly jealous. After giving it considerable thought over the weekend, he'd determined that the only reason Harper had kissed him in the first place was due to Betsy. Betsy had been bold in her wants, and not shy about sharing them—or letting others hear. That had fired a need in Harper to prove herself more desirable. And she'd done an admirable job.

"Buckle bunnies definitely have their place," he teased. Then he reached over and took Harper's hand. Her arm tensed next to his, but she didn't immediately pull away. So he left her fingers in his, and together they stared off into the distance. They could hear murmured sounds coming from climbers on the same face as them and the occasional shifting of a branch in a tree down below. It was so quiet up here that they could pick out random noises traveling from thousands of feet away.

"You're really good, aren't you?" Harper asked. She glanced over at him—and she also took her hand back. "At bull riding, I mean. Like . . . really good? The commercials and everything aren't just because you're so pretty?"

He winced at the word "pretty." "Yeah. I'm really good."

"Then what's stopping you?" She nodded to the view in front of them. "Is it really just this? You'd be traveling more, but it's not like you'd never come home."

It wasn't just this, but he had yet to pinpoint the exact reason. He answered with a shrug.

"Does it have anything to do with those secrets you mentioned?"

Again, he didn't comment. Because what she didn't realize was that he'd shared one of those secrets with her today. Everyone in the business was aware that he'd been delaying joining the PBR for a long time. They'd assumed the timing wasn't right, or that he feared he couldn't run with the big dogs. As if. But what they didn't know, what he'd never said out loud until just now, was that he hadn't gone simply because he didn't want to.

He rose and held a hand down to her. "Come on. We have more rock to climb."

Chapter Nine

Harper turned into the Wilde driveway later that afternoon, replaying the day in her head and deciding that she was glad she'd let Nick talk her into going. Kissing aside, it had been a good day. The reality was, the kissing had made it better. Not that she'd tell Nick that. His ego was already big enough.

She slowed to a stop at the end of his driveway, then put the jeep into park, and when Nick turned to her, she didn't know what to say. Would he try to kiss her again?

Would she stop him?

"Let's do this again," he said.

It wasn't that easy. "Probably not a good idea."

Nick studied her in the silence. "Can we if I promise not to kiss you anymore?" There was a solemnness to his eyes. "I'd miss it, though. Because I happen to like kissing you." He gave her a wry twist of his lips, as if embarrassed by his words. "I like doing *more* than kissing. But everything else aside, I've also discovered that hanging out with you is as much fun as any of it."

The words touched her heart.

"I . . ." she began, but paused to gather her thoughts. What was she supposed to say to that? "I had a good time today, Nick. Thank you for suggesting it. And Friday night was fun, too," she added. "But maybe we should slow down."

"Slow down being friends?"

She shook her head, because she feared he might change her mind by doing nothing more than training his blue gaze on hers.

"My youngest sister graduates from high school tomorrow night," she told him. "Then I have a full day of flights Thursday and Friday, and I'll be with Jewel on Saturday." That weekend's rodeo was a one-day event not far from there, but the day would still be busy. "I don't have time," she finished.

He gave her hand a light squeeze. "Then I'll keep an eye out for when you do."

The light came on in the jeep when he opened the door and stepped out. Harper watched until he'd disappeared around the back corner of the house, then put the jeep into gear and circled around, heading back down the drive. She couldn't hang out with Nick again because she'd had too much fun with him today. And because—when she got right down to it—if they did something else together, she'd want it to end with neither of them wearing clothes. Again.

And though she'd been fine with doing it once, something told her that a second time would bother her. Because a second would turn into a third. And then a fourth.

And that might just be more than she could handle.

"Patti Jackson."

Harper rose to her feet with her family, clapping for her baby sister who was graduating at the top of her class. The youngest Jackson was the brain of the group. All of her siblings were in attendance today, as well as their parents, and the group of them made a lot of noise as Patti walked across the stage. She accepted her diploma and turned to wave it toward her family. Then she gave a big, sweeping bow. Which made all of them hoot even louder. The raucousness had Harper laughing out loud.

As they sat back down, the grin remained on her face, and she caught both Jewel and her mother sliding glances her way. Jewel nudged Chastity, the sister exactly halfway in age between Jewel and Harper, and then Chastity cut a look her way, too.

"What?" Harper mouthed.

All three of them shook their heads and popped innocent expressions on their faces. Harper frowned at them and went back to watching the proceedings. But once the program ended and they'd moved off the stands, she cornered her two sisters.

"What was that about?" she asked.

"What?" Jewel and Chastity chorused together. They even blinked in unison.

"Why were you three talking about me? What were you saying?"

Chastity blinked again, owl-like, and Jewel suddenly looked everywhere but at her.

"Quit talking about me," Harper growled under her breath. They'd whispered about her too much over the last year and a half, and she was beyond tired of it. *How's Harper? Is she doing better yet? What should we do for her?*

Of course, there had been nothing they'd been able to *do* for her, and she'd hated their sad, woe-is-Harper looks even more than their whispers. But their direct questions had been the worst. Harper had grown especially good at fielding them.

I'm fine.

Yes, I've moved on.

No, of course I'm not suicidal.

Thankfully, she'd only had to force the last one for a short time, but there *had* been a few seriously rough months. Yet their whispers today seemed different. Their looks weren't the same.

Their mother joined them, slipping away from their dad to stand between Chastity and Jewel. She slid an arm around both of Harper's sisters, and suddenly the three of them were no longer ignoring her, instead standing as a united wall. In front of her. The sight made her nervous.

"You're different today," her mother informed her—direct and to the point as usual.

"How so?" Harper looked down at herself as if seeking out the changes.

"Your smile," Chastity added.

That brought Harper's head up. Her smile? She forced one. "What's wrong with my smile?"

"Nothing is wrong with it," Jewel explained. "It's just that it's . . . *real.*"

"My smile has always been real."

The three of them exchanged glances.

"It *has.*"

Chastity was the one to shake her head. As a park ranger in Yellowstone, Chastity usually only made it home for Jackson Sunday dinners once a month. A tradition started, Harper suspected, purely for her benefit. "You've had to remind yourself to smile for a long time," Chastity explained. "Today"—she lifted her hands, palms up—"you're simply smiling."

Harper frowned at all of them. Maybe she hadn't been pretending to be okay as well as she'd thought. "None of you know what you're talking about," she mumbled.

"What's different?" her mom questioned. Their mother never beat around the bush.

And Nick was what was different. Not that Harper would say that, or even mean it completely. She had changed in the last few days, and yes, Nick had played a role in that. But that didn't mean she hadn't been smiling for months.

"Did you meet somebody?" The question was asked hesitantly, and Chastity had the grace to look embarrassed at voicing it.

"Do you honestly believe I can't be happy without a man in my life?"

"No!" they all three denied quickly.

Jewel tilted her head as if an idea had just occurred to her, and her eyebrows inched slowly up. Her expression seemed *too* innocent. "Did something"—she shrugged her shoulders casually—"*happen* at the rodeo last weekend?"

Their mother's eyes rounded, and Harper's narrowed. Innocent, her ass.

"Nothing happened anywhere," Harper informed them as her gaze locked onto Jewel's. Harper had worried that her sister might have overheard her and Nick through the motel room wall Friday night, but when nothing had been said about it the next day, she'd decided her worries were for nothing.

However, she now suspected otherwise.

"You're all wrong," she stressed, looking purposefully away from Jewel. "I'm not different. Nothing is different."

And she most definitely didn't need a man in order to be happy.

"I'm fine," she continued when everyone remained silent. They were all simply watching her. "I've been fine for a long time, and nothing is different now."

"Only," Chastity murmured under her breath, "something *is* different."

"*Mom.*" Harper looked to her mother as if expecting her mom to chastise Chastity.

"Is it Nick?"

At a man's name coming from Jewel's mouth, both Chastity and their mother looked at Jewel. "Who's Nick?" they asked in unison.

Jewel's face gave nothing away. "Nick Wilde. You remember him. Used to hang out with me at the house a lot. He had a big crush on Harper when he was a kid. She flew him home a couple of weekends ago."

Chastity and their mom swiveled back to Harper.

"He needed a ride," Harper gritted out. She pointed a finger at Jewel. "And it was *her* idea."

"But he was also in Great Falls."

"Because he's a *bull* rider. And we were at a *rodeo*." Embarrassment filled her, but she passed it off as anger. Jewel knew. There was no doubt. And she'd saved that nugget of information for just the right time. "I don't need this crap." She turned away from them. "You three carry on without me. I'm going to go stand with Dad."

She stormed off, refusing to look back at her mother and siblings, but she couldn't help wondering what Jewel thought of her actions. Or if she would tell everyone else.

Harper also questioned the subject that had started the conversation to begin with. Did she really seem different? Nick was fun, sure. And a good guy. He was easy to talk to and be around, and they'd had a good time the day before.

And, holy smokes, could he kiss.

But being around him hadn't really changed the way she smiled, had it?

She reached her dad's side and dropped her head to his shoulder when he shot her a wink and slid an arm around her waist. Her dad wouldn't grill her over her happiness. Not because he didn't worry about her, though. She'd seen it in his eyes as often as she'd witnessed it in everyone else's. In fact, her dad probably worried about her the most. But he provided support in ways other than badgering her with questions. Like simply being there when she needed him.

The way Thomas once had.

Chapter Ten

"Why aren't you out there, Uncle Nick?"

Nick looked down at the dark-haired beauty in his lap and wrinkled his nose at the five-year-old. "Because bull riding is *better* than calf roping."

Haley wrinkled her nose in return and stared at him, her green eyes seeming to be assessing him, sorting through whether he was serious or not. When he winked at her, her confusion cleared and her giggles rang free. She snuggled in tighter against his chest. "You're silly, Uncle Nick."

They were at a charity rodeo in Missoula, only an hour from home, and Dani, Ben, and Haley had come down for the event.

"My friend Leslie's uncle ropes the cows, and she says he's the best ever."

"Yeah?" Nick drawled. "Well, has he ever ridden a bull?"

"Reel your macho back in, big guy," his sister muttered at his side.

Nick looked at her. "I'm just saying, there's a difference."

"And each sport is perfectly acceptable."

Nick shot his sister a bored look, then once again winked at Haley. "I'm sure Leslie's uncle is great at roping, sweetheart. But just wait until you see me ride tonight. You'll *love* bull riding then."

The corners of her mouth turned up. "I already love it. Because that's what you do. And you're my favorite uncle."

Dang. He was head over heels for this kid.

The action in the arena switched as the next group of ropers began making their way to the chutes, and Nick stood, Haley on his hip. "How about we find ourselves some hot dogs?"

"I love hot dogs!" Haley shouted.

Ben and Dani chuckled, rising to follow them out of the stands. Nick had been thrilled to get a text from his sister that the three of them would be there tonight. Though she'd stopped by the house earlier in the week, they hadn't had time to stay long, and Nick hadn't seen them since.

"Hey, Wilde," another rider greeted him as they approached the concession area. He tipped his hat at Haley. "Looks like your taste in women has improved."

Haley wrapped an arm around Nick's neck.

"I'd say my taste is about perfect these days," Nick confirmed. Which also included a certain blue-haired woman he hadn't seen in days. "Haley Denton"—he looked at his niece and nodded toward James—"I'd like you to meet the *worst* bull rider you're going to see tonight."

"Hey." James straightened. "That's not right." He faced Haley, his tone serious. "I'd suggest you root for me tonight, darlin'. I'm actually better than this one. *And* I'm better looking."

"My uncle's the best," Haley informed the other man without pause.

Nick grinned with triumph. He'd known James since the other man had joined the circuit six years ago. He was a good guy, and he not only rode bulls, but he would complete a master's program the following spring at Montana State. He'd been working at his father's apparel company since graduating high school—his intention to take over someday—and while both working and going to school, he'd managed to pull in enough money from riding to pay for his education.

And as if lightning struck him where he stood, it occurred to Nick that he, too, could do something at the same time as riding. Something other than volunteering and taking random jobs in his downtime. He could work toward an actual career. He'd gotten a semester of college under his belt back in the day. Maybe he should consider going back.

James got a drink and left, and Nick stood silently, remaining deep in thought as Ben and Dani stepped to the window in front of him. When he'd turned eighteen, he'd headed off to college as his sister and dad had presumed he would. As all of his brothers had done. Only, he'd had more to prove than getting an education, so he'd ditched that plan after one semester and gone to bull-riding school. It had felt more like the real him. He'd once pushed all the limits as a kid. Breaking bones, getting into fights. Always up for the biggest, baddest things. He'd been intent on showing the world how tough he was.

But when his mom died, Nick lost the urge to fight. Dani didn't need that crap from him. She had too many other issues to deal with. So he'd calmed down. At least, until he'd dropped out of school and started climbing onto bulls.

When Dani looked back at him now, a question on her face, his thoughts came to a screeching halt. "What?" he snapped.

He had no idea what he'd missed, and thoughts of his mom threatened a bad mood.

Dani eyed him carefully. "Did you want something to eat or not?"

"Oh." He glanced at Haley, who remained in his arms, and caught her smiling oddly at him.

"What was you thinking about, Uncle Nick? My Momma said your name three times."

"Just"—he tucked his chin, pulling in a breath and banishing thoughts of his mother from his mind—"whether I wanted a hot dog or pizza." He brought his gaze up, aware that his breathing had grown ragged, and found his sister still watching him.

Nick ignored her and leaned in to place his order. Dani knew him well, she'd practically raised him, after all, but that didn't mean he'd spill his guts to her simply because she gave him a look.

"How about we sit at that table over there," Ben said. He pointed toward a long bench already half full of people that was situated directly in front of the balloon-animal booth.

"Can we get me a balloon, too?"

Ben picked up the tray of food. "A rodeo wouldn't be complete without one."

He led the way to the table, but before Dani followed, she stopped Nick. "Are you okay?"

"Couldn't be better," he answered.

Her mouth turned down in a frown, and when she opened it as if to question him further, Nick pushed past her and moved to the table. He settled in beside Ben, and the two of them talked about manly things. Not feelings and whatever other shit he could see sitting inside his sister's head. Ever since she'd come back from New York, she'd made it a point to call each of them on a regular basis. She was seeing a shrink to work on her remaining issues with their mom, and she'd gotten it into her head that the rest of them needed to talk about their feelings, as well.

But Nick didn't need to talk about anything. He was good.

The flat stance of being "good" reminded him of Harper. Didn't she claim to be "fine"? At the same time that she crossed his mind, his gaze landed on her. She stood beside Jewel a couple of buildings down, her jeans outlining her perfectly tight rear and her hands propped on her hips. He'd given her space the last few days. She'd been busy, and he got that. She'd needed to sort through her thoughts. So he hadn't bothered her.

But looking at her now, he was suddenly in the mood to bother.

She might say they needed to slow down, but he couldn't stop thinking about her. Or wanting her. Or wanting to make sure she was thinking of and wanting him.

He hadn't lied when he'd said he'd enjoyed hanging out with her as much as kissing her. Or, it had only been a partial lie. He enjoyed the kissing a hell of a lot. But it had been a long time since he'd run into anyone whose company he truly enjoyed. Harper was smart and didn't mince words. She called it like she saw it—and her seeing *him* made him want to open up and show her more.

Which was scary in its own right. He'd never wanted anyone to talk to.

"We didn't just come to watch your ride tonight," Dani said, pulling his attention away from Harper. His sister scooped up some baked beans with her fork but paused before shoving them into her mouth. "We wanted to invite you to dinner tomorrow. We're heading out of town for the next few weeks, going to be spending some time traveling across Canada."

"A few weeks?" Nick parroted.

Dani nodded. "We'll be back in July."

"So you won't be home until after I'm gone?" He suddenly felt even more alone than he did at the house all by himself.

"Well, yeah, but"—worry crossed Dani's face—"you'll be back for harvest, right? We'll see you then."

"Sure." Nick tried to remove the look of sulking from his face. This was good for his sister. He knew that. She'd been stuck here in Montana watching after them for years. She deserved to travel. And it wasn't as if he'd gotten to see her much since he'd been home, anyway.

Still. Knowing that family was near had been nice.

"Say yes." Ben spoke around his hot dog. "I'm cooking."

"Daddy's a good cooker now. The last time it was good."

Nick eyed his brother-in-law. The last time was good?

"They got me a grill for my birthday," Ben explained. "I've been practicing."

Laughter from two buildings down caught Nick's attention, and he flicked a quick glance at Harper. "Sure," he agreed. "I'll be there." He took a casual sip of his drink. "Okay if I bring someone?"

"Who would you bring?" The question burst out of Dani.

"Bring whoever you want," Ben answered. He shot Dani a look.

Nick's sister ignored her husband and peered at the area around them, as if expecting someone to show up at their table at that very moment. Nick worked on his food and gave nothing away. He might not ask Harper, anyway.

"Is she pretty?" Haley asked.

His back went straight at the unexpected question.

"Leave your uncle alone," Ben said, his words coming before Nick could figure out how to politely dodge the question.

"But, Dad . . ."

Ben nudged his chin toward his daughter's plate. "Finish your food so we're ready to watch when it's Nick's turn to ride."

The little girl's face twisted up in irritation, but she shoveled a bite of hot dog into her mouth. "I just wanted to know if she's pretty," she muttered softly, but she continued eating without additional complaint. However, when she cut a look in Nick's direction a few minutes later, and gave him the kind of smile that melted an uncle's heart, he couldn't help but smile back. Then she leaned into his arm, her warm body melting against his, and whispered, as if to no one, "I'll bet she's very pretty."

Nick couldn't help it. He caved. She *had* said he was her favorite uncle, after all. So why not play the role of favorite uncle? He leaned down and whispered, "If I tell you, will you keep it a secret?"

Haley nodded, her enthusiasm restored.

He glanced around the table as if making sure no one else was listening—ignoring his sister's curious stare as he did so—then cupped his hand over his mouth and Haley's ear. "She's gorgeous," he confirmed. "And she has *blue hair*."

Haley's eyes went wide.

"But remember, you can't tell anyone." He puckered his lips and put a finger to them in the universal sign of silence. "Just between you and me."

She nodded again and mimicked his motion with her finger, and Nick rose from the table.

"And speaking of riding, I need to head off to do just that." He pinched Haley on the tip of her nose as he stepped over the bench seating. "I'll be listening for you to yell the loudest for me."

"I will, too." She jumped up on the bench and wrapped her arms around his neck, and Nick wondered for the first time in his life what it would be like to have this kind of love waiting for him at the end of every day.

He confirmed the time for dinner after Haley released him, then headed away from the table. Harper still stood with Jewel, but he didn't move in their direction. Ben might have given him an out with Dani by shutting down her line of questioning, but that didn't mean she wouldn't watch him with an eagle eye for the remainder of the night. She'd probably grill her stepdaughter, as well, to find out what he'd said to her. And all Haley would have to do was mention blue hair.

He definitely should have kept that one to himself, no matter how cute and imploring his niece could be. He simply wanted to spend more time hanging out with Harper. Not have his sister wearing him out with questions about what Harper might or might not mean to him.

A bead of sweat trickled down the front of Harper's shirt as she tugged at the metal door of the trailer. The danged thing kept getting stuck. She yanked once more and the rod slid out, moving with such ease that she almost landed on her backside in the dirt.

"You mad about something?" Jewel asked. She'd just come around the side of the truck.

"Only at the pigheadedness of this gate," Harper muttered.

And maybe a little bit at herself. Because she kept watching for Nick.

She'd seen him earlier as he'd been getting ready to ride, and she'd been unable to take her eyes off him. The man wore good looks effortlessly, and it wasn't fair. It made a rational person like her think irrational thoughts. Toss in the fact that *he* no longer seemed to have an issue with checking *her* out—he'd not done it all day from what she could tell—and her mood had soured. She wouldn't be surprised if he'd already forgotten her.

And why would he do anything else? She'd turned him down when he'd suggested they get together again. She'd made it clear she wasn't looking for another roll in the hay.

He had no reason to hunt her down.

Yet absence makes the libido grow fonder, and all that.

But hadn't he said he'd wait until she wasn't so busy? That, alone, implied he'd seek her out again, didn't it? She growled under her breath. Not only had he not paid the slightest bit of attention to her tonight, but she'd also checked her phone for missed calls or text messages too many times over the last few days to count. And she'd called herself an idiot every time she'd done it.

She was seriously messed up. She didn't even want to go out with him again.

Except she did.

She ignored her sister, who now wordlessly watched her, and together they worked to get everything set to load the bulls. With a path secured to the waiting trailer, Jewel released the two animals they'd brought with them, one by one, and guided them into their individual compartments. The last guy was a bit more ornery than the first, but she and Jewel were getting good at this and took it all in stride.

Dusting her hands off after they'd finished, Harper scoped out the area to see if any of the other stock contractors needed help, but paused in her search at the sight of Nick. He stood with his family in the distance, and Harper once again couldn't pull her gaze from him. What was it about this guy?

Was it just the sex? The torturously amazing kissing? The fact that he'd said he liked hanging out with her? It had been a long time since someone had simply enjoyed the pure pleasure of her company.

"He'll make a great dad someday."

Harper's insides seized up at the sound of her sister's words. Jewel now stood beside her, and without looking, Harper knew that her sister was taking in the same sight as she.

"I suspect he will," Harper agreed. Nick currently had his niece on his shoulders, and the child was laughing with uninhibited glee. Additionally, Harper and her sister weren't the only women watching. Nick directed female attention without trying.

"So . . ." Jewel drew the word out as they continued to watch. "About those noises I heard last weekend."

Humiliation doused Harper. "I don't know what you're talking about."

Denial was her best friend. Her second closest was avoidance, which Harper had used every time Jewel had called her since Patti's graduation. Thus, the reason this conversation was only now coming up.

"I'm talking about the *noises*," Jewel repeated. "From your *motel* room." She apparently would no longer let the fact that she knew what Harper and Nick had done go unnoticed. "A lot of noises," she added. She began to moan under her breath, and soon the moans turned into panting. Harper kept her gaze straight ahead and pretended that her sister wasn't being an embarrassing nuisance at her side, and as quickly as the sounds started, they stopped. Jewel leaned in and whispered, "I'm pretty sure I heard the headboard bang against the wall a few times, too."

Harper hung her head.

"Then there was the pleading."

She covered her face with her hands.

"And I do believe there was something about a condom . . . on his body, maybe? But what part of his body, is what I wanted to know."

"Jewel," Harper hissed. "Please stop.

"*Hmmm.* Nope. I don't recall hearing 'stop' at all. Was there a 'more' in there, though? I'm not sure."

Harper glared at her sister from between her fingers, and embarrassment heated her words. "Did you honestly lay over there listening to us the whole time?"

"What else was I supposed to do? Bang on the wall and ask you to keep it down?"

"Ah, geez. I can't believe—"

"You're not beating yourself up over it, are you?" Jewel's teasing evaporated. "Because you know you did nothing wrong. He's gone, sweetie," her voice softened even more. "And that's not your fault. You can't punish yourself forever."

Harper crossed her arms over her chest and turned her back to her sister.

"Harper," Jewel said from behind her.

Harper needed this to stop. Now. She didn't want to talk about the past or what she'd done or not done that day. And she didn't want to talk about what she'd done with Nick, either. So she peered over her shoulder and gave her sister a tight smile and forced a normal voice. "I'm not beating myself up. I swear. But *that* makes me feel bad. You have to see that. He was my husband. I should feel guilty about being with another man."

"Maybe." Jewel wrapped an arm around Harper's waist. "But it's also okay for you to move on."

"I know."

"Do you?" She studied Harper. "Because you've seemed kind of stuck for a while now."

"I'm not stuck. I'm . . ." How did she explain it? And did she even want to?

Maybe Jewel was right. Maybe she *had* been stuck. But it wasn't because she felt guilty for moving on. It was because of the anger. It festered inside her. They shouldn't have even been there that day. Thomas shouldn't have died.

And he shouldn't have had to save *her*.

But Harper didn't know how to explain any of that to her sister. Not without telling her everything.

"I'm not stuck," she repeated. "I slept with Nick, and I don't feel bad about it. Doesn't that prove to you that I've moved on?"

"So you're going to sleep with him again?"

White-hot lust shot through Harper. She didn't answer Jewel, but both of them turned to watch Nick once again. Instead of playing with his niece, he was now entertaining a couple of the women who'd been eyeing him earlier. Making *them* laugh. One put a hand to his arm, leaning toward him, and the other stepped in closer, as if to compete. Nick simply grinned wider in return.

A couple of minutes later, he tipped his hat to both women and headed off with his family. Harper watched the other females fan themselves as he retreated, knowing exactly how they felt.

"I don't think so," she said, in answer to Jewel's question.

"Why not?"

Because she suspected that he'd already lost interest. "I just don't see the need."

A snort burst from Jewel. "Honey, I'm happily married, but even I can see the *need*. He's *fine*, Harp. Capital *F* kind of fine. And I'd be willing to bet he knows how to make things sing down there, too."

Once again, Harper covered her face. For crying out loud, why did her younger sister insist on talking to her about this?

"Tell me it wasn't amazing," Jewel urged. "A body like that? It had to rock your world."

A partial sigh, partial groan escaped Harper, and she finally made eye contact with Jewel. She intended to deny all charges, but when her mouth opened, what came out shocked her. "My world was rocked, okay? Completely off its axis. He's ripped and hard, and"—she blew out a frustrated breath—"and I could have spent *days* exploring that."

A hundred-watt grin covered Jewel's face. "Then do it again. For me, if not for you. Screw his brains out. As many times as he'll let you. Then do it once more for good measure."

Harper gaped at her. "I don't even know who you are anymore."

"I'm the sister who's on hormone overload and whose husband won't be home for weeks."

"Can we just drop it?" Harper begged. Because though Jewel made a good argument—as many times as he'd let her, and then once more—Harper didn't plan on partaking anymore.

"Will you at least consider it?"

Hadn't she been considering it since she'd run him from her room?

"Want me to make the noises again?" Jewel asked.

"No!"

Laughter rang from her sister. "Just have some fun, Harp. We all need it from time to time. And you deserve it. You've had a rough year."

It had been longer than a year.

They turned and headed to the truck, and Harper found herself grumbling under her breath. "If I *do* do it again, you can bet I won't tell you about it."

"I'll still know."

She stopped walking. "How?"

Jewel grinned. "It's all in the smile, babe. Didn't we all notice it had changed?"

Harper sighed. This conversation was not what she'd expected. Nothing in her life lately was what she'd expected. She pulled up short. She needed a minute alone. "You go ahead and pull the truck out. I'm going back to see if I can snag us something to eat for the ride home."

Too much thinking and talking about Nick had gotten in her head, and she needed to reorient herself. She wouldn't be sleeping with him again. End of story. So no reason to fantasize about it. But she was also hungry, and they had a long ride home. Jewel hadn't been as sick today as she had been last weekend, but the one time her queasiness had made an appearance had been when they'd had a moment for dinner. In fact, Jewel had to be as hungry as Harper. A woman couldn't exist on saltines alone.

Harper hurried back through the concession area, finding most everyone either already gone or within minutes of leaving, but her gaze finally landed on one seller who hadn't quite packed everything up. Only, when she made it to his cart, he had exactly one hot dog and one package of cotton candy remaining. She took what he had, knowing she'd insist Jewel eat it all, and headed back the way she'd come. But as she made her way across the dirt floor, her feet slowed at the sight of the tall, lean cowboy leaning against the far post. His hat was pulled low, and she could feel his eyes on her.

Her pulse sped up.

Nick didn't push off the side of the building, so Harper kept moving in his direction—trying not to look excited to see him. When she reached his side, her eyes went to the funnel cake in his hand, and her mouth watered. And not just for the deep-fried sugary snack.

"Hey," she said causally. She swallowed. "I figured you'd be off with Betsy by now."

His brows inched up. "Betsy wasn't here tonight."

"Some other woman, then?" She set her features to unconcerned, but she wanted to smack herself for momentarily letting her jealousy show. What did it matter who he slept with?

Instead of letting himself be baited, Nick held up his paper plate. "Want a bite?"

She wanted a bite, a lick, and a whole lot of other things.

She wanted the funnel cake, too. Her stomach growled.

"I know you like it," he murmured, waving it beneath her nose.

"And how do you know that?"

"Because it's what you tasted like the night you kissed me." He popped a bite into his mouth and chewed around a smile, while heat teased at her cheeks. But she didn't take any of the funnel cake. Her stubborn streak had sparked to life with the mischievous gleam in his eyes, and she wouldn't give him the satisfaction.

"Then I'd say I've tasted like a lot of things over the years," she taunted. "Doesn't mean I like all of them."

His laugh was low and sexy. "So you still busy?"

"Jewel's waiting for me." She accidentally eyed the funnel cake in his hands before jerking her gaze back up. It was a shame when her head was torn between flirting with a hot cowboy or begging for his high-calorie treat. "But we've already got the bulls loaded," she finished lamely.

"I meant *after* tonight." The mischievousness faded. "What are you doing tomorrow?"

Oh. He was referring to her being too busy this week to do anything with him. She bit back a smile. "Depends on what you have in mind."

And damn, hadn't she made that sound inviting?

She swallowed and pretended not to notice her unintentional come-on, but the corners of his mouth hitched up. He finally pushed off the post, but he didn't go far. Just far enough to stand directly in front of her. He kept the funnel cake between them.

"Dinner at my sister's house?"

Harper's eyes went wide. "Dinner? I thought you meant . . ." She trailed off. She'd thought he might mean a number of things, but none of them had involved dinner with his sister.

"What?" he asked. Then his own eyes widened. "You thought I meant sex?"

"*No!*" She gulped. At least, she'd been trying not to think that. "I thought you meant doing something *fun*. Like you suggested the other day."

Another low chuckle hit her ears. "Sex *is* fun."

"*Nick.*"

He tugged off another bite of the snack and wiggled his brows at her. "*Harper.*"

She couldn't quite pull her eyes from his mouth as he chewed. When had chewing become sexy? And why did she now want to be that bite of funnel cake? "You know what I mean," she breathed out.

"Yeah, I know what you mean." He licked the sugar off his fingers, and she feared a groan might slip out of her. "So you doing okay?" he asked.

She frowned at the subject change. "I'm fine." Were they now going to small talk? "Looks like you are, too. Nice riding tonight." She flailed about, looking for something else to say. "I saw Ben and Dani here watching you."

Surprise lit his eyes. "You know Ben and Dani?"

"Sure. I knew your brother Cord in school—he was a couple years ahead of me—and I'd see Dani at football games cheering him on. I see Dani around town now, too. And I know Ben because I've taken him up a couple of times."

Ben had once been a celebrity photographer, but had changed direction when he'd discovered he had a daughter last year. He was currently working on his second coffee table book. She'd put him down in several gorgeous locations for nature shots during those two trips.

"Then you should fit right in." Nick disarmed her with his made-for-sin smile. He pulled off another bite and moaned as his teeth sank into it. A small dot of confectioner's sugar now clung to his upper lip. "So, dinner?" he asked around the treat. "Tomorrow night?"

"You were serious about that?" Why would he ask her to dinner with his family?

"Sure. I was told I could bring a date."

"But I wouldn't be a date."

He tilted his head then, but he didn't say anything. His eyes simply stayed on hers. So long that she began to twitch in place. He could somehow say so much without saying anything at all.

"I told you that I don't want to date," she reminded him. Her fingers itched to swipe the sugar off his lips.

"So now you're telling me that you don't eat steak either?"

"I don't go to random guys' family dinners to eat steak."

Hurt flashed across his face. "And you're saying I'm a random guy?"

"I'm saying"—she sighed—"that me showing up at Dani's with you would be odd."

He suddenly focused more on his food than her, and Harper didn't know what to do. She wasn't sure why her pointing out the obvious would have offended him, but she was fairly certain that's exactly what she'd done.

"I'm just saying," she tried again, "that they might read more into it than is there."

"Or maybe they'd read into it that I don't want to be a third wheel." He wiped off his mouth, and the sprinkling of white disappeared. "You know how weird that can be. And as a bonus, I have it on good authority that Ben can grill a mean steak."

"Yeah? And who told you that?"

"His daughter." He smiled again, and danged if her chest didn't squeeze tight at the sight. "I'm her favorite uncle, so she wouldn't mislead me."

Harper couldn't get over the softness that overcame him simply by talking about the little girl. Jewel had been right. He would make a great father someday. "Then it sounds to me like *she* should be your date. Imagine how thrilled she'd be with that."

"She's cute," Nick acknowledged. "But I prefer my women older. Preferably with blue hair." He lifted a hand, capturing several strands of her hair, while the backs of his fingers grazed over her ear. "I remember pink when I was just a kid. There was the summer of red. Then your rainbow phase." His gaze returned to hers. "I always wondered if you were making a personal statement with that one."

"Simply a statement," she said, filling in the space when he paused. Since the day her mother had insisted Harper and her sisters wear matching dresses for Easter Sunday, Harper had started dying her hair random colors.

"But I do have to admit," Nick continued. He released her hair, and his eyes fastened on her lips. "Blue is my favorite."

"Quit trying to charm your way back into my pants, Nick Wilde," she breathed.

"But I like your pants, Harper Stone." His eyes inched lower. "Those jeans fit you really, *really* nicely." When he finally dragged his gaze back up her body, she literally throbbed in front of him.

And oh, sweet Lordy goodness. That fast, and he had her completely undone.

"Come with me tomorrow night," he urged.

She *would* like to get out of the house.

"I'll even ply you with beer," he said. "I know you like beer."

"I do like beer." And if she *did* go with him, that wouldn't necessarily make it a date. Just a night out with two other people she already knew.

"What else do you like?" He slid the tip of a finger over her bottom lip, his voice lowering to that belly-quivering octave he was capable of. "Tell me, and I promise I'll make it happen."

Her tongue touched the spot where his finger had traced, and she found a path of powdered sugar in its wake. She licked at it while considering him. Because she didn't for a second think they were still talking about a steak dinner.

"I'm still not sleeping with you again," she finally managed, but her voice had turned shaky. And she wasn't 100 percent certain she could back up her statement. Not if she found herself alone with him.

"So you're saying your steam situation remains under control?"

This time there was definite heat in her cheeks at the reminder of their prior conversation. "My steam is definitely in check."

His gaze lowered to his plate, and one corner of his mouth hitched up in a tiny smile, and Harper found herself squirming in front of him. He was laughing at her.

When he picked up another piece of the fried bread and her stomach growled a third time, his gaze shifted back to hers. The devil danced in the blue depths as he hovered the bite a half inch from her mouth. "Sure you don't want any of my treat?"

"I'm positive I don't want any of your treat," she whispered hoarsely.

"Okay," he said. He slid the bite between his lips then, and after he swallowed, he once again licked his fingers clean. "But feel free to call me if your steam situation changes."

Harper's throat went dry. The man was evil. Yet his taunting only cranked her stubbornness higher. She lifted one hand slowly and waggled her fingers in his face. "It's been a while," she began, the boldness in her voice misleading, "but I'm quite confident I could remember how to use these if my *steam* needs to be released."

Deep laughter instantly circled her, and she almost died of embarrassment. Good Lord, she'd just blatantly told the man that she wouldn't have a problem masturbating.

Jewel's truck and trailer pulled up at that moment, and Harper quickly glanced over Nick's shoulder in relief. She was breathing heavy, her nipples had hardened, and a few more seconds of this particular form of foreplay, and she might have agreed to anything the man suggested.

Nick followed her gaze, and at the sight of Jewel, he waved. Then he turned back to Harper. The humor disappeared from his eyes, replaced with pure heat, and he leaned in—so close that she could smell the sweetness on his breath and feel the faintest touch of his chest rub against hers. And danged if her legs didn't quiver.

His mouth brushed across her ear. "You be sure to let me know if those fingers don't quite do the trick."

She nodded.

Then she groaned as she realized what she'd agreed to.

Nick straightened, heat still the only thing on his features, and slipped a bite of the funnel cake between her lips before she could even guess at his intent. His fingers lingered for an extra second, and this time, he was the one who watched her chew. And she had no doubt that the action turned him on just as much as it had her. There was something innately hot about watching someone's mouth. Especially when that someone's mouth had been on your body.

After she swallowed, he pulled his gaze back to hers. His eyes looked drugged. "Let me know what you decide about that steak," he scratched out. Then he turned and walked away, and Harper slumped where she stood. Because what he hadn't figured out was that at that very second, he'd had her.

Chapter Eleven

Incredible steak, Ben." Nick gave his brother-in-law a slap on the back. He grabbed the loaded-down bag of leftovers his sister had packed for him and winked at his favorite person in the room.

Haley giggled and climbed onto an island barstool to wrap her arms around his neck. She planted a sloppy kiss on his cheek and turned to whisper in his ear, "I didn't tell no one about your blue-haired girlfriend."

"Thank you," he whispered back. He didn't correct her on the girl-friend part. "I knew I could count on you."

"And I'm sorry she didn't come with you."

"Me, too." Nick ignored his sister's clearly nosy look. Sometimes a man and his niece had to have secrets.

And sometimes a man kept his own secrets. About blue-haired women who were too chicken to come to dinner with him. Harper had texted an hour before he'd left the house to tell him that she couldn't make it. Which had been a letdown. Yet not surprising.

He pulled back from Haley and winked at her, changing from a whisper back to normal volume. "You have a good trip to Canada, okay? Your Uncle Gabe will be very sad that he missed you."

"Gabe's coming in?" Dani asked.

"Yeah." Nick glanced at her, surprised their oldest brother hadn't shared his plans. "Next week sometime." Gabe had let him know a few days ago.

Dani glanced toward Haley, and Nick noted the girl's suddenly long face and felt guilty for bringing it up. Gabe's daughter, Jenna, was Haley's best friend. The two girls had only met the year before, but the friendship had been instantaneous. However, since Jenna's mother had pretty much forced Gabe into relocating to Los Angeles before the school year started, the girls had rarely gotten to see each other.

"But from what I understand," he began, once again talking to Haley, and hoping his words would cheer her up, "they're planning to stay all summer."

Her mouth formed an *O*. "All summer?" she whispered. She looked at Dani. "Does that mean I'll get to see Jenna?"

"It sure does." Dani scooped Haley onto her hip. "And she can spend as many nights here with you as you want."

"And I can spend nights there with her, too? And with Pops and Gloria." She shot a toothy grin Nick's way. "And with Uncle Nick?"

Nick chuckled. The child could get anything from him that she wanted. "I won't actually be around all summer, sport. I go home in a few weeks, remember? But I'm sure Pops and Gloria will love to have you. And I'll be back to visit, too. I'd miss you too much if I didn't." He gave Haley another wink, making her giggle again, then turned back to Dani. "Been a while since you talked to Gabe?" Dani typically badgered all of them weekly.

"She's a slave to the job these days," Ben said. He moved to stand behind his wife and daughter. "It's sad when she's too busy to harass her own brothers."

Nick agreed.

"My workload has definitely increased." Dani owned her own marketing company. "Which is great. Happy clients talk, and I like them talking. But part of the problem is that I've been trying to get ahead due to this upcoming trip, and I've yet to hire a receptionist to field some of the calls."

"Hiring someone is first on the list for when we return," Ben told him. "If she doesn't get on it herself, I'll take that one over."

"My hero." Dani patted Ben on the cheek and smiled up at him, and he gave her a look that Nick—frankly—wished he wasn't able to interpret. But thankfully, Dani remembered they weren't alone in the room, and returned her focus to Nick. "Are Gabe and Jenna coming *alone?*" Her tone changed from hero worship to subdued.

"Who knows?" No one was a fan of their sister-in-law. Gabe's marriage had been on the rocks for as long as they could remember, and Nick and the rest of them were pretty much holding their breaths, waiting for it to collapse. "All I know is what I got in the text. They'll be in by the end of next week. Before Dad gets home."

Dani nodded as if a decision had been made. "Then I'll call him before we leave. Nate, too. We never know if Nate will make it in for harvest, so I'll start bugging him now."

"Of course you will." Nick rubbed his knuckles on the top of his sister's head. "But don't be surprised if he doesn't answer."

"I never am."

He headed to the door, reaching it and looking back in time to catch Haley's yawn. Her face was now tucked into the side of Dani's neck, and Dani peered down at her.

"We let you stay up way too late, didn't we?" Dani spoke softly to the little girl.

"I'm not tired," Haley denied around an even larger yawn.

Dani smiled fondly at her stepdaughter, and Nick felt a pang of jealousy as he stood there. The utter look of contentment on his sister's face knocked him for a loop. She'd found it all here with Ben and Haley. While Nick still struggled to believe "all" existed.

He pinned Haley with a look. "You be sure to bring me back a present, okay? Since you're going to Canada, I'd like an igloo."

Giggles once again filled Nick's ears. He loved her laugh. "I can't bring home an igloo, silly."

"Then how about you just don't forget that I'm your favorite uncle while you're gone?"

Berry-colored lips curled up. "I could never forget that."

Dani moved toward him then, Haley still in her arms, and caught him in a hug before he could get away. "You'll be okay while we're gone?"

"I'm always okay." He kissed both her and Haley on the tops of their heads. "Have fun and don't worry about any of us." Then he turned to Ben. "Take good care of her."

"Priority number one."

Nick knew Ben would see to it that Dani was fine, but he was continually caught unaware at how much he worried about his sister these days. He'd always worried, but until their skeletons had come out of the closet, he'd been a master at ignoring it. Yet now he found himself wanting to check in on her as much as she did him.

He left and slid behind the wheel of his truck but took a minute before driving away to take in the setting sun. That pang of jealousy hit again. This was nice. And not just the lakefront view. It had been interesting watching Dani and Ben together tonight. They'd grown closer over the months they'd been together. So close that they seemed like a fully contained unit now. They fit. And Haley only complemented what the two of them had.

Nick couldn't wait until his sister had more children. She would thrive as a mother. And he needed more nieces—and wouldn't complain if he had a nephew or two running around.

And if kids had great parents, then they wouldn't grow up to be messed up in the head.

He put the truck into gear and pulled out onto the highway. Even bad parents had their purposes, he supposed. He shoved his mother from his head, choosing to fill it with Harper instead. And what came to mind wasn't only the thrill he'd seen in her eyes the night before when she'd found him waiting on her, but her sexy stubbornness, as well. She'd wanted him. As much as she'd wanted his funnel cake. And though she'd refused to give in—to either offering—she hadn't been able to keep from flirting with him. It had fired his need to a new level.

Until she'd called him some random guy.

His ire rose. Random guy, his ass. He wasn't just some Joe off the street. He was the man who'd recently been buried deep inside her. Who wanted to be there again.

Who already knew how to make her fall apart in his hands, and who knew they could have a heck of a lot of fun together both in *and* out of bed. He sighed with frustration, and his fingers clenched around the steering wheel. She might want him, but she wasn't merely saying no to *him*. He still understood that, no matter how much his hormones tried to convince him otherwise. Harper had crap to sort through. And he didn't need to add to it.

Only . . . she'd waved her danged fingers in his face, and he'd thought of little other than her own hands touching herself since.

He groaned and flipped on his turn signal, slowing to make a right turn into the driveway, but at the sight of a shadow up ahead he turned on his brights. A dark truck sat where he normally parked, and he couldn't help but wonder if Cord had come home. Cord was a doctor in Billings, and the last Nick had been aware, he drove a dark Chevy similar to the one that sat silently in the dark. He'd bought it a year ago as a birthday present to himself. Maybe he'd gotten a few days off and had wanted to get away.

Or it could be Nate. Nick hadn't talked to his twin in almost two weeks, and given that Nate wasn't always one to report in *before* he headed out to pastures unknown, he could very well be making Birch Bay stop one on whatever leave he'd decided to take.

Whoever it was, it didn't matter. A thrill shot through Nick at the thought of having either of his brothers home. He pulled behind the truck and stopped, acknowledging that he'd be just as thrilled at having *anyone* here. As he exited the vehicle, he took in the house and noted that the only light burning inside was the one he'd left on earlier. Whoever was here hadn't seen fit to light the place up. He pocketed his keys and grabbed the doggie bag, then headed for the back deck. But when he rounded the corner, he stopped. It wasn't Cord or Nate.

It was Harper.

She stood stiffly beside the back door, her eyes glued to his and her arms crossed over her chest. Desire fired through Nick like a rocket taking off into the night sky. In two seconds, he'd taken inventory. Trim denim skirt hitting a couple of inches above the knee, turquoise cowboy boots with silver toe caps, and a black sleeveless shirt with a zipper running the length of the front.

And he suddenly couldn't care less about his brothers.

He took the steps two at a time, but when he reached her, uncertainty took hold. He held up the bag of food. "You missed a good dinner."

Harper nodded. Then licked her lips. She looked nervous.

She glanced away from him, and he saw her chest rise with the breath she pulled in. When she brought her gaze back to his, she blew out the breath. "It wasn't steak I was hungry for."

That was all he needed to hear.

Blood roared through Nick's head. He reached around her, not touching her, and not looking down, as he focused all his attention on the door. He had to get the key into the lock. Then he had to turn the knob. As the door swung silently open, he finally dropped his gaze back to Harper's. She hadn't moved. She stood with her face turned up to his, and he fought to maintain control until he made certain he wasn't mistaken about her purpose for being there.

"Are you telling me that your steam situation has changed?" he asked in a low growl.

And finally, her features eased. She smiled at him, her intent written into that simple move of her lips, and his jeans grew instantly tight. "It's leaking out my ears," she replied.

Nick dropped the bag of food and backed Harper into the house. They made it just inside the door before he shoved her against the wall and his palms landed under the hem of her skirt. Her thighs were hot and smooth, and he crushed his mouth to hers. They grunted at the same time, and as Harper's arms wrapped around his neck, he discovered that her skirt was the only article of clothing she wore below the waist.

"Condom," she murmured. "There's one in my back pocket."

"We're going to need more than one."

Her legs wrapped around his hips before he could say anything more, and when the heels of her boots hit the backs of his thighs, his body rocked into hers. He could feel her heat through his jeans. She whispered something and bit into his neck, but he couldn't make out the words. All he could hear was his blood pounding in his ears.

His fingers found the zipper of her shirt and jerked it open, and lo and behold, she wasn't wearing anything under the shirt, either. So he filled one hand with a breast while the other once again slipped under her skirt. Meanwhile, the situation behind his zipper was fast becoming painful.

"Undo my jeans," he begged. "And promise me that you won't run out the minute we're done. Because I'm going to make this one fast." He kissed her again, his lips as demanding as his words. "And when I'm finished here, I'm going to spread you out on my bed and start all over. Working my way up from your toes."

He slid on the condom after she'd freed him, his breaths coming out as short gasps as he took her in. Then he positioned himself at her opening. They were still up against the wall, no clothes removed and everything in disarray.

Grabbing her chin, he brought her face to his. "Promise me," he demanded.

"I'm not going anywhere." She was as out of breath as him, her voice just as raspy, and when she thrust her hips forward and her heat surrounded the tip of him, he was done.

He shoved inside her with a loud groan, relishing in the similar sound being returned from her. Then he pulled out and pushed in again. Harder this time. He gripped her butt in both hands and buried his face in her neck. He couldn't slow things down. They both moved fast, each touching, thrusting, rubbing. They'd be done within seconds if they kept this up. But he was powerless to change course, and she didn't seem to be in any better shape.

When the muscles of her thighs clenched tighter, whatever blood that remained in his head went south.

"Nick," she whispered.

Her chest arched toward him and her entire body grew tight. He dug his fingers deeper into the curves of her rear. "Me, too," he panted.

A shout ripped from her, quickly joined by the one from him, and he pumped himself dry, his hips clenching rhythmically with his release. When he was finally empty, he collapsed, pinning her between him and the wall. Her legs remained around his hips—now trapped there by his weight—but they hung as boneless as his entire body felt.

Ninety minutes later, they were in Nick's bed, propped up against the headboard. Harper had a beer in her hand—with an eye on Nick's hand as his fingers stroked along her inner thigh. He didn't seem to be aware that he was touching her. On his other side, he worked the remote, and she'd swear all his attention was focused on that task. Yet those fingers . . .

For someone who'd not only had one mind-blowing orgasm at the front door but another after Nick had brought her upstairs, his fingers shouldn't be messing with her the way they were. Yet she was about to toss both beer and remote and climb back on top of him if he didn't put a stop to it.

"I just got this today," Nick said as a picture finally filled the screen.

"Is it any good?" It was a preview copy of his latest commercial.

"Haven't watched it yet." He hit "Pause," then reached over and stole her beer and took a deep pull. "I was saving it until I was in a better mood."

"You were in a bad mood before?"

He handed back the bottle and waggled his brows. "I was sexually frustrated before."

He hit "Play," and the screen filled with a nasty-looking bull standing in a chute, its head the size of a small country, and its horns nothing short of terrifying. The animal snorted and reared back, and then a single leg dropped down over its side. At the glimpse of the denim and chaps, Harper caught her breath. Now it only took the sight of the man's *leg* to turn her on.

She shook her head at the absurdity and tried to block out the burn of Nick's fingers, where they were still drawing circles on her thigh. She watched the remaining forty seconds of the commercial, and as it ended, with Nick's naughty smile front and center, she couldn't help but laugh.

"What?" The grin he directed her way was cute, but she detected embarrassment as well as humor.

"Isn't this commercial to promote clothing? That other *men* wear?" She pointed the tip of her beer bottle at the screen. "Yet that whole thing was about sex. Or made to make women think about sex."

"Who do you think buys those men most of their clothes?" He smirked. He leaned over and nuzzled her behind the ear. "Women eat this stuff up."

"I can see why."

"So you like it, do you?" He pulled back slightly, and his gaze landed on her lips. And his fingers inched farther north.

"We still talking about the commercial, Wilde?"

He shook his head. "Not the commercial. Tell me you like it," he murmured. He nibbled at the corner of her mouth.

"Well, the man in it *has* gotten me naked twice now, so"—she gasped when a finger slipped inside her—"I'd say I like it at least a little," she finished on a whisper. She slid a couple of inches back down on the bed and opened her legs a little wider. He had really good technique with his fingers.

"I like it a *lot*." He went back to nuzzling her ear. "You." His fingers continued to work her down below. "Sex with you." He sucked her earlobe between his teeth. "Anything I can get with you."

His words had her edging away from him, the need to make sure they were on the same page suddenly paramount. "This *is* just sex, right? Because I don't want anything else."

Nick didn't pause. "I'm right there with you."

He brought his mouth to hers and kissed her, his tongue mimicking the action of his, now *two*, fingers inside of her, and he made her forget everything else. When he ended the kiss, they were both out of breath.

"I'm just saying that I want a *lot* of sex," he clarified. His lips closed over hers again.

"A lot of sex," she agreed when they next came up for air. They were both once again horizontal, and getting naked with Nick as often as possible suddenly made perfect sense. "I can do that. As long as you're okay with the fact that I'm a little too old for you."

He pulled back. "How do you figure that?"

"I'm not one of your rodeo girls, Nick. I'll be thirty in a couple of years."

His thumb rubbed a tight circle between her legs. "Are you saying you can't keep up with me?"

"Oh, I can keep up."

"Then I don't see a problem." His mouth returned to her neck, and he mumbled, "And you're far from too old for me."

"Yeah, but," she panted, "I'm also saying—"

He gripped both of her hips and dragged her under him, and her words snapped off like a twig. The man's body touched hers from head to toe. His thighs stretched just on the outside of hers, trapping her into immobility, with his thick, nudging erection pressing hard against her belly. He planted his elbows directly above her shoulders, then he held her head steady between his large hands. She tried to concentrate on what else she'd wanted to say, but as he angled his head and took her lips in a slow, exploratory kiss, focus became impossible.

So she closed her eyes and enjoyed the moment.

He kissed her for a long time, seeming to put all his attention into that single act, and when he finally lifted his mouth, she was left staring up at him in wonder. That had been a hell of a kiss. He'd slowed them down, but she knew it would be only temporary. This man wasn't made for slow.

The slight break, though, let her previous thought return.

"The other thing I wanted to say," she breathed out, "was that *because* I'm older, I'm not simply going to stand around and fawn over you at rodeos. We may not be dating, but I did have fun with you the other day. As friends. So, consider this your warning. I might try to talk you into doing things *other* than sex." She gave him a crooked smile. "In fact, that's actually why I came over here tonight. I had an idea for something fun we could do."

His hand once again headed south. "That isn't why you came over here tonight."

His deep rumbling words had her chuckling. "Maybe not. But it is the excuse I'd planned to use."

"Is it?" He nibbled her shoulder.

Her eyes fluttered closed as he slid off her, and his fingers returned to tweaking and probing and touching her in all the ways she liked best. And it occurred to her that he'd certainly learned the needs of her body awfully fast.

"Lay it on me," he murmured as his mouth made its way to her breast. "This great plan of yours. The one you have to talk me into."

She sucked in a deep breath as moist heat covered her nipple. "Racecar driving," she whispered. At his surprised glance, she nodded, unconcerned with her unladylike panting. "There's a track about thirty minutes from here. We could go Tuesday."

He rose to one elbow. "Or I could clear my day tomorrow."

"I can't tomorrow. I'm taking a couple to the top of Mount Cleveland in the morning for a marriage proposal." She gasped when he suddenly picked her up, and she landed on top of him. Her thighs straddled his waist.

"I didn't think it was standard to fly up that high." Though he continued talking, his hands remained focused on her body. He inched her higher on his torso until she covered his chest, then lifted her rear off him and directed her hands to his headboard. She now leaned over his face, her breasts swinging free, and he groaned like a man who'd just discovered the female anatomy for the very first time.

"It's fine," she answered. The look on his face could only be described as rapturous. "I've flown up there many times."

His teeth closed around the tip of her breast, and at the same time his thumbs spread her open below the waist. And again, she gasped at his touch. He kept her trapped between his teeth as she squirmed due to his finger movements, pulling at her in an almost painful—yet highly pleasurable—way.

"Scoot up," he mumbled a few minutes later.

She looked down at him, her eyes almost completely glazed over now, willing to do anything he asked. But when she saw the intent in his eyes, she paused. And though she had the thought to refuse the act out of sheer respect—Thomas had been the only one who'd ever touched her in that way—she couldn't bring herself to see what they were about to do as wrong.

Nerve-racking, yes. But not wrong.

Nick nudged her rear, and she lifted fully to her knees. She repositioned her knees above his shoulders, breathing hard as she stared down at his mouth. It was only inches away. But he clearly felt her nerves, because he didn't immediately put his lips on her. Instead he spent several minutes running his palms over her arms and thighs, down her back. He even caressed her calves and the bottoms of her feet. He soothed her in a way she hadn't realized she'd needed. And when he reached up to bring her face down to his for a soul-searching kiss, she melted in his hands.

When he pulled back and looked into her eyes, she nodded. She'd never have guessed she needed gentleness like this.

Nick took his time, bringing his attention to her center. He nudged her back up to her knees—she'd dropped to his chest while he'd kissed her—and he once again slid his palms up and over her body. He stroked along the sides of her waist, across her shoulders, and down her arms to where she once again had a firm grip on the headboard. And when she looked down at him, he kissed her right at her belly button.

She shivered, and suddenly she was the one no longer wanting to keep things slow. She edged closer to his mouth, and at the move, she caught the slash of masculine pride across his lips.

He spread her apart, but then he did no more than take her in.

"Please," she whispered.

His mouth pursed and she felt a stream of air slide over her. She dropped her head, and the muscles in her thighs tensed.

"Nick," she pleaded again when he still didn't put his mouth on her.

"Will you promise to be careful tomorrow?"

"What?" Dazed, she looked at him. "When?"

"On your flight."

She nodded. She would have a man and woman in the aircraft with her, their hopes high for a beautiful, long life ahead of them. Of course she'd be careful. "I promise."

"Then come find me when you're done. I don't want to wait two days to see you again."

She nodded once more, and when he stopped talking, he finally touched his lips to her body, and she got lost in the pure pleasure of how Nick could make her feel.

Chapter Twelve

On Monday afternoon, Nick once again sat at the worn wooden desk in the family study, working on cleaning up the farm's books. He'd been through the last twelve months and confirmed that the problems hadn't started until after his dad had taken over. So he'd saved a copy of the original before beginning the changes—in case he made things even worse—but as of that moment, the numbers once again balanced. He saved a backup copy of the updated file and shut down the accounting software. Then he brought up the website for the University of Montana.

Should he really consider going back? He hadn't given it much thought since the idea had formed, but it *had* sat in the back of his mind.

If he did go, though, how would that even work? He needed to move forward in his career, not continue sitting still. His agent wouldn't stick with him much longer if nothing changed. Commercials or not, Charlie had signed on with the intention of bigger things.

Yet attending school would require Nick to be in Montana. Unless he did online classes.

He thought about the one semester he'd spent on campus when he was eighteen. He'd enjoyed it. He might be older than everyone now, but he couldn't help but think he'd get more out of the atmosphere by attending in person.

Or, hell, maybe he should just forget the whole idea. He'd chosen his path years ago, hadn't he? He loved bull riding. He wouldn't even know what to study at this point.

He clicked the link for the fall schedule and found the application deadline. There was still plenty of time to decide. Next he brought up a list of degrees and scanned it. Nothing stood out.

What kind of degree could bring me back to Birch Bay?

He blew out a breath at the thought. He hadn't realized he wanted to come home for good. But he did. He missed it.

A ding sounded through the speakers, and he clicked over to his e-mail. His first thought was that it might be Harper e-mailing him. About what, he didn't know. He just knew he wanted to hear from her. She hadn't stayed over last night. She'd blamed it on her early flight, but, a couple of hours after she'd shown up, he'd seen the need in her to get out of there.

Once dressed, she'd practically run from the house, stopping only when she'd come upon the remains of the leftovers he'd brought home from Dani's. Not that there was any food to be found. There'd been a couple of empty containers, a shred of the plastic from the bag it had all been carried in, and bear prints. But thankfully no sign of the bear.

But even though Harper had run, she would be back. Soon, actually. Her flight should have ended thirty minutes earlier, and the minute she returned, Nick intended to hustle her off to Kalispell. It might not be as exciting as tomorrow's plans for the raceway, but he'd lined up a couple of horses for them to ride that afternoon.

Scanning his e-mail, he wasn't surprised to see the incoming message from Charlie, and he opened it to find the same old thing. Pressure to make a decision. Giving it no thought, he went back to the university website, but there were too many what-ifs and not enough answers running through his mind to be able to focus. So he pulled out his phone and called his brother.

"It's two o'clock in the afternoon there," Nate said by way of greeting. "Shouldn't you be watering a tree or something?"

Nick grunted. "The trees are being watered as we speak."

"Sounds like you can barely keep the place running without me," his brother returned sarcastically. "What's up?"

Nick leaned back in the chair. "There's something I need to talk through."

"And you called me for advice? Smart man. About time you grew a brain. Is this about your girlfriend?"

"My what?" Nick shot up in the seat. "Who told you—"

He stopped talking and thought *Haley* at the exact second Nate said, "Haley."

Nick narrowed his eyes. His darling niece had ratted him out. So much for keeping her favorite uncle's secrets. Not that he'd ever actually *told* her that Harper was his girlfriend.

"So who is it?" Nate asked.

"Who is what?"

"Clever. Play stupid. But you have to know that once she mentioned 'girlfriend,' I wouldn't let it go at that."

"And you have to know that the kid loves to make stuff up. Her favorite pastime is playing pretend. You can't believe anything that comes out of her mouth."

"I believed her when she said the girl has blue hair."

Nick clamped his mouth shut.

"She also claims to have seen her."

"No, she hasn't."

Nate laughed, and Nick could see the smirk that went along with it. "Still want to deny this woman exists?"

Nick sighed. "I don't have a girlfriend. Where did Haley claim to have seen her?"

"You mean this blue-haired woman that doesn't exist?"

"Just answer the damned question," Nick gritted out.

Nate laughed again. "Said she saw her at the rodeo. Something about her being in the bathroom throwing up and begging for crackers." There was a slight pause before Nate asked, "You're not dating some pregnant chick, are you?"

"I'm not dating anyone." And probably the throwing up had been Jewel. But he hadn't realized that Haley had seen them. "She say anything else?"

"Only that she agrees with you. The girl is pretty. So who is she?"

"Nobody."

"*Hmpf.* Just one of your groupies?"

"I don't have groupies." At least, never more than one at a time. Regardless of reputation, he didn't switch up like some of the other guys. "And that was supposed to be my and Haley's secret," he grumbled.

"Well, she is only five. From what I've seen from both of our nieces, I'm not sure secrets are a high priority at that age. And anyway, she told me about her because I'm her favorite uncle."

Nick frowned. Cute smile or not, that kid knew how to wheedle information out of people. "And the other night *I* was her favorite uncle," he told his brother. "Right before she got a secret out of me. You reveal anything to her?"

"Do you think *I'm* an idiot?"

"Well—"

"Wrong," Nate interjected. "If I were an idiot, I wouldn't already know who this mysterious beauty is, now would I?"

Nick went silent. Because he suspected that Nate could easily figure out who she was. His brother's memory had always been good, and no doubt he'd recall the one girl in town who Nick had crushed on, who'd also once been prone to uniquely colored hair.

"I thought she'd gotten married." Nate said, his lowered tone showing his concern.

"Her husband died a year and a half ago."

"Ouch." They both fell silent before Nate added, "And what? You just happened to run into her? Figured you'd finally scratch that itch?"

"Something like that." Though Nick didn't personally like that phrasing when it came to Harper. "But that's not why I called, so can we drop it?"

"For now. But if you didn't call to discuss woman problems, then why did you call? Don't tell me that you've finally fallen in love with cherry farming and decided to move back home to do it full time."

Nick remained silent, if for no other reason than to annoy his brother.

"You're kidding me."

Nick grunted again. "Moron. Of course I haven't." But he did keep his mouth shut about his newfound desire to come home. "I did call to talk about my career, though." He waited, already questioning if he should have even brought it up.

"You're finally signing on with the PBR?"

"No," he answered bluntly. "I haven't made a decision on that yet. But I *am* considering going back to school. Or, at least taking some classes on the side."

"Yes," Nate replied without hesitation.

"Yes, what?"

"Yes, go."

"But then how do I fit it all in? If I register—honestly—I'd prefer to take a full load. Otherwise it'll take me forever to earn a degree. But the logical thing is for me to go national. It's time. Yet . . ." He sighed. "I can't do that and go to school, as well."

"Why not?"

"Because I can't do everything."

Such heavy silence came from on the other end of the phone that Nick pulled his cell away from his ear to make sure they hadn't lost connection. When Nate finally spoke, his tone had grown serious. "Are you still letting her control your actions?"

"Letting who control my actions?" The hair rose on the back of Nick's neck.

"Mom."

"What are you talking about?" Anger sliced through him. "She never controlled my actions."

"She always did."

"Bullsh—"

"You used to take every risk in the book just to get her attention."

"No, I didn't." But his childhood flashed through his head. Hadn't he come home with more than one cut or broken bone over the years? And he knew why. Because he'd learned it from her. He'd seen *her* do the exact same thing to get attention.

Only she'd never wanted *his* attention.

He swallowed his disgust, but he kept his mouth shut. Nate didn't know what Nick had seen their mother do. Nick had never told anyone.

"Yet that all stopped after she died." Nate's words rang softly in Nick's ear, and as clear as day, Nick understood that it had stopped after his mother died, not because Dani didn't need the additional hassle but because he hadn't had to do anything to get Dani's attention. Because *she* had loved him. Just as he was.

Shit. Why had he never seen that before?

"You know you're full of it," Nick growled out. Nate might know him better than anyone else, but some things they kept to themselves. And would go to their graves denying.

"And you know I'm right. And that nothing you tried got her attention. She always berated you for not being good enough. Not tough enough."

"I did not call you to talk about her," Nick bit out. He also hadn't called to get into an argument, but he couldn't stop the anger or the heated words. "I called because I, *stupidly*, wanted your thoughts on the matter of me going back to school."

"And I gave them to you. Go. It's about time that you went back." Nate's words remained calm, which only irritated Nick more. "In fact, you should never have quit. I always thought you wanted to do more with your life than chasing girls and trying to kill yourself on a bull."

"Unlike you, who got a business degree and became a fisherman?" Nick sneered.

"Kiss my ass."

"Dare to come home for once and I will."

"I was home twice last year," Nate snapped out. And finally, Nick could hear his brother's annoyance. It made him feel better to know he wasn't alone.

"Only because our entire family was on the brink of collapse," Nick pointed out. The heat of his anger suddenly disappeared, leaving him drained. They were both so messed up. All of them were. And sometimes that came out by way of fights. But it didn't keep them from having each other's backs when the need arose. He crossed to the front window and dropped his forehead to the cool glass. "Isn't it time to deal with your own crap, Nate? Quit hiding away in Alaska. It's time for all of us to do more than spin in circles."

"Yet it's easier said than done, isn't it?"

They both went silent. Being a Wilde had never been as black or white as outsiders might have believed. They hadn't had a perfect family. And trying to dig out from that wouldn't come easy. For any of them.

"We're all doing just fine," Nate said. "No need to mix things up simply because we're not hiding from reality anymore."

"Yet, you're not happy stuck away up there."

"Big deal. None of us are happy."

Nick thought about the moment the night before when he'd been leaving Dani's house. As he'd stood at the door and looked back at her. She'd seemed completely content for the first time in her life. "I think Dani might be," he said, nearly under his breath.

Nate went silent for several seconds. "She deserves to be."

"Maybe we all deserve it."

Nick could hear Nate's steady breathing, and he caught himself counting the exhalations. "Maybe we do," Nate conceded after the count rose to seven. "And if going back to school is what will start you down that path, then do it. Everything else will fall into place somehow. And as for bull riding . . . I know it's your life. I was only teasing with the crack about killing yourself. I get that you enjoy it and that you're good at it."

"I'm great at it."

"Right. But have you never found it odd that you didn't even get into the sport until after you graduated from high school? What I'm saying is, it wasn't a dream of yours since childhood."

The problem was, Nick had had no dreams. "I dislocated a shoulder when I was seven because I fell off a sheep," he reminded his brother. "Of course I wasn't excited to jump back on after that." Especially given how that entire incident had played out afterward.

"But you didn't even want to be on the sheep," Nate pointed out. "I was there. She dared you. You only did it to win her approval."

A jeep came into sight at the far end of the driveway, and Nick had never been so relieved to see signs of another human being in his life. This was supposed to have been a conversation about his potential future. Not about their mother or how she'd been living in their heads their whole lives. He left the room and headed for the front door, stepping onto the porch before Harper made it to the house. She waved when she saw him, and pleasure flooded him.

"I've got to go," he said into the phone.

"Come on. Don't hang up because I brought up a bad memory."

"I'm not. I just have to go."

Harper stepped out of her vehicle, slamming the door behind her, and Nate cut off whatever he'd been about to say. "Is that her?" he asked instead.

"I don't know what you're talking about."

Good Lord, she looked good enough to eat. She had on skintight tan riding pants tucked into knee-high black boots, and her black tank top showed off the biceps he'd grown to love. He'd still win in an arm-wrestling match, but those babies could sure give him a run for his money.

She stepped onto the porch and looked him up and down, and he gulped in response.

"Send me a picture of her," Nate said in his ear. "As hot as she was as a teenager, I'll bet she's lethal now. Let me see."

"Not on your life." Nick hung up on his brother. Then he reached for Harper and pulled her into a kiss to let her know just how much he'd missed her since she'd left him the night before.

Harper stared up at the ceiling of Nick's bedroom, her chest still heaving from the very satisfying calisthenics they'd just performed, while Nick lay facedown beside her.

"You okay?" she asked.

"Never. Been. Better."

She chuckled. The third time was the charm with them. She'd swear she'd heard the angels sing with this one.

"Give me two minutes and I can go again," Nick mumbled into his pillow.

She laughed again. He'd given her the same pledge while riding horses earlier today, after she'd dared him to an all-out sprint. A challenge he'd lost.

She looked over at him. "Not that I'm saying you're a liar, but I'm calling bullshit. You're going to need at least five minutes after that particular sprint."

A heavy arm dropped across her stomach and slid her over the damp sheets until she bumped into Nick's side. Then Nick buried his nose into her neck. "I love how you always smell like baby powder," he mumbled after several minutes.

"That's because it is baby powder." She peered down at his arm and wiggled under the weight of it. He'd trapped her against him.

And she didn't like being trapped in any situation.

When he went to reposition himself, and the muscles in his arm tightened as if to pull her even closer, she quickly slipped out of the hold and rolled to her side. Nick eyed her from where he now rested on her pillow before shoving up to mimic her pose. They lay facing each other, a good eight inches of sheet between them, and as Harper's gaze inadvertently traveled to her favorite body part, she had to amend her earlier prediction that it would take a full five minutes.

"My apologies to your manhood," she said.

Nick stared down at his now-erect penis. "Hmmm. Now that impresses even me."

She giggled when he made it bounce in the air at her, and shoved at his shoulder. "Behave yourself."

Nick brought his gaze back to hers and grinned, and his twinkling blue eyes suddenly had her right there, as ready to go again as he was. He cupped a hand around the back of her head and brought her mouth to his, and another twenty minutes passed in a blur.

This time, both of them ended up facedown.

"I give," she muttered into the down feathers cushioning her nose.

"You can't give. I already did. You win this round."

She turned her face to his, smiling, and found him watching her, and she silently thanked her sister for needing her help over the next few weeks. If not, she wouldn't have run into Nick again, and she would still be sitting all alone in her giant, empty house every second of every night.

But even thankful, reservations remained.

"You," she began, then had to stop and lick her lips as nerves hit. She closed her eyes before continuing. "You're not still sleeping with Betsy, are you? Or anyone else?"

Silence was her answer, and after several deafening seconds, she pried her eyelids back open.

Nick was on his side again, his eyes on hers. "Are you asking if we're exclusive?"

She nodded her head on the pillow. "Not *serious*, but exclusive. Though, I understand you might have been with her after our first time. Since that was supposed to have been a onetime thing and all. So I get it if—"

"I haven't slept with Betsy since you kissed her out of my mind that first night," Nick said. "Though I will admit that she texted me Friday night. She was in the area."

Harper waited, holding her breath and hoping he'd answer without making her voice the next question. This was embarrassing enough. She also wished she'd been able to ask the question purely due to sexual health.

And not ridiculous jealousy.

"I told her that we needed to cool it," he said.

She exhaled. She wouldn't name the gush of emotion that rushed through her. "Thank you." She hid her threatening smile with words. "Potential diseases make me nervous," she explained. "You just never know these days. And Thomas is the only other man I've ever been with, so . . ."

She pressed her lips together and stared down at the sheet. Why had she told him that?

Why this entire conversation was so mortifying, she couldn't say. She wasn't a prude. But she did currently wish the floor would open up and swallow her whole.

Nick touched a finger to the underside of her chin and lifted her face. He stared at her for way too long, and she knew he was replaying her words in his head. Thomas was the only other man she'd been with. *Don't ask.*

She silently begged him not to make a big deal of it. Because it wasn't a big deal. She'd had more important things to do in high school than let herself get caught up in love, and then when Thomas had come along . . . she'd been unable to keep from falling in love.

This thing between her and Nick, of course, was a totally different situation. *This* was just sex.

"I'm clean," he finally said, giving her the only words she wanted to hear. "And this definitely is exclusive. I know rodeo guys have reputations, but I don't play that way. When I hook up with a woman, I have a good time until I don't anymore. And then I move on. No Betsy or anyone else." He kissed her tenderly. "Only you."

Good. She nodded. "That works for me."

She then rolled over and climbed from the bed with no grace whatsoever. Because she'd been embarrassed enough for one evening. She grabbed her pants off the bedpost and scanned the room for her bra.

"Where are you going?"

"I thought I'd go home." She dropped to all fours to look for her bra. She'd been up against the wall when he'd taken it off her. Could it have ended up under the bed?

Nick rolled to the edge of the mattress and peered down. "You could stay, you know? You don't have to go."

She looked up and gulped. She didn't want to stay.

"I know," she said. "But I have a job in the morning." She found her bra and stood to put it on, praying that Nick wouldn't push about her reasoning. Sex was one thing, but overnight felt too personal. Too *real.* "I'm doing some stunt work for a movie, so I need to be there early."

Nick's eyes narrowed, but he climbed from the bed without another word. He scooped up her panties and tossed them to her on his way to the connected bathroom, and when he returned—sans condom—he stepped into his jeans.

"So, I'm curious," he began, and Harper paused in the act of dressing to watch the man's denim slide over his well-muscled legs. Geez, he was nice to look at.

When she brought her gaze back up to his, he had one eyebrow up and a question on his face.

"Sorry," she muttered. She pulled her shirt over her head. "Your question was?"

"My question was, do you purposefully look for the biggest risks out there, or do they just have a way of finding you?"

"What do you mean?"

"Stunt work?" he asked. "Who does that?"

"It's for a producer out of Hollywood I know. I've worked with him before."

"Okay. But is it safe?"

She shrugged. "As safe as stunt work can be. I'll be doing some tricky maneuvers, but nothing I can't handle."

"And how about that wedding proposal this morning? How did that go?"

Oh. She slowed her movements. This was about him looking out for her. Trying to *protect* her. "It went fine."

"Fine?" He stared at her from the other side of the bed, but instead of immediately voicing whatever else was on his mind, he retrieved her boots and brought them over to her. "I was worried about you, so I read up on it."

Irritation fired. "You read up on it?"

"Yes. You shouldn't be going up there. That peak is too—"

"Nick." She held up a hand and took a step back. "Stop right there. We're having a good time here, right? And I'd like to keep having it. I was under the impression that you would, too."

He stood immobile, his arms now hanging at his side. "I would."

"Then you need to keep one thing in mind. And that's that I'm very good at my job. I not only am an excellent pilot and scored top of the class in my unit, but I also do things as pedestrian as check the weather before I take my helicopter up. Every single time. I'm aware of what I can and can't do."

"I was just—"

"I know what you were doing. But the fact is, my job isn't your business. *I* am not your business."

He looked sufficiently mollified—and marginally pissed. Which pleased her, because she was beyond ticked, herself. She thought she'd made it clear that she didn't need him or anyone else trying to keep her safe.

"Duly noted," Nick monotoned.

Since she was now fully dressed, she moved in front of him when he motioned for her to proceed him out of the room. She led the way down the hallway, to the bottom of the steps, and to the front door. But she stopped before Nick could open the door and turned back to him, uncertain what to say to break the tension.

He took care of that for her. He closed the distance and kissed the breath out of her.

When they parted, he swung the door open to the dark night. "We still on for racing tomorrow?"

She blinked. "You still want to go?"

"I want to hang out with you, yes." His gaze locked onto hers, and his features finally softened. "I want to do whatever you have in mind. Racing or otherwise."

"Racing," She nodded. She was glad she hadn't pushed him away. And that thought, alone, should be a warning to her. They weren't dating. They were just hanging out. And having sex. But the mood suddenly had the distinct feel of something different, and she'd been holding her breath all the way to the door, hoping this wasn't the end of it. "I'll have a surprise for you there," she told him.

"What kind of surprise?"

"You'll have to wait and see." She went up on her toes to kiss him then. One last time before she turned and left his house.

Chapter Thirteen

The Ferrari that rolled onto the racetrack was a solid red, low-slung exotic machine, and it was the hottest thing Nick had ever seen. He didn't take his eyes off the vehicle as its nose inched forward and came to a slow stop twenty feet in front of them. The engine growled like an untamed animal.

The owner climbed out through the window, wearing the glow of a man who knew he had something that everyone else in the world wanted, and Nick looked down at Harper. She wore the same expression on her face.

"You going first?" he asked. They'd been here for a couple of hours, but the Ferrari had only now arrived.

Her eyes turned up to his. "You don't mind?"

"This baby was your idea. It's only right that you get first crack at it."

She rubbed her hands together and licked her lips, then she strode straight to the car.

Nick chuckled under his breath and cast a glance at the manager of the racetrack, who stood on the other side of him. "How in the hell did you get that thing here, anyway?" Nick asked.

"Owner's a buddy of mine." Dean didn't take his eyes off the other two. "He uses the track several times a year. Used to race with Harper's husband. When she called to tell me she was coming up and asked if I had anything extra special for a friend of hers, I knew just who to call." The man looked Nick up and down. "You must be a good friend."

"And you might note that I'm not the one about to climb into the belly of that beast."

"There is that," Dean agreed.

They both went quiet as they watched Harper talk to the owner. Like Nick, she'd changed into a racing suit for the day, and she fully looked the part. She nodded at the owner occasionally as he spoke, looked into the interior a couple of times, and practically bounced on her toes as she waited for the man to get through his spiel.

Finally, instructions were over, and the owner helped Harper on with her helmet and into the seat. Nerves flared inside Nick. They'd both spent time in several different cars since they'd arrived that day, and though there'd been no true mishaps, he had held his breath on more than one occasion. Always because of Harper. The woman didn't do anything halfway, and if he were made to swear in a court of law, he'd have to say that she was borderline unsafe. She'd taken curves too fast, had gotten too close to the danger zones, and there had been a couple of times he hadn't known if her brakes had gone out or if she was simply waiting until the very last second to tap them.

Sure, professional drivers maintained speeds higher than they had today, but there was a reason for that. They did this for a living. Yet Harper had attacked the sport as if she, too, made a habit of climbing behind the wheel. It had reminded Nick too many times throughout the morning of how he used to push the envelope to get his mother's attention.

As Harper now sat in a car far more powerful than any they'd sat in during the last two hours, Nick had second thoughts.

"You think this is wise?" he asked Dean.

"I did before I called my buddy to bring his car over."

The way he phrased the sentence worried Nick. "You don't now?"

Dean gave a one-shoulder shrug and chewed on a piece of straw he'd had in his shirt pocket. "Can't say as she's been the most careful person I've ever seen."

Damn. It wasn't only him.

Nick gritted his teeth and strode to the door of the vehicle. Harper looked up at him when he reached her side, and the pure glee on her face stopped him in his tracks. Crap. He couldn't keep her from doing this. She was having a great time.

She revved the engine and the thing gave a deep, throaty rumble, the noise so saturated with power that it vibrated in his belly. "Isn't that the hottest sound you've ever heard?" Harper shouted.

The hottest sound he'd ever heard was a particular high-pitched noise *she* made when she came apart in his hands. But instead of telling her that, he squatted and stared through her tinted visor. "Please be careful. I'd like to see you back in one piece."

He didn't miss the quick narrowing of her eyes.

"I'm perfectly fine."

"I know. But this car"—he looked down its length—"it's not like the other ones. Just be careful."

She revved the engine again and stared straight ahead. And with that, Nick understood that he'd been dismissed. Kind of like the night before when she'd shut him down due to his questioning her safety of this morning's stunt work. The woman had made herself clear. His concern was unwarranted and unwanted.

And that irritated the piss out of him.

He stepped away and then walked with the owner to stand with Dean. The few other people who'd been at the track that day were also standing off to the side. They'd been removed from the track, but they wouldn't get the pleasure of driving the Ferrari. Nick had no idea what

Harper had paid for the pleasure, but it wasn't a price most people would be willing to part with.

The high-school kid that waited several hundred yards down the track moved into position, and after Dean gave him the word through a handheld radio, a green flag flew, and Harper was off.

The sound was unlike any Nick had heard, and he'd swear his balls tightened as the motor went from growl to snarl to wail. That was one fine machine. And Harper *did* seem to have it under control. She'd started out slower than he'd expected. As if respecting the power between her hands. She made several laps, throttling higher with each rotation, but maintaining a reasonable speed at each pass. Nick had just begun to relax when she zoomed past a fourth time, and suddenly the vehicle shot forward. The engine emitted a sexy, high-pitched scream, and there was no longer anything respectable about what was going on out on the track.

"She's got it wide open," Dean muttered at Nick's side, and Nick glanced over to see that Dean's body language matched his tight words. The owner of the Ferrari seemed equally tense.

But Harper still seemed to be handling the car just fine. She made several more laps, and Nick had to admit a bit of jealousy. He was ready to be the one behind that wheel. But then she went into the last curve, and all three of them sucked in a breath as the car swung out too far, barely sliding back to the center of the track before it hit the wall.

"Tell her to stop," Nick ordered when the car swerved once again. He looked at Dean, who wore a headset connected to Harper. "Now," he growled.

But the grimace that filled Dean's face told Nick that it was already too late. He turned back to the track and the world in front of him seemed to come to a crawl. Everything moved in slow motion as the car left the track and shot airborne, sailing over the sandpit meant to slow down out-of-control vehicles. The tires thudded to the grass on the other side of the pit, but forward motion didn't stop until it crashed into the protective barrier about forty feet away. Water sprayed from the large grouping of filled barrels as the car finally came to a stop.

In the next instant, all three of them took off. Nick sprinted out ahead, and almost dropped to his feet in relief when Harper crawled from the driver's seat. She backed away from the vehicle, her movements jerky. She was okay.

And now Nick was going to kill her.

He reached her side and whipped her around. "Are you hurt?"

Through the visor Nick could see that her eyes were wide with terror, but she quickly recovered. She pulled her arm from his grasp and tugged off the helmet. "I'm fine," she said with a forced laugh. Her face was pale. She ran a hand through her flattened hair and gave him a wide smile. "Did you see that? I went airborne."

Nick stared at her in shock. She was laughing about this? "You could have been killed."

"But I wasn't."

The two other men reached them, Dean gasping as if he'd sprinted up ten flights of stairs instead of across a nearly flat surface, and Nick forced himself to move away and attempt to calm down.

She was right. She was fine; she hadn't died.

But he nearly had.

Good Lord, what was wrong with the woman that she had the constant need to risk her life? Even yesterday when they'd been riding horses, she'd taken it to the extreme. She'd pushed her animal hard, but the real issue had arisen when they'd gone up into the mountains and she'd insisted on riding along the edge of the ledge. One slip of a hoof, and both she and the animal would have been gone.

She was nuts. That's all he could figure out. Certifiable.

An adrenaline rush could be had without the constant need to put her life on the line.

And at the same time that he told himself to walk away from her, to leave her madness for someone else, he was reminded of the anger he still saw simmer behind her eyes so easily. Of the sadness he caught etched in the tightness of her mouth when she thought no one was looking.

She needed to face her pain.

Nick waited silently, just out of reach, as she assured everyone that she was not only perfectly okay, but that she'd cover any damage she might have caused. The car didn't seem to have suffered much more than a few scratches and one rather impressive dent, though, and the owner claimed all was fine. He was covered for this sort of thing.

No one chewed her out for taking unnecessary risks, and no one seemed overly concerned that she could have perished right in front of them. Which made Nick mad all over again.

Once the excitement died down, and it was determined that a mechanic would look the car over before it was driven again, Nick led the way off the track. He'd had enough, and if Harper tried to convince him otherwise, they would have a knockdown, drag-out fight right there for everyone to watch.

Not that he'd ever hit a woman, but he'd sure as sin yell at her.

But she didn't utter a word. In fact, she acted as if nothing out of the ordinary had happened as she grabbed her handbag from the storage locker and chatted up Dean. So Nick put on the same face. After changing out of their racing suits, they finally headed to the parking lot where Nick opened and held the truck door for her before rounding the front to the driver's side. The fact that he'd insisted on being the one to drive today had riled her, but he'd won that battle. Just as he was about to win the one ahead.

He climbed behind the wheel, but sat unmoving. "Where to?"

He'd planned on taking her to a local pizza joint that served a one-of-a-kind cherry pizza made from fruit from their farm, but at the moment, he didn't feel a public place would be appropriate. Because they were going to discuss this whether she wanted to pretend all was well or not.

She glanced at him before answering, and after eyeing him quietly, she said, "You know what?" She put a hand over the top of her purse as if to pick it up. "Maybe we should call it a day. I live not too far from here. I'll just take a cab."

She reached for the door handle but stopped at the sound of the locks being thrown.

"Are you kidding me?" She jerked her gaze back to his. "Like I can't simply open the door and get out."

"You could, but I'd follow you."

"I just want to go home, Nick. There's no need for us to argue."

She reached for the door again, and this time he put his hand over hers, his fingers trapping hers against the cool metal of the handle. He was directly in her face now and caught her heated breaths on his chin.

"Let me out of your truck," she gritted out.

"Not going to happen." He stared at her. "Your place or mine?"

They had a stare-off, but apparently she saw the error of her ways. He would not be backing down from this one. He might give in when it wasn't a battle that needed to be fought at the moment, but this particular war wouldn't wait.

"Fine," she ground out. "Take me home. I'll pick up my car later— and don't you *dare* be all manly and have it taken care of for me."

"I wouldn't *dream* of it."

He returned to his side of the truck and she turned her head to look out the window. But she did give him directions, heading him toward the west side of the lake. He'd wondered where she lived, but given that nothing personal seemed to cross her lips when she was around him, he hadn't yet broached the subject. Clearly she didn't want him at her house, so he'd steered clear.

But he had gotten one personal thing out of her the night before. And he hadn't even had to try. Thomas had been the only other man she'd been with.

That had surprised him—not only that she'd had only one other lover but that she'd then allowed *him* to be her second—but what had shocked him even more was her sharing that information with him. Other than the day she'd shown up at the house to make arrangements to take him back to get his truck, she'd never once spoken her husband's name. Yet last night it had slipped out naturally.

Of course, she'd then climbed from his bed and left his house.

He fought the urge to roll his eyes. The woman was a master at emotional distance. Had she never heard of cuddling after screwing someone's brains out?

And when had he turned into such a pansy-ass that he wanted to cuddle?

He followed her directions as they sped down the highway, as both of them continued to fume in silence. In between the anger, he worked through scenarios for starting the conversation when they got to her house. He didn't want to come across as attacking her. That would be a bad move. *Or* looking out for her. He definitely had more sense than that by this point. But he also refused let her walk away without discussing her recklessness.

As the mailbox numbers grew closer to hers, Nick decided it would be best to simply take the plunge. And he might as well start now. "You scared me out there today." He recalled his fear as the car had left the track. "In fact, you terrified me."

She shook her head. "It was *nothing*. I barely even crashed."

"Harper. *Honey*." At the endearment, she jerked her gaze his way, her brows pulled in tight. "You lost control at nearly two hundred miles per hour. You're going to sit there and tell me that was nothing? That it didn't scare you?"

"I don't get scared."

He bit his tongue at her words. He'd seen the terror on her face, but he didn't point that out because she'd deny it. Instead, he shut his mouth and drove the remainder of the distance in silence. When he pulled into her driveway, he was floored at the sight of her home. But again, he kept his comments to himself.

"Thomas had it built," Harper said, as if to explain the ostentatious size of the building sitting in front of them. "He didn't want us to want for anything."

"It's nice," Nick replied. And he'd say the man had accomplished what he set out to do.

Harper huffed out a breath and grumbled, "It's too big."

Well, there was that. He didn't know why anyone would need such a large place to live. He pulled up beside the garage and stopped the truck, and she had her purse on her lap before he could shift into park.

"Thanks for the ride." Her tone wasn't polite, but as least she hadn't jumped from the truck with it still moving. However, when she opened her door, Nick opened his, as well. She stopped and looked back at him. "What are you doing?"

"Coming in. We need to talk about what happened today."

"No, we don't." She made another move to exit, and Nick once again followed suit. He slid his left foot to the ground, and Harper sighed and dropped back to her seat. "I'm trying not to be rude, Nick, but the fact is, I don't want you to come in."

"That's fine. We can talk here."

"We're not going to talk anywhere, because there's nothing to talk about."

When her look turned even more belligerent, he merely shrugged. "We can either talk out here or I'm following you into the house."

"Then I'll call the cops."

"Really?" His own anger rose to a new level. "You want to avoid your issues so much that you'd call the cops on me?"

"I'm not avoiding anything. I just don't want unwelcome people in my home."

"Well, at least you didn't call me a random stranger again."

She jutted out her chin, and he matched her look. So she turned away from him to glare out the windshield. The both of them were acting like children, pouting because they couldn't have their way, but Nick was powerless to change things. He remained furious, she remained stubborn, and somehow, one of them was going to win this argument. But honestly, he wouldn't bet on either one of them at that point.

Yet when she pushed her hair behind her ear, and he saw her fingers shaking, he couldn't help the concern that washed over him. She'd scared herself today. Badly. She was crashing from the adrenaline rush now, and all of that fear was wrapped around a pain that he so clearly recognized. Her walls may have been thick, but that didn't keep him from seeing straight through them to know that she was hurting. And that *that* was the basis for her recklessness.

He gentled his voice. "You're too risky, Harper. And I'm certain it comes from the loss you experienced a year and a half ago."

"You know nothing about my loss."

"Then tell me about it."

Her shoulders curled in on herself, but nothing else about her changed. Face remained forward. Silence stony.

"I've told you before that I have broad shoulders," he reminded her. "Let me help. You're lashing out. Daring something to happen to you because you're hurting. Maybe because you lived and he didn't."

Her throat moved as she swallowed, and Nick wondered if he'd called it right. Was it survivor's guilt?

"No, I'm not," she whispered heatedly.

"And you're stubborn as sin on top of it," he muttered. But he shifted in his seat, bringing one leg up so he could face her, and hoping that if he opened up a little, then maybe she would, too. "I've had my share of heartaches, as well," he told her. "Not like yours. Definitely. But bad enough that it permanently damaged me on the inside. I understand the need for anger. The desire to hurt in the present just so you don't have to hurt from the past."

A muscle jerked in her jaw.

"My mother hated me," he said softly. "She died never once implying that I made her world brighter in any way. That she even so much as cared."

Harper stared at him.

"I'm just saying that I recognize pain when I see it, and especially in you. And that I truly do want to help."

"But I don't need help." Her voice shook.

"I know. You keep saying that. And I never thought I did, either. Until—"

She shook her head as if she didn't want to hear any more, and Nick stopped talking, almost thankful for the interruption. He didn't want to talk about his mother, anyway. Christ, what had he been thinking?

"I'm sorry I scared you today," she said. "Truly, I am." The words came out soft, and he watched as she seemed to try to force the tension in her shoulders to ease. She unclasped her fingers where they gripped her purse. "I didn't mean to wreck. I wasn't trying to hurt myself. I was just having fun. And really, everything did end up okay. I didn't hurt me or anyone else."

"But you didn't have it under control."

"Things happen sometimes, Nick. It was an accident."

"You're too risky."

"No, I'm not. I'm just living my life. Experiencing things. It's what Thomas and I did." And again, the anger Nick had become so familiar with flashed through her eyes and stared back at him, and a light began to dawn inside Nick.

"You're acting this way *because* of Thomas?" he said. "Because of something he did?"

"I'm acting no way."

Was it not survivor's guilt, but something her husband had done?

This time when she reached for the handle, Nick didn't try to follow her. She opened her door and slid to the ground. "I'm fine," she told him once more. "I've got everything under control. I always do."

"But what if one day you don't? People mess up. Accidents turn deadly."

Her body jerked with his words, and he felt bad for bringing up her memories. She'd definitely been in an accident that had turned deadly.

But he didn't feel bad enough to keep from finishing his point.

"What if you push too far?" he asked her. "Panic instead of maintain control? It could kill you."

Pure anger filled her eyes now, and it was definitely directed at him. "I never panic."

Then she slammed the door and walked away.

Harper stopped at the corner of her house and turned to watch Nick drive away. How dare he say that accidents could turn deadly. She, out of everyone, knew that. And he was a callous, spiteful person to say that to her just because he was mad.

His truck disappeared from sight, and she whirled around and stomped up the front steps. What did he know about accidents, anyway? Or heartache. His one big beef with the world was that his mother hadn't liked him.

Well, boohoo.

A hint of guilt over her thoughts niggled at her as she shoved open the heavy wooden door and stared into the empty house. She had a few more battle scars than Nicholas Wilde did, so he could just deal. Dead husband. Dead baby. Destroyed life.

Dropping her purse, she slammed the door and stormed through the house, and suddenly, all the fire drained from her and she found herself sinking to the floor. She crawled on all fours to the corner and put her back against the wall. And for the first time since Thomas had left her, she wished she could cry. Maybe shedding a few tears would lessen the never-ending weight that sat in her chest. The weight had gotten really heavy lately. And she was so tired of carrying it.

But the tears didn't come. They never did.

Dropping her head back, she stared up at the ceiling, her eyes roaming over the smooth white finishes. In a fit of frenzy, she'd had everything on the first floor redone in white. White walls, white fixtures, white cabinetry. She'd even replaced the countertops with white marble—as well as the floors. The entire place was now a mausoleum. And it was depressing as hell.

She hated it.

She hated everything.

Her gazed moved to the center of the ceiling and landed on the elaborate crystal chandelier that she'd paid way too much money for. The light hung directly under what she now considered Thomas's room. The space that housed all of his stuff. She'd originally removed everything of his from the house, but her mom had gathered it from the pile in the backyard and brought it back in.

After her mom had not only lugged Thomas's belongings back inside the house but had also packed them into totes, Harper hadn't had the energy to fight her over it. So she'd eventually stored everything in the room above where she now sat. Then she'd shut the door, and she hadn't stepped foot back in it since.

She closed her eyes and let herself picture Thomas as he'd been before that last day. Man, she'd loved him. And he'd loved her.

She thought about their wedding day, her white lace dress handed down from her grandmother, and him in his dress blues. There had been so many dreams between the two of them. And they'd been fulfilling them, too. They'd been helping people, loving each other. Honoring his brother.

They'd even been bringing a new life into the world—not that the pregnancy had been discovered until after Thomas had died.

Their lives together were all they'd ever wanted, and despite protests from his parents, they'd never veered from their paths. But now she sat in the corner of their sterile kitchen, all alone, with nothing but herself and her loneliness to keep her warm at night. And her fear. This was not the life she was supposed to have.

Nick's words came back to her. *You're lashing out. Daring something to happen to you because you're hurting. Maybe because you lived and he didn't.*

No, she wasn't. It was more complicated than that.

But he *had* been right about one thing. She'd been scared today. When the car had gone airborne, she'd honestly thought her time had come. That she was finally going to kill herself.

Because, yeah, maybe she did dare fate. She had ever since she'd crawled out of that really dark place she'd gone to those first few weeks. Yet she hadn't realized any of that until today—when she'd thought that fate was about to put her six feet under.

She didn't want to die.

She just wanted to quit being so angry.

Chapter Fourteen

Ohmygoodness. I wish she'd hurry up before I pee on myself!"
Harper peered up from her phone where she was scrolling through Facebook and eyed her sister, who was lying flat on the ultrasound table. They'd arrived at the obstetrician's office more than an hour before and had been waiting in the patient room for a good twenty minutes. "Maybe you should just go," she suggested. She nodded toward a closed door. "There's a bathroom connected to this room."

"I can't just go." Jewel groaned. She pulled her knees up on the table and cupped her hands over her lower belly. "They told me to drink water before I showed up, so they could see the baby better."

"Well, maybe you drank too much. You could get rid of a little of it."

Jewel shot her an irritated glare and added in an eye roll, as if asking what Harper could possibly know about it, and Harper silently agreed. She knew nothing.

She returned her attention to her phone and slunk down even farther in her corner chair. She *really* wished Bobby had been able to make it home for this appointment. He'd tried. Arrangements had been made to fly in late last night so he could be here, with the intent of leaving in the morning. He'd planned to help them load up for this weekend's rodeo, then they'd drop him at the airport on their way out of town.

But at the last minute, dangerous thunderstorms had cancelled several flights out of Boston, and the earliest flight he could rebook would have been too late to make the ultrasound. So they'd gone to plan B. Harper would FaceTime him when the technician arrived.

The door opened, and a twentysomething woman in pink scrubs and a bouncy blonde ponytail walked in. And she was *also* pregnant. Noticeably so.

Harper squelched her irritation. The last thing she wanted to do was be around pregnant women, and now she was in a building full of them. They were everywhere. Not to mention, she was about to get a close-up look at one on a monitor. It was a crappy kind of day. The last *two* days had been.

"And how are you feeling today, Mrs. Brandon?"

Jewel's eyes narrowed on the woman. "I feel like I need to pee. You kept me waiting too long."

"My apologies," the technician murmured. She shifted her gaze quickly from Jewel and reached out a hand to Harper. "Hi. I'm Claire." At Harper's less-than-enthusiastic reception, Claire timidly returned to Jewel. Jewel merely snarled at her, so Claire turned her attention to readying her machine.

Once the other woman had looked away from them, Jewel flapped her fingers toward Harper. "Hurry up," she hissed. "Call him."

Harper scowled and held the phone up for her sister to see. The call was already going through. And clearly, pregnancy hormones had turned her sister into the devil. Bobby didn't answer, which helped nothing, and Harper swore under her breath as tears welled up and spilled over Jewel's cheeks.

"Try him again," she sobbed.

Claire peeked up from a folder of paperwork to eye both of them at the sound of Jewel's wails, and Harper once again held up her phone. She pointed to the screen, where another call was going through. "I'm trying to get her husband on the line. His flight got cancelled and he couldn't make it home for the appointment."

"Awww," Claire murmured. She immediately had complete sympathy for the nut-job pregnant lady about to pee all over her table. She patted Jewel's hand. "Don't worry, sweetie. We'll get him on the phone. We can wait a couple of minutes to start if we need to."

"What I *need* is to *pee!*" Jewel yelped.

Bobby answered as Jewel shouted, and with a relieved look, Claire once again turned away. Harper thrust her cell at Jewel, and instantly, her sister's entire demeanor changed. She was once again the sweet woman Harper knew her to be.

Harper shook her head at the Jekyll-and-Hyde impersonation and returned to her seat. She felt uncomfortable enough being there. The last thing she wanted was to intrude on Jewel and Bobby's moment. So she crossed her arms over her chest and sank down, making no attempt to hide the fact that her sister wasn't the only one in a foul mood. She'd been like this since Nick had dropped her off at her house two days before.

She hadn't bothered to pick up her car yet, nor had she reached out to tell him when she would. She'd just sulked.

And she remained angry over their argument. Granted, she could understand his worry over her safety. Those had been a few tense moments. And she even got his need to discuss the situation afterward. He seemed to be like that. In her face about everything he deemed an "issue."

And in a better frame of mind she might even be inclined to appreciate that characteristic.

But right now she remained ticked.

Jewel's light laughter permeated Harper's fog of bad mood, and Harper found herself silently watching her sister and Bobby as they stared wide-eyed at the monitor together. Jewel's belly was still flat, but that didn't stop the technician from finding hidden tissue underneath. Harper couldn't make out anything specific in the grainy black-and-white images, but she understood that it represented a life. She found herself suddenly thinking about Thomas again. She missed him. And if he couldn't have been at her first ultrasound, then she would also have wanted to FaceTime him during it. They would have had this same first moment together in a similar low-lit room, each softly murmuring words of wonder to the other.

Harper smiled slightly as another tear rolled over her sister's cheek. It was a single tear this time, and Harper understood that it was a happy one.

Then she thought about how she'd told Nick that she never panicked. That had been a lie. She had panicked. In the worst possible way.

She suddenly wanted to apologize to Nick for being so angry with him. He hadn't done anything wrong. She'd been rude and tried to push him away when he'd just been attempting to help. Thomas would have been doing the same thing as Nick.

"And that right there," Claire began, reaching over and turning up the volume on the machine, "is your baby's heartbeat."

Harper wanted to die. Right there in the middle of the office building as she listened to the steady whop-whop from the machine. She didn't want to draw another breath.

Unable to be in the room any longer, she made an excuse and left. She didn't stop moving until she got outside, and then she continued until she found herself standing in the middle of the parking lot. A car horn honked, trying to get around her, and she held up a hand in apology. She stumbled out of the way and ended up leaning against the trunk of another vehicle, dragging in gasps of air.

She didn't know how long she stood there, bent over like that, but eventually a light hand touched her shoulder. She looked up.

"Are you okay?" Jewel asked.

Harper nodded. She pushed off the car and looked around as if uncertain where she was. She hadn't even come to the right parking lot. "Sorry," she mumbled. She took her phone when Jewel held it out to her, and ignored the pinched concern on her sister's face. "You ready to go?"

Jewel cast a shrewd eye in Harper's direction before leading the way to her car. She'd driven today, with the plan being to drop Harper at Nick's after the appointment so she could get her jeep. They slid into the front seat of the car, but instead of starting the ignition, Jewel looked over at her. Worry lined her face. "I'm sorry I was such a bear in there."

Harper laughed tiredly. "Honey, you're pregnant. You're allowed."

"Then if you're not upset about me . . . what's going on with *you*?"

Harper shook her head. "Just a bad day." She couldn't bring herself to make direct eye contact. She reached over and took the key from her sister, sliding it into the ignition and starting the car. "Can we just go?"

"Sure." Jewel backed out of the space and made it to the edge of the parking lot before she tried again. "Really, are you okay, Harp? Because you don't look so good. What happened?"

"I'm fine. I promise." In truth, she was about to fall completely apart.

"We could go to my house. I could make us some lunch?"

"I'm not hungry."

"Then how about—"

"Jewel." Harper heard the noticeable shake in her voice. "Please. Just take me to get my car. I have things to do this afternoon, and no time to . . ." She pressed her lips together and shook her head instead of finishing the sentence. She knew Jewel just wanted to help. Her whole family would be there in an instant if she'd only let them.

But she couldn't. She was too ashamed.

"I'm not sure—"

"I'm just tired," Harper interrupted again, this time forcing a smile. "Really. I'll be fine."

Nick wiped sweat from his brow before he attacked the next tree, once again cursing the bears that had a cherry fetish as he worked to minimize the damage. It looked as if more than one bear had managed to break through the fence barrier that had been erected several years ago—probably a mama and her cubs—and they'd literally shredded ten mature trees. The plumping green cherries were gone, branches hanging at odd angles. And Nick found himself wishing curses upon the animals, hoping the unripe fruit made them sick.

He also grudgingly thanked them for only taking out ten trees. It could have been worse.

He'd already fixed the fence, and was now on the last tree. Once he had it sheered down into manageable pieces, he'd drag the limbs to the pile where he'd stacked the others, then he'd come back with a trailer to pick them up. They'd hit the chipper before the afternoon was over.

Danged bears.

He grumbled under his breath as he finished up, and recognized that his bad mood wasn't solely due to the wildlife. He hadn't heard from Harper since he'd dropped her off at her house, and his patience was wearing thin. Her jeep still sat in the driveway, and though he'd considered having it delivered to her house just to get a rise out of her, he'd decided to wait her out instead. He'd pushed her pretty hard the other day. Now it was up to her. They were either through . . . or they were due for a serious conversation.

And the truth was, with any other woman he'd be done. But this time, his fingers were crossed for that conversation.

When he finished with the branches, he climbed on the four-wheeler and headed back along the path that took him nearest the lake. It passed the spot where he and Harper had walked the day she'd told him about her late husband. It was also where Nick had admitted to her that he wasn't sure he'd be ready to leave when his dad returned.

He was even more conflicted on that topic today.

He brought the all-terrain vehicle to a stop at the edge of the ridge and spent a moment taking in the lake. It was a clear, warm day, and from this viewpoint, it seemed as if he could see all the way across the water. He couldn't, of course. The distance was too far.

He thought about his years growing up here . . . about growing up with his mom.

His sister used to sneak out to the dock simply to get away from her, but Nick and his brothers had been able to escape with their dad on a more regular basis. If they weren't helping him with something in the fields, then they were running errands in town or working on machinery in the barn.

It hadn't been Nick's favorite way to spend the time, but it had been a heck of a lot better than staying inside. The best thing to ever happen to him had been his mother dying.

And how completely sad was that?

If Harper hadn't stopped his runaway mouth when she had the other day, he probably would have shared that bit of info with her, as well. Along with the fact that his mother had hated him. She hadn't loved him because he hadn't been enough. And he'd been about to share *all* his baggage with Harper.

That knowledge amazed him on a number of levels. He'd not only never talked about his mother with another woman, but the idea had never even crossed his mind to do so.

He climbed back on the ATV and headed to the barn. But before he could hook up the wagon to retrieve the limbs, the sound of an approaching vehicle stopped him in his tracks. He straightened and watched as a dark-blue sedan headed up the driveway. He didn't recognize the car, but he had an inkling of who sat in the passenger seat.

The car stopped, and Harper opened the passenger door, and Nick finally recognized Jewel in the driver's seat. He tossed up a hand to Jewel. She waved, then drove off. Harper didn't look his way as she got into her jeep.

Nick's chest ached. Was she seriously going to leave without saying a word?

The jeep remained silent, the engine not turning over—but neither did Harper get back out. Nick maintained his position by the barn. Any discussion at this point had to be initiated by her. When the vehicle's door once again opened, Nick released a sigh of relief. She stepped out, and the minute her footfalls headed in his direction, he moved toward the house. They met about thirty feet from the deck.

"Can we talk?" Harper asked. She shaded her eyes as she looked up at him.

"Of course."

They walked side by side to the deck, and when Harper lowered to a wicker chair sitting in the corner by itself, Nick kept his opinion on her choice of seating to himself. He pulled out a chair at the patio table and waited. They'd not parted on the best of terms, and he had zero idea where to start. He'd let her figure that out.

"First of all," she finally began. She licked her lips and scrubbed her palms down over the denim covering her thighs. "Don't call me honey."

He lifted a brow. "Excuse me?"

"You called me honey the other day when we were fighting. I'm not your honey. We're just having sex."

He held his palms up as if in surrender. "My bad. I will never again call you honey. It was an unacceptable crime on my part to indicate through words that I like you."

She rolled her eyes at him, and for the first time since she'd lost control at the wheel of the Ferrari, he began to breathe marginally easier. "And don't make me laugh while I'm still mad," she grumbled.

"That one I can't promise." He gave her a small smile. "It's part of my charm."

She blew out a breath then, and a slight curve finally found her lips. She shook her head at him, as if unsure where to start, then opened her mouth and her words tumbled out. "I scared myself the other day. When I wrecked. You were right. I was terrified. I thought I was going to die. And I swear, I don't want to die. But my life flashed before my eyes in that moment. All the things I once wanted. All the things I haven't done."

Her voice broke, and Nick rose and dragged his chair over to sit in front of her.

"But you *didn't* die," he said calmly.

"And then there's . . ." She blew out another breath and looked away, and Nick reached out and captured her hand.

"Look at me. Tell me what's going on in your head."

"You weren't wrong, okay?" Her eyes were hollow when they turned back. "I do tempt fate. I do. I know it. But the thing is, I had no idea that's what I was doing. Because I'm so angry." Her fingers squeezed his. "Thomas died, and he shouldn't have."

He nodded. He understood that kind of anger. "Do you want to tell me about the accident?" he offered. "Would that help?"

He knew of the details because he'd read about it in the news. But she'd actually been there. She'd jumped from the plane with him, and her husband had died in front of her. Nick couldn't imagine that kind of experience, nor its impact on a person.

"I'm so tired," she whispered. "All this anger . . . it's exhausting. But I can't figure out how to move past it. Or if I even want to. And I lied to you." She stared at him, the intensity on her face breaking his heart. "I did panic. Once. Just once in my whole life. And because of it, Thomas is dead."

"No," he began, but she covered his mouth with her fingers.

She nodded. "It was my fault. He would be here today if not for me." She let out a dry chuckle. "Or he'd be in California if he'd never met me."

Nick no longer cared if she wanted her space or not. She needed him. And he was here for her. He picked her up and resettled them both in the chair she'd been sitting in.

Chapter Fifteen

Fear had dried out Harper's throat, but now that she was here—now that she'd started talking—she didn't want to stop. She'd kept so much bottled up, maybe sharing *would* help. And if not, she certainly couldn't imagine it would hurt at this point.

"As you can guess," she began, "Thomas's death was hard on me."

Nick's arms hugged her tight, and she tilted her head to look up at him.

"You know how he died, right? And that I was there?"

"I do. And I'm so sorry."

"Yeah, well. We all have burdens to bear," she said softly. "This is mine." She tucked herself back against his chest. "Anyway, it was a gorgeous day that morning. Perfect jumping weather. We jumped all the time, and had for years. But that morning, our jump was a celebration."

"What were you celebrating?" Nick asked.

She looked up at him again, trying to decide how much to share, and settled on the facts as they'd been known at the time. "The start of our family."

"You were pregnant?"

"We planned to get pregnant. We'd been playing for years, living our lives for the moment, but we'd always promised each other that when the time was right, we'd settle down and focus on a family. Less about adventure. And the time was right."

"So you jumped as one last hoorah?" he guessed.

"Exactly."

Only, she hadn't told Thomas that morning that her period was late. And she was like clockwork. It had only been one day, but she'd known.

She'd just known.

So she'd picked up a pregnancy test before heading out, intending to take it with Thomas after they'd made it back to the ground. She swallowed the details that she wasn't willing to part with and continued. "It's a simple story, really. My chute didn't open."

"And your backup chute?"

She grimaced. "That's when I panicked. All I could think . . ." Was that she was going to kill the baby that might be growing inside her. That she shouldn't have jumped given her suspicions. That they could have celebrated by having a nice romantic dinner, instead.

But she'd always wanted to do things big. Hadn't that been the basis for her in-laws' hatred? Not only had she convinced Thomas to live *here*, but she'd then encouraged his irresponsibility.

"I couldn't think straight," she said, forcing herself to continue. "It didn't even occur to me to open my backup chute. My mind just froze. Thomas saw what was happening and dove through the air to get to me. I was flailing. Literally. As if it were my first solo jump and I had no clue what to do. It was ridiculous."

Nick gave her a squeeze, and the reminder that she was in his arms soothed her.

"He calmed me. He caught up with me and held on to me. Kissed me." She stared off in the distance toward the lake as she told the story. Her nose burned. "He looked me in the eye and got me focused. We'd dropped low at this point, but we still had time to get down safely. He got the cord for my backup chute in my hand, then he gripped his cord. On the count of three he pushed off, and we both opened our chutes. Only . . ."

She blinked as the lake went unfocused.

"Only, our chutes got tangled," she said more softly. "I'm not sure why. He didn't get far enough away before I opened mine, I guess. But we got tangled up, and though both partially opened and they did slow us, we were still dropping too fast. And we weren't heading for open land any longer. When we looked down, it was trees or power cords. With no time to avoid both.

"We tried again to get apart, but . . ." She had to pause and catch her breath. Her breathing had sped up.

"Stop," Nick said. "You don't have to finish."

"No." She shook her head, almost frantic with the need to get through the story. "He died because of me. Because I panicked. If I'd just pulled the backup chute, he wouldn't have been there beside me. We wouldn't have gotten tangled. And then"—she gulped—"when we headed for the tree, the idiot wrapped his entire body around mine so *he* would be the one to take the brunt of the fall. Stupid—"

"He saved you," Nick interrupted.

"Yes." The word came out as hard as she felt. Thomas shouldn't have died. Not for her.

She thought about his last words. *Don't quit living because of this. Promise me. Don't ever let anything slow you down.*

She'd refused to make that promise. She'd refused to consider life without him.

When they'd crashed, and she'd heard so many snapping sounds, she'd sworn to herself that none of them were from him. That she hadn't honestly just heard her husband's body breaking into pieces.

But she'd been pretty sure she was wrong.

She scrubbed at her face with the heel of her hands as if expecting to find tears there, but her skin came away dry. She stared at her palms, holding them up in front of her. As if the lines marking her skin had the answers. Thomas had died. And on the very same day, she'd gotten confirmation that she was pregnant. That the baby was fine.

"I'm sorry for the things I said the other day," Nick said, and Harper looked up at him. Dazed. She'd forgotten that he was there. "About you panicking," he added. His skin seemed pale, and she put her fingers to his cheek. "I'm so sorry," he finished on a whisper.

"You don't need to apologize for that."

"I do. I didn't know what I was talking about. I shouldn't have—" His jaw clenched, and he pressed into her hand. "I hurt you with my words."

"You were just trying to help." She traced her thumb over the line of his jaw. "I get that. And I actually think it did help. I mean, I'm here now, aren't I? I'm facing my anger. I'm talking about the accident. It's the first time I have, by the way. I did rant to my mom *about* the accident at one point, but I didn't talk about it. Not like this. I could never talk about it like this."

He didn't say anything else, so she put her head back on his shoulder and enjoyed the feel of his heartbeat underneath her body.

"Tell me about him," Nick said after a few minutes.

"About Thomas?"

"Facing the accident brought back awful memories. It's hard on you." He glanced down at her, and she saw concern in the tenderness of his gaze. "You should remember the good things, too. Tell me about him."

Her hand shook as she touched a single finger to the center of Nick's mouth. It had softened along with his eyes. "Okay." She nodded. She liked that idea. "Where should I start?'

He pressed a kiss to her forehead. "Tell me what you loved most about him."

That was easy. "That he was willing to try anything." Though she'd sometimes questioned if his parents had been right in their accusations. "And that he had a heart of gold."

She shifted on Nick's lap, bringing her legs up and draping them over the arm of the chair. Her move pulled her away from his chest, but he left his arm behind her. He dropped his other hand to her lap, and she leaned back and tilted her face up to the sky. There were no clouds today, only blue as far as the eye could see. And she couldn't help but think that Thomas was looking down on them.

Would he be happy to see her sitting in another man's lap? To see her less sad for once?

She brought her eyes back to Nick's. "I once told you that he had no siblings, but that's not quite true. He had an older brother who died. Thomas idolized him as a kid. Harry died when Thomas was ten, and Thomas decided on the spot to spend the rest of his life honoring his brother. Harry had wanted to go into the army, so Thomas went for him. Harry had never seen a challenge that he wouldn't take, so you couldn't have made Thomas back down."

"What killed him?"

She swept a hand out in front of her. "This place. He was in the area with a buddy for a birthday trip. He'd just turned sixteen, and his parents had let the two of them stay at the lake house for the week. They'd gone to Huckleberry Canyon but got trapped in a thunderstorm. He broke a leg trying to get to shelter. Clear through the skin. So his buddy went for help. Search and rescue was called out, but by the time they found him, Harry had apparently tried to move again. Possibly he'd been dazed due to his pain. They found him seventy feet below a nearby ledge." She recalled Thomas's pain as he'd told her the story. "His body had been so broken. I don't think any of them ever recovered from his death."

"I can imagine. The elements here can be brutal."

"When Thomas first told me about it, I remembered hearing about the accident. I'd been ten at the time, too. And I'd wanted more than anything to go out and help find that missing boy. I was certain I could locate him if only Mom and Dad would let me go."

Nick's fingers danced lightly along the skin of her arm. "You used to do similar things a lot, didn't you? Rescue animals, raise money for needy people. All kinds of causes you led the charge for, if I'm remembering correctly."

"I always had a mission."

Until lately. These days, she merely flew her helicopter when she felt like it. And pretty much sat in her house the rest of the time.

"Anyway," she continued, pushing *that* thought away to reexamine later, "after his brother's death, his parents sold their vacation home and refused to come back."

"Thomas falling for you . . . that had to be tough."

"For them," she said. "Thomas had actually always intended to come back; they just didn't know it. Thomas tried to change his parents' minds about this place. About me. But they wouldn't listen. Threatened to disown him. But he had a trust fund from his great-grandfather. His parents couldn't keep him from it. And to rub salt in their wounds, when Harry died, *his* trust transferred to Thomas, too. The day Thomas got access, he bought the helicopter. We came home and started volunteering in the Flathead Valley Search and Rescue program right after."

She saw the surprise on Nick's face. "He was a pilot, too?"

"No, he was a flight medic. But we made a good team. Of course, we had paying jobs, as well. I had my flight business, and he'd gotten hired locally as a paramedic until he could get on full time with the SAR program. We refused to simply live off his trust. That's not who either of us was." Her voice grew melancholy. "I'd had interest in SAR most of my life. It's why I wanted to fly in the army. Then I met Thomas and learned about his brother, and our dreams became one. It seemed like what we were meant to be, you know? Fate," she finished on a whisper.

She pressed her cheek into Nick's palm as he brushed a piece of her hair behind her ear. "Are you still involved with search and rescue?"

"No." She squeezed up her shoulders in a tight shrug. "I can't. Not without him."

And that made her feel hollow inside.

Nick put his arms around her and held her tight, and as she sat there in the comfort of his lap, she became grateful for two things. That he'd pushed her to talk about Thomas. And that he'd been here when she'd needed him. She'd had no idea that simply talking would help ease her grief.

Not that it was gone.

But for the first time since Thomas had died, she could feel the good of what they'd once been. Her anger sat behind her memories now. Instead of front and center.

She tilted her mouth up and touched the warm skin on the underside of Nick's chin, and when his caring eyes peered down at her, she said, "Make love to me."

He didn't immediately respond. Just studied her as if trying to determine her reasoning.

"You make me feel," she explained. "More things than anger and pain. That's what I need. That's why I invited you into my room that first night. No one has done that for me since Thomas."

He stroked his hand over her hair. "You're okay? We can keep talking."

"I don't want to talk anymore."

There might be more to the story, but not more she was willing to share.

She stared at Nick. Waiting. She needed him to understand. She'd given him all she could. When he finally nodded, she wanted to wrap her arms around him and never let go.

"Then that's what we'll do," he said. He kissed her. His lips gently touching hers. Clinging. But he kept it PG. And when he lifted his head, she could see such tenderness in his eyes. "You're sure?" he asked.

"I am."

So he kissed her again, and this time didn't pull away nearly as fast. One hand slid along her outer thigh, and she felt like a cat, readying to stretch in the sun. "Where to?" he muttered against her lips. "It's private back here. No one would see us. Or we could go inside."

Out here?

She pulled back and looked around. The idea had merit. And it turned her on. She caught Nick's chin with her fingers, then rubbed the pad of her thumb over the length of his bottom lip. He was a good man.

"Out here," she said. A shiver shook her when he sucked the tip of her thumb into his mouth. "It's a beautiful day," she continued. "And I want to live right in the middle of it."

He nodded in agreement and stood with her in his arms. He moved them both to the matching sectional and stretched her out before him, but when she reached for the top button of her shirt, he stopped her.

"Let me." His words were low and heavy, and he sat beside her and moved her hands to her sides. "Let me take care of everything."

His motions were slow, but Harper felt every one of them to her core. He cupped her face in both of his hands and took his time making love to her mouth. Then he kissed her eyelids and grazed his lips across her temple and to her ear.

He pressed soft nibbles along the shell of her ear as his fingers inched down the front of her shirt and slipped the buttons free one by one. After sliding the last free, he leaned back and slowly spread the material wide. She wore a tiny pale-green lace bra that closed in the front, and at that moment, she couldn't have been happier with her selection.

Nick seemed pretty pleased with it himself, as his thumb scraped along the dip in the center of her stomach and slipped under the bra's hook. His gaze found hers, and her lips parted on a breath. His slow and gentle moves were more than she was used to with him, but she found it was exactly what she wanted. The clasp slipped free, and she sucked in a breath as he parted that material, as well. The cooler afternoon air brushed over her, but Nick didn't look down at her body. Not yet. He kept his attention focused on her face.

He kissed her again, taking his time once more, while his hands stroked over her. He touched her in a way she might have guessed him incapable of before she'd gotten to know him, and though his careful, easy moves had her more than ready to progress to the next step, she also found herself with the desire to go even slower. Nick seemed to want that, too, as after he tugged the remainder of her clothing from her body, he shed his own and carefully eased down beside her. No condom appeared, and he moved as if they had all night.

He continued doing exactly as she'd asked. Making love to her. And her eyes grew hot with surprising pressure. So hot that she thought her long-awaited tears were about to make an appearance. But she didn't cry. Not with Nick. She simply soaked in every touch and heartfelt move he made.

And when he finally pulled a condom from his wallet, there were still no hurried movements. He kissed her while he rolled it on, and when he stretched his body over hers, he lifted her arms above her head. He slid his rougher palms down the length of her, from her hands to the sides of her hips. And only then did he finally lift her gently and position himself between her legs.

And when he pushed in, fitting to her so perfectly, it seemed in that second as if he'd been made for that very spot.

Chapter Sixteen

A cool breeze brushed over them later that evening, and Nick found himself lifting the blue strands of Harper's hair and running the chunks, one by one, through his fingers. The two of them were tucked under a blanket he'd brought out earlier, and they'd just made love again.

"Your hair was the first thing that attracted you to me," he told her. "I'd never seen a girl with pink hair before."

She lay draped on top of him, and her lazy smile implied his revelation was no surprise.

"I take it you've heard that from guys before?"

The corners of her lips inched higher. "Boys think girls with funky hair are funky in other ways, too. They were always bummed to learn that my hair was more about my rebellion over frilly dresses and being made to look like my younger sisters than an announcement of my wanton ways."

"I'm sure you broke many hearts with that news."

"Maybe. But I rarely cared. I had more important things to worry about."

"Like saving puppies and feeding the hungry?" At her nod, he asked, "That why Thomas was your first?" He'd wondered how she'd gotten out of high school a virgin. "Because you were always too busy with a cause?"

She lay perfectly still on top of him. "Thomas was my first because I loved him."

Her sincere words proved to Nick yet again that she was far more than met the eye. And he was lucky to have the honor of being her second. He slid his palm up her spine, enjoying the silk of her skin and reveling in the fact that he could roll her over and go yet again. He couldn't get enough of this woman.

Her fingers trailed down his bare arm. Across the lake, the sun began to set.

"This afternoon," Harper began, her words as soft as the moment. "It was different between you and me."

This, from the woman who, until today, hadn't let him hold her unless he'd been inside her. He was surprised she'd acknowledged it. He slid his palm back down her body, not stopping until he reached the top curve of her rear.

"Are you okay with that?" he asked.

"I don't know," she admitted. She lifted her head and looked at him. "It's scary."

"It doesn't have to be," he told her. But he wasn't so sure that was true. Today had been a lot more than sex, and it scared the crap out of him, too. "It was just a new thing for us."

Harper watched him as if waiting for him to change his mind, but he kept his fears to himself. He'd never done more than sex before. He had no idea what this afternoon meant, if anything, and honestly, he didn't want to think about the implications.

Finally, she settled her cheek back to his chest, and her breaths danced through his chest hair. He closed his eyes and let his senses enjoy the moment. He could feel her soft breasts just above his waistband, the remaining heat between her thighs, and her toes wiggling along the tops of his feet. It was a moment he suspected would stay with him forever.

"This is a gorgeous view," she said.

He didn't open his eyes. "Yes, it is." He let both hands reach to the underside of her rear, and he cupped her in his fingers. "And I'm eventually going to come home to it."

Once again, revelations he hadn't intended to share came out, but this time he didn't care. He *did* intend to return to Birch Bay, and saying the words out loud made it feel more real.

Harper didn't respond to his statement, as if understanding that he didn't really want to talk about it, and they both grew quiet. His breaths deepened as the night edged toward black, and he told himself they should move inside. If not, he'd be asleep within minutes, and as comfortable as he currently was, he didn't think either of them would appreciate the accommodations after spending a night out on the deck.

"I was brutal to my family afterward." Harper's tone matched the quietness of the night, but her words immediately woke Nick back up. He opened his eyes. She was talking about after the accident.

"How so?"

"I tried to run everyone off."

He felt her body tense.

"They came over every day the first week. After that I wouldn't let them in the house, and I only answered the phone so they'd stay away. But a few weeks into it, I got angry. I yelled at anyone who called. I tried hard to shove them away."

Nick soothed her with his hands, not knowing how else to help. He sensed her need to get more out, so he remained silent.

"After a week of that, my mom showed up and wouldn't leave. I ignored her, but when she made a bed on my porch, I couldn't stand it. So I let her in. She stayed four nights before I would talk to her." A puff of air tickled his chest with her soft laugh. "I love my mother, but I was so angry with her for being there. Then a report of a missing hiker came on the news, and I just started talking. I didn't seem to have control of my words. I yelled about how unfair life could be, and I spewed hate. But it was cathartic. I didn't provide details of the accident, but I showed her what I felt." She lifted her head and shot him a smirk. "And then I made her leave and I redecorated the house, turning the entire first floor white."

His eyed went wide. "White?"

"Everything," she stressed. "It's ghastly. I don't know why white. I had all this stupid money that I didn't want, and I was in a giant house all alone. We'd decorated those rooms together, Thomas and I. And everything we'd picked out suddenly made me furious every time I saw it. So I turned it all white."

He touched a knuckle to her chin. "You're a strong woman, Harper Stone."

"Yeah. But I might be borderline nuts."

He grinned. "Probably. "

A gorgeous smile was his reward before she rested her hands on his chest, and propped her chin on top of them. "Now it's your turn," she announced.

"My turn to what?"

"To tell me your secrets."

Her quick change caught him off guard. "Maybe I just have one secret," he hedged. He assumed she wanted to know about his mother.

"Save the denial, cowboy. You're not the only one who can read people. You're a good man, a charming one, and you have lots of happy groupies."

He looked down his nose at her. "You are so jealous of my groupies."

She grinned wide. "I might be. But that's not the point."

"And what is the point?"

"You are. You have a charmed life. Or on the outside, you seem to. Yet you long for a home you could have returned to years ago,

something holds you back from taking your career to the next level"—
she gave him a tender smile—"and you hurt because of your mother."

Her ability to read him so well moved him. And he found that he
liked that she'd been able to do that.

"So tell me about your mother."

He grunted. "Now?"

"Seems the time for it, doesn't it? No one is around to interrupt us.
Plus"—she touched one fingertip to his lips—"I shared mine."

He kissed her finger. "You did share yours." And because she had,
he figured he owed her one. But it was more than the payment that
made him willing to talk. He *wanted* to share his past with Harper.

The realization made him think of that first night he'd run into her
at the rodeo. He'd just walked away from Betsy and had been wondering
if he were missing a key ingredient to being "normal." To being able to
react in a "typical" fashion toward the woman he was sleeping with. Yet
with Harper, it wasn't a question at all. He wouldn't even let himself
entertain the idea of Harper having sex with anyone else—at least not
while he was having sex with her—and he found himself *wanting* to
tell her his secrets. He'd never had the desire for anything more than a
physical experience with any other woman in his life. The knowledge
was both worrisome and comforting. He held on to the comfort and
ignored the worry.

"Okay," he finally said, returning to the here and now. He would
give her what she asked.

But before uttering another word, the large windows that made up
the back of the house captured his attention. He couldn't see through
the dark panes at the moment, but he could easily picture his mother
standing just on the other side. She'd been beautiful. Always. Polished
in clothes and appearance, with never a single dark hair out of place.

Yet appearances could be misleading. Just as their rustic home had
deceivingly implied warmth and love, on the inside, his mother had
been as cold as ice.

He turned back to Harper. "My mother had issues," he blurted out. She nodded as if in understanding. "What kind of issues?"

"The kind you want to run away from." He closed his eyes and began his story. He couldn't talk about his mother with Harper directly in his face.

"Everyone in town thought we were a perfect family," he explained. "Parents in love, thriving family business, six happy kids. But the reality was, none of that was true." Even the business had been a struggle a lot of the time. "Our lives might have looked pretty from the outside, but they were rough at home. And that was all because of her."

He waited for Harper to comment, but when she didn't, he opened his eyes and stared at the stars coming out above them.

"I was ten when she died, and at that point, I had no idea that anything was wrong with her. I just knew that she didn't love me. And the thing was, not only did she *not* love me, but she made it a point to tell me that she loved my brothers more."

A soft inhalation hit his ears, and Harper cupped his cheek in her hand. "How cruel," she whispered. Her words were harsh. "You deserved better than that."

He swallowed. They'd all deserved better.

"Then there was the fact that she would hurt herself sometimes." He lost focus on the stars as he remembered what his life had been like. "It was only a handful of times. Three, I think. But she'd put herself in danger to get the attention she wanted.

"No. That's not right. To get the *control* she wanted." He looked down at Harper. "She had something called narcissistic personality disorder. If attention wasn't on her, then she found a way to make it so. People worrying about her gave her that attention." He thought about how as a small boy, he'd worried about her more than anyone had known. He'd tried to help, to make her happy. He'd wanted her not to feel bad and be stressed all the time.

But he'd never been able to figure out what he could do to make it better.

"I actually caught her hurting herself once," he shared. A lump formed in his throat. "I was five."

"Oh, Nick. I'm so sorry. What happened?"

He could feel Harper's heart pounding against his chest. "She cut off the tip of her finger," he said. His words were flat. "Literally, cut it off. She caught me watching from the hallway, and screamed that I couldn't tell anyone. So I ran away and hid in my closet, afraid that if I did tell, then she'd *never* love me."

Harper slid her arms around him and pressed her cheek to his chest.

"Only, guilt ate at me," he continued. "Maybe if she'd loved me to begin with, she wouldn't have done it. Or maybe I should have run immediately and told someone in order to show her how much I cared."

He groaned and put the back of his hand to his forehead as he once again stared at the sky. "But then I figured out that she'd cut herself only because she wanted my sister to come home. Dani was in New York City with our aunt. She was having fun, and Mom couldn't stand it. She would have done anything to get Dani back at that moment, and the sad thing was, *I* hadn't mattered in the least. I'd worried myself sick—to the point that I threw up while hiding in my closet—and I had never factored into the equation at all."

"Your mom was ill."

"Yes. Very. But I didn't get any of that at the time. That she brought the problems on herself. That she had a mental issue." And then he realized what Harper had said. He peered down at her. "You sound like you know something about NPD."

"I had a friend in the army. Her mother was similar."

"It wasn't Thomas?" He asked the question carefully, praying he wasn't stepping into another minefield.

"No. Though, his parents had other issues. But I did some research on the matter after I learned about it, and from what I remember, I doubt your mom really loved anybody but herself."

"You're right, that's typical. And no, she didn't."

"But you didn't understand that at the time?"

"Right."

"And you still aren't convinced of it now?"

Nick stared at her, appreciative of her intuitiveness, and finding that he needed to make her see how he felt. He'd never been able to share these things with Nate. How could he? His mother had beaten into his head that she'd loved Nate more. And though the wedge that had once been driven between the two of them had long since disappeared, he still struggled to talk specifics with his closest brother. "I am convinced of it now," he finally answered. "I know it. I've known it for years."

"But . . ."

He didn't take his eyes off Harper. "But at ten years old, I just wanted her to love me. And instead, she died. I took that as my fault."

"No!" She pushed up off his chest. "It wasn't your fault."

"If only I'd made her love me enough," he said. "If only I'd been tough enough." He shook his head, feeling like the little boy he'd once been. "Then she wouldn't have left us."

"She *couldn't* love you, Nick."

"I know. Logically, I get it. But I was ripped apart when she died. I should have saved her."

Pain sliced across Harper's face as she studied him. He could tell she was trying to figure out what to say next. How to make it better. And he could have told her that talking about it was already making it better. But it still wasn't enough, so he waited. Hoping she'd say something so brilliant that he could suddenly rewrite his emotions from fifteen years ago.

"Refresh my memory . . . how did she die?" When Harper finally spoke, her words came out so softly that Nick could barely hear them in the stillness of the night.

"Car crash."

"And were you in the car with her?"

He shook his head.

"Then—"

"It doesn't have to make sense, does it?" He took her hand in his and kissed her palm. "I get that it wasn't my fault. Yet . . . it still was. I found out years later that she'd caused the crash herself, because she once again wanted Dani's attention. Dani had gone off to college—back to New York—and Mom couldn't get her to come home. So she planned the crash to get her to rush home. Only, it didn't go quite as planned. Mom ended up hitting another car, and died from internal bleeding before anyone even knew it was happening. Cord found her. He says she was asking for Dani up until the end."

Understanding dawned. "And that bothered you that she asked for your sister?"

He couldn't answer. Dani's life had been far worse than his, yet he'd spent years being jealous of her. Angry at her.

"But you know it's not because she loved Dani more," Harper said.

He nodded, then looked away. He couldn't stare into those eyes any longer. That only made it worse. "Hell," he muttered. He dragged his hand down over his face. "How messed up is that, huh? She had it ten times worse. Yet I was jealous of a sister who—with my own eyes—I saw being treated more unfairly than me."

"Like you said, it doesn't have to make sense. Mothers are supposed to love their kids. When that doesn't happen, I'd suspect a lot of wires get crossed."

"I suspect you're right."

They both grew quiet as he thought back over the years after she'd died. Their mother had hurt her own daughter so much, that at eighteen, Dani had blocked the memories. She'd ended up repainting the past, putting their mother on a pedestal. The rest of them had gone along with it. Why force her to remember? To hurt like they did? And hey, maybe if they all tried hard enough, then they might remember differently, as well. But that never happened. And though he'd been thankful for everything Dani had done, he'd had to get away from *her*, too.

"I left home at eighteen because I couldn't stand the thought of being in this house one minute longer," he told Harper. "My mother was still here. Her presence, anyway. And that presence overshadowed everything. I couldn't be here. And I never wanted to come back."

"Yet you do now."

He gave a single, dry chuckle. "Does that mean I'm maturing?"

"Or just that you have enough distance to finally deal with it."

Nick gave her a sad smile—knowing she was talking about herself, too—and returned to staring at the stars. He kept a hand on Harper's back, stroking the length of her spine, and she once again tucked in against his chest. He liked them this way.

And he liked that they were talking.

"I never expected to share all that," he told her. "And certainly not with someone outside the family."

"I hope it helped."

"*You* help," he said.

She captured his free hand and kissed his palm the way he'd done hers. "I'm glad." Then she snuggled in even tighter, and they lay there, the sun fully set now and no lights on in the house, and let the darkness surround them.

At the sound of her stomach rumbling, he suggested going in to forage for food.

"In a minute."

So he kept her wrapped up in his arms, his wrists crossed at the small of her back.

"Can I ask you something?" she asked a few minutes later.

He kissed the top of her head. "At this point, I'd say either of us could ask the other anything." He tilted her face up to his. "Lay it on me."

Her mouth twisted into a half grimace, half smile, and she said, "Will you come to dinner with my family on Sunday?"

At his surprised stare, she continued.

"I *know*. I totally ditched you when you wanted me to go to Dani's. I don't deserve you to even consider it. Yet I'm asking. And not as my date." She made a face before adding, "Well, I guess *technically* you'd be my date, but not like a *date*."

"Like a not-a-third-wheel kind of date?"

"Well, not that, either. You'd actually be the only man other than my dad there."

Nick shot her a bored look. "You make it really hard to resist, Stone."

"I know." She laughed lightly. "But I swear it wouldn't be horrible. And it's not like you don't already know all of them. Plus, my mom is a really great cook. I'd just tell everyone that you're coming as a friend. But I need you there because I want them to see that I'm better," she added. "That I'm trying. They do this dinner once a month to force me out of the house, so if I were to show up with someone, that would take some of the pressure off."

He studied her for a moment, trying hard not to read too much into what she was asking of him. She wanted to take him to dinner with her family, to show that she was what? Moving on? Getting out there?

Caring about someone else?

And he did think she cared. Though, to what extent he had no idea.

"And my showing up would say to them that you're better?" he asked.

She nodded. He could see her nerves in the tightness around her eyes. This was important to her.

"Okay. I'll do it. But on one condition." He added the last sentence at the exact moment that she looked relieved.

"And what's that?" She eyed him carefully.

"That you repay me the following Sunday."

"Dinner with Dani again?"

He shook his head. "They're out of town. But Dad and Gloria will be back, and apparently my oldest brother will be home, too. I'll be leaving soon after, so Gloria wants to make dinner a 'thing' that night. She's already e-mailed me about it."

"Then maybe I shouldn't be there if it's going to be a thing."

"Tit for tat, gorgeous." He grinned. He had her. "You actually can't say no."

"Fine." She groaned, but she smiled as she said it. "I'll be there." She reached up and kissed him. "Actually, I'd love to. I haven't seen your dad in years, and I'd be honored to meet his new wife."

"Then it's a date."

"Two of them," she said wryly.

Chapter Seventeen

For someone who didn't want to date, Harper found it odd that she'd not only invited a man to her parents' house but that she'd also agreed to have dinner at his. Sometimes her common sense made no sense.

She pulled open her mother's knife drawer and walked her fingers over the handles until she found the chef's knife. Then she tugged the basket of zucchini closer and plucked one out. As she made the first cut, the clothes dryer sang a tune from the adjoining room.

"My sheets," her mother mumbled. She dropped the lid back on the pot she'd been stirring and hustled out of the room.

Harper smiled to herself as her mother disappeared. Sunday was sheets day. Every bed in the house got stripped whether it had been slept in that week or not. The practice struck her as a complete waste of time, given that three of the four children who'd grown up there no longer slept in most of those beds.

She continued chopping while listening to the light humming now coming from the laundry room. She loved spending time with her mom. And even better, she'd been at the house for the last two hours, and not once had she been grilled about "how she was doing." She'd also barely let herself think about Nick. Or the fact that they'd had a fantastic time together the last few days.

They hadn't done much of anything—she'd helped with chores at the farm and they'd failed at making Parmesan chicken. He'd kissed her on the back of her neck, right at the base where it got her every time, and by the time she'd remembered the chicken . . . it had been too late. They'd also flown down to Big Sky and gone fly-fishing the day before. Her contracted flight had cancelled, so she'd offered to take Nick wherever he'd wanted to go.

Then there had been the nights. She almost groaned out loud at the thought of what they'd done during those nights. She'd stayed at the house with Nick the whole time. It hadn't even crossed her mind to go home that first night after they'd both shared so much of themselves, and other than a quick trip for clean clothes and necessities, she hadn't left Nick's side since. Which was mildly disturbing now that she thought about it.

"I'm not here." This came from Patti as the eighteen-year-old ducked inside the kitchen and poked her head into the fridge. Every month, the four children rotated helping in the kitchen, and this month, cooking fell on Harper. "Just need something to drink," Patti said. She grabbed an orange juice and left as quickly as she'd shown up. Harper's youngest sister hated anything to do with being in the kitchen.

She finished slicing the zucchini at the same time that her mother breezed back into the room. "Only one more load to do, but I'll save that one until later," her mom said. She turned on the faucet to rinse her hands and spoke over the running water. "Wouldn't want to have the machines running while your new man is here."

Harper rolled her eyes. "You know he's not my man, Mom."

"Well, is he coming over for dinner or isn't he?"

"As a friend." She handed her mother a clean towel. "*Only.* Not as my man."

Instead of immediately replying, her mother took her time drying her hands, then opened the oven door and peered in. She closed it, the snapper remaining inside, but as she returned to the stovetop, she cast a glance Harper's way. "So are you telling me that you haven't slept with him?"

"Mom!" Harper yelped. She was horrified. "Why would you even . . ." She stopped talking and gaped at her mother. Was nothing sacred anymore? Mothers and daughters weren't supposed to talk about such things. Her cheeks flamed.

"I'm just saying, that new color in your cheeks looks nice on you," her mom added.

"That color is embarrassment." Harper pointed to her burning cheeks. "I can't believe you just asked me that."

Her mom's eyes suddenly twinkled. "You have, haven't you?" She nodded knowingly. "I can tell. I remember what it was like when your father and I first got together. *Mmmm.* That man. I practically floated on air."

"Really, Mom." Harper shook her head and wanted to disappear. Jewel definitely got her outrageousness from their mother. "It's nothing. We're not *together*. Not in the way you mean. We're just—" She shrugged, going for casual, but in the end she couldn't stop the grin that stretched across her cheeks. She hung her head in shame. "We're just having some fun," she finished.

"Well, fun looks good on you." Her mom kissed her cheek. "It's what you *need*." She winked when Harper peeked back up at her. "Even if it is just temporary."

"Well, it is just temporary," Harper grumbled. "Don't make the mistake of thinking it could be anything else. I don't—" Her voice cracked, and she took a moment to clear her throat as she thought about all she'd never have. "It's all it'll ever be, Mom. I can't . . ." She ended with a shake of her head and a tight-lipped frown.

"It's okay, sweetie." Her mom gave her a warm hug. "This is good. Anything other than sitting home alone is *good*."

"I know." And she did. Her mom might say that fun looked good on her, but Harper knew the changes had come from more than the last three nights of sex. It was because she'd finally begun to heal. Not that she'd ever be completely healed. Her husband was dead. Her child never to be born. Those were burdens she'd forever bear.

But she *was* able to breathe freely for the first time since the accident, and that was due to Nick. She owed the man a huge thanks for getting in her face and not letting her push him away.

And for the first time, she thought about just how temporary all of this was. His dad would be home in a week. Which meant only seven more days.

Her mother took the vegetables to the stove while Harper opened cabinet doors and pulled down dinnerware, and together, they fell into silence as they finished preparations. Harper set the table in the dining room, taking extra care to make everything look just right, and when the doorbell rang on her last trip into the kitchen, her heart skipped a beat.

She looked at her mom, and cracked up at the sight of her mother giving her a naughty brow waggle.

"Mom," she groaned out. She wiped off her hands and pulled the apron from her waist.

"I'm just saying," her mother murmured. "Don't think that temporary means you can't have a heck of a good time."

That darned smile returned to Harper's face, and she decided to give her mother a piece of her own medicine. "Oh, I can definitely promise you I'll have a good time. In fact"—she leaned in so Patti or her dad wouldn't hear if either wandered through—"I plan to have *multiple* good times every night. And maybe again each morning."

She headed to the front door to the sound of her mother's laughter.

Pulling the door open, she was surprised to find not only Nick waiting outside, but Jewel and Chastity, as well. The three of them were deep in conversation, debating the merits of male versus female pregnancy, and she caught Nick's eye over her sisters' heads. Their shared smile made her feel all warm inside.

"The human race would end if men had to go through this," Jewel declared. She entered the house, with Chastity on her heels.

"And I'm saying that until you walk in a man's shoes, give your poor husband a break."

Jewel laughed good-naturedly at Nick's words, and as he stepped into the house, he leaned in, and with his hand on the small of Harper's back, pressed a kiss to her lips. The move shut up both her sisters instantly as they stood there, mouths agape.

Harper flushed at the comfortable intimacy that had developed between her and Nick.

"I'm sorry," Nick murmured. His ears turned pink. "I didn't even think."

"It's not like we didn't know—"

"Jewel," Harper bit out.

"I'm just saying—"

"Out." Harper pointed to the hallway, hoping her sister would actually obey for once. And shockingly, when Chastity grabbed their mouthy, younger sibling by the elbow, Jewel allowed herself to be led from the room.

As silence descended, Harper turned back to Nick. He looked as embarrassed as she felt.

"I really am sorry," he said. "I didn't even think. I just"—he shrugged—"it came naturally."

"I know." She took the two bottles of wine from him. It had come naturally to her, too. "Don't think anything of it. I'll have to take some teasing from everyone later on, but it's already set the tone that I wanted to create tonight."

She looked up at him as they both remained in the open doorway and ignored the tiny voice in her head telling her that he was even better for her than she'd thought. That he could fix her if only she'd let him.

Because she knew that to be untrue. She neither *could* be fixed nor did she deserve to be.

"I'll put these on ice," she said, still staring up at him. Her feet didn't want to move.

"How about we set the tone a bit more first," he murmured.

She nodded as if her neck and brain weren't connected, and made an embarrassing little breathy sound when Nick pulled her to him. He kissed her again, right there in her parents' foyer, as if the two of them hadn't just spent nearly every minute of the last seventy-two hours together.

"And then there was the time the neighbor's cat had seven kittens," Chastity said.

"They were going to turn them all in to the shelter!" Harper exclaimed. "I had to do something."

Nick laughed as Harper's dad went into the story about how an eight-year-old Harper worked tirelessly to talk everyone she'd known into taking a kitten. The man spoke with his entire being, putting much animation into the story, and Nick also picked up on the fact that his eyes never went long without seeking out his wife at the other end of the table. There was love in this room. The real kind of love.

"We ended up with two of them," Glen Jackson finished.

"I remember them," Nick said. He looked across the table to Jewel for confirmation. He'd played with those cats when he'd visited. "Bert and Ernie, right?"

Jewel nodded with a small tip of her head. "Excellent memory."

"Jewel hated those cats," Chastity added.

"I know!" This came from Harper, who sat at Nick's side. "But that's because *they* hated her first. They liked everyone in the family but Jewel."

Nick sipped his wine as he listened to the conversation continue around him. They were all so normal. So real. The kind of family that would have been nice to grow up with. And this dinner was a great idea—just having a standard, once-a-month thing. It was special in a way they probably didn't fully recognize yet. The tradition might have started due to Harper's loss, but something told him that it would continue for years to come. Her mom and dad practically beamed as the girls batted insults and memories back and forth. It was a welcoming space to be in.

He wondered if maybe it wasn't too late to do something similar with his own family. They didn't all live in the same area, but possibly they could make an effort to get together three or four times a year. He had no skills in the kitchen, of course, but that didn't mean he couldn't start the tradition once he moved back home. Potluck at Nick's house.

He smiled into his wineglass as he imagined the outcome. Probably four bags of chips, a store-bought tray of some sort of meat, and whatever Nate decided to prepare. Nate was the only legitimate cook among the boys, and Dani had pretty much given up kitchen duties after handling it all herself for years. Of course, Gloria would be good for something.

But still, maybe it would be better to hold it at the farm with Gloria in charge. It was time to move beyond what that house used to be, and his dad and Gloria had already made good headway in that direction. It was no longer simply the house his mom had lived in.

Chastity started a new story, her hands waving as she got into the guts of it, telling everyone about the time that Harper talked Chastity's boyfriend into jumping off of Harper's favorite diving cliff. "If I remember correctly"—Chastity turned to Nick—"you once saw her jump off that very spot."

Nick stared at Chastity, unsure what to say. How did she . . .

She laughed. "Oh yeah, we all knew you had a crush on her. I was out there that day, too—though you probably never saw me, given that you were only looking at Harp."

Humiliation burned the back of Nick's neck, and he fired a look at Jewel.

"I didn't tell them," she said. "You were an open book. Your tongue hung out whenever she walked into the room."

"I even knew," Patti muttered from her seat down by her mom. "And I was in elementary school."

Harper snorted into her hand. "I will admit that Patti knew because *I* told her. I said that if any boy ever looked at her like that, she should kick him in the nuts and run."

"Harper Ann," Harper's mother chastised.

"I know." Harper spoke with a bored monotone and hung her head. "Don't say 'nuts' at the table."

They all laughed, and Chastity picked her story back up where she'd been interrupted. When she finished, their dad lifted his glass in a toast. "To good wine and better company. Thank you for coming over with our Harper today."

"And thank you for having me." Nick lifted his glass in return. "I'm not much of a cook, so anytime I can get a good meal, I'm in."

Harper's fingers landed on his thigh, and he slipped his hand under the table to cover hers.

Chairs were scraped back after that, and her Dad stood. "Time to do the dishes," he announced. "One of the girls helps Marg cook each month, and another helps me clean up."

Jewel rose with her dad. "I'm up, Dad. Let's get this done before my dinner decides to make a reappearance."

Nick rose, as well. "Let me help. You take the night off, Mr. Jackson. Put your feet up."

"Well, there's no need," her father started. He looked flustered. "You're our guest."

Nick picked up his and Harper's plates. "I'd love to help, really. I haven't gotten to harass Jewel enough today. It'll give me time to make up for that."

Harper's father paused, unsure what to do. Finally, he looked to his wife for answers. She nodded in permission, and the man put his palms up in surrender. "Then thank you, young man. I'll take you up on it. And given that I have a free few minutes, I think I'll take my woman out for a walk. Been a while since we've done that."

The older Jacksons headed out the front door while Chastity, Patti, and Harper stood awkwardly, all seemingly unsure whether they should offer to help since Nick was, or not.

"Get out," he told them. He waved a hand toward the door. "You wouldn't be on dish duty if I wasn't here, right?"

"Absolutely not," Patti agreed. "It was my turn last month, and that's when we had lasagna. Baked-on cheese is *not* my friend."

"Then go." He looked at Harper and nudged his head, telling her to leave, too. With a small nod, she and her sisters took off, same as their parents. The Jacksons lived in an upscale subdivision near the lake, and there was a walking path that wound through a park and play area before ending at the water. At this time in the evening, it would be a lovely walk. He wished he could take it with Harper.

"I'll be back soon," she told him before disappearing out the door.

Nick lifted the plates in his hand. "I'll be here."

As he and Jewel made several passes from dining room to kitchen, he couldn't help but glance through the windows on each trip. The girls hadn't gone far. They'd stopped at the tree he and Jewel used to climb when they were kids. And he couldn't pull his eyes off Harper as she shimmied her way up to a high branch. The smile on her face was contagious.

"You still like her, huh?"

Nick froze, unwilling to look at Jewel, though she now stood directly at his elbow.

She laughed. "I know you're sleeping with her."

"Oh." The word slipped out. What the crap was he supposed to say to that? "I . . ."

"She didn't tell you that I heard you two going at it at the motel?"

Horror washed over Nick as he finally turned to his friend. He knew his mouth hung open, but he seemed to have lost the ability to close it.

"Hey, feel proud. Those were some hella-good noises coming from that room. In fact, if Bobby hadn't been asleep on the other side of the country, I'd have called him up. We could have rung our own bells while you were ringing Harper's."

Nick stared down at her. "Are you going to talk like that when your kid gets here?"

"Maybe." She eyed him with a sweet smile, but that sweetness was deceptive. "Depends on if I have to hear you banging my sister again." She glanced out the window at the sound of Harper's laughter, before turning her gaze back to Nick. "I wasn't sure if you two had hooked up any more since that night until now. But that laugh?" She shook her head with something akin to awe on her face. "I haven't heard it in eighteen months."

"We're just having some fun," Nick muttered, unsure what else to say. He grabbed the last of the glasses and returned to the kitchen.

Jewel followed. "She needs some fun." She peered out the window again. "You may not realize how bad it was for her. Those first few months"—she bit off her words as her eyes filled with tears, and Nick crossed the room and put an arm around her shoulders.

"She told me," he said.

Jewel looked up. "Really?"

It occurred to him that he might have just admitted to something he shouldn't have—he and Harper had done more than have sex. They'd talked. And she'd yet to talk to her family about the accident. "Just that it was a rough time for her," he added, hoping to soften any hurt.

"It's *still* a rough time for her," Jewel told him. She watched Harper through the window for a few more minutes, before turning back to the sink and narrowing her gaze on Nick.

He'd bent to load plates into the dishwasher and tried to ignore her, but when she stayed put he slowly straightened and faced her. Her look pinned him in place.

"It is still just a crush, right?" Jewel asked. "You're not thinking serious? Because she's just now beginning to come out of it. I don't want her hurt any more."

"And what if she hurts me?"

"Nick." Jewel gasped his name. "Really?"

He didn't even know where that thought had come from. "I'm teasing, J. No. It's not serious. I know that's not what she wants or needs. It's not what I want, either."

Jewel nodded, but she looked less than convinced. She glanced over her shoulder to take in Harper once more. "Just be careful with her. I see the way you look at her."

He didn't even want to know how he looked at her.

"We can see that she's better." Jewel turned back to him and they began to work in sync as she handed him dishes and he loaded them. "And we assume you're at the root of it. But at the same time, I still feel like she's hanging on by a thread. As if the wrong word or thought could make her snap. She ran out of my doctor's appointment the other day as if something was after her, and I have no idea why. So I'm just saying, I'm not sure how bad that snap will be if it happens."

Nick made a promise to himself that he'd do his best to be there if the thread broke.

"I'd never do anything to hurt her, Jewel. You know that. You know me."

"I know. And thank you." She hugged him, her head barely hitting him midchest, then she smiled guilelessly up at him like the brat that she was. "And now I'm going to leave you to finish this mess all by yourself. I'm going outside to play with my sisters."

Chapter Eighteen

Nick and Harper sat at the end of the dock on Wilde property Wednesday afternoon, feet dangling over the edge, faces turned toward the sun. It was the end of a long day, and they'd come down to the beach with a couple of beers and a need for nothing more taxing than lifting the bottles to their mouths. They'd spent the last three nights at his place, same as before, though this time they'd done little more than they were doing right then. But Nick *had* taken her into town for dinner last night. And this morning he'd noticed her toothbrush in the holder next to his.

He'd paused at the sight of it. Struck by the simplicity of the moment but at the same time by the difference a week could make. Less than a week, actually. And he'd wondered if she would consider extending this thing between them beyond next weekend. She might be willing to come to Butte occasionally. Or to meet up with him at whatever rodeo he'd be attending.

Or he could come back here. There were no rules on having a fling.

"You talked to your parents since Sunday?" he asked. He turned his head toward her, scanning the length of her body as she brought her legs up and stretched out on the dock.

"Only once. Which is shocking in its own right. Dad called before we went hiking yesterday. I think you convinced them. You were the perfect fake date."

Nick didn't want to burst her bubble, but nothing that had gone on on Sunday had been fake. Nor anything the rest of the time. "You were the one who did the convincing," he told her. "But don't think that my lack of being needed excuses you from returning the favor. Sunday night. Here." He squinted down at her, trying to look menacing. "Don't back out."

She stretched her arms over her head and yawned. "As long as you're not cooking."

He laughed.

She remained stretched out beside him, and he wondered if he could talk her into getting naked right where they were. With boaters out, it wouldn't be possible to ensure privacy.

Still.

He lowered to lie beside her.

"You'll be riding at Augusta this weekend, right?" she asked.

Neither of them had been scheduled for a rodeo the weekend before. "I am." He trailed his fingers up her inner thigh. "You going to watch me ride? Cheer for me?"

Her eyes found his. "I'm not one of your buckle bunnies."

"I know. Because you're far too old."

The corners of her mouth twitched, and she closed her eyes. She looked utterly at peace. "I'll be watching," she said quietly.

He leaned in and brushed his mouth just below her ear. "And cheering?"

"You *are* the man I want to see win."

"And if I win, will you spend the night in my room?" he whispered. He nipped at her earlobe, taking pleasure in her soft moans and the way her lower body reached for his fingers as he continued to toy at her thigh. She had on a sweet pair of cutoffs today that he was ready to take off her.

"Or you could come to mine," she answered.

Her words had him pulling away. "Yeah, that won't happen." He'd forgotten to mention his conversation with Jewel to her. "I'm never staying in your room again when your sister is around."

Harper's laugh rang out. She stared up at him, her smile beautiful. "Jewel told you?"

Nick rolled to his back. "Christ, woman. You could have warned me. Give a man a chance to prepare a response."

"It didn't occur to me that she'd bring it up."

He raised his head to look at her. "You have *met* your sister, right? The girl who'll do or say anything to get a rise out of someone?"

"You're right. My bad. The next time she explains to me just what I sound like when you put your hands all over my naked body, I'll be sure to warn you."

"I could make those noises for you now if you need a refresher course," he offered. Then he rolled back over and tugged up the edge of her shirt. He went to work at the snap of her shorts.

"*Or* you could just make me sound like that now," she murmured.

"I could." Determination sprouted, and he wanted her naked. "If you give me a good reason."

"And what kind of reason would you need?"

He unzipped her shorts and tugged them until they rode just below her hip bones. He could make out a pink sliver of panties, which gave him a nice buzz that started low in his body. Then he straddled her and shoved her T-shirt up over her chest, and growled at what he found. She had on another one of those lacy numbers that had the clasp in the front.

"Tell me that you like watching me ride bulls," he said. He bent and put his mouth to her stomach. "That it turns you on to see me get whipped around by a wild animal"—his fingers slid up and closed over her lace—"that your panties grow wet at the thought of how strong I must be to stay on top of that big bad bull"—he worked his way upward—"and that all those same muscles will later be holding *you*."

"The last time I watched you ride," she said on a gasp, "those muscles didn't hold me at all. You didn't even touch me."

"Oh, but I wanted to." He kissed her neck. "And I did touch your lips."

"Only because you fed me funnel cake." Her breaths were coming hard, and he was ready to be inside her.

"I wish I had some funnel cake now." He unhooked her bra with a single flick, and his dick sang hallelujah. "I'd sprinkle the powdered sugar all over your body"—he dragged a finger over the inside curve of one breast—"and I wouldn't stop licking you until I had every last speck of it off."

He cursed under his breath at the sight of her nipples tightening into sharp, hard buds, and leaned down, intent on having one in his mouth.

"Uncle Nick!"

He and Harper both froze, his face three inches over her chest, and both of their eyes went as round as saucers. Then Harper shoved him out of the way and sat up, her hands going immediately to the front of her clothes.

"I didn't find you at the house," came the child's voice again. And that's when Nick saw her, just coming over the rise with her dad. Jenna and Gabe stopped at the top of the hill, both of them eyeing him and Harper curiously.

"Oh my God," Harper moaned. "Is that your brother?"

"And my niece."

"What did they see?"

He climbed to his feet. "I'm thinking nothing. Otherwise Gabe would have turned her away." Nick stood directly behind Harper as she finished righting her clothes, and he thought every frigid, unsexy thought in the book to get his own situation back under control.

While Gabe remained at the top of the hill eyeing him.

"I'm going to murder him," Nick muttered.

Harper finally stood, her legs seeming unstable, and Nick took her hand. Together they headed toward the others, and when they made it to the top, Gabe and Jenna both stared at her.

"Who are you?" Jenna asked.

"Jenna," Nick began before casting a dry look toward his brother. "*Gabe.* This is my friend, Harper."

"Harper," Gabe said. His eyes narrowed in concentration as they took in both her face and her hair. "I think I remember you from school. Were you in Cord's class?"

"Two years behind him." She reached out and shook his hand. "You're looking well."

"You, too." Gabe glanced at Nick. "I didn't realize you two were friends."

"I know her through her sister."

Nick turned his attention to Jenna, and Harper followed suit. Jenna stuck out her hand. "Nice to meet you. I like your name."

Harper's entire body relaxed. "And I like yours. I also love your doll."

Jenna had a pink-clad baby under one arm, and she went into an instant litany of details for Harper as they moved toward the house: the doll's name, why she had on the clothes she wore, what she liked to do when she woke up every morning.

As they moved toward the house, the two females walked a few steps ahead, while Gabe hung back. "I'd heard a rumor about a woman with blue hair." Gabe spoke low, but Harper still looked over her shoulder at them.

Nick ignored her. "You must have talked to Nate."

"I haven't talked to Nate in weeks. Haley told me."

Jenna turned at the sound of her best friend's name. "Is Haley back home?"

"Not yet, sweetheart," Gabe answered. "I was just telling Uncle Nick that Haley told me all about Harper."

"She did?" Harper questioned. She eyed Nick. "Why would Ben's daughter be talking about me?"

"Because *he's* been talking about you." Gabe smiled unabashedly.

A question landed on Harper's face, and Nick rolled his eyes, nudging them all to start moving again. "When I asked you to dinner at their house," he explained. "I asked if I could bring someone, and Haley wanted to know if you were pretty."

Jenna peered up at Harper. "You are pretty."

"Thank you, sweetie." She turned back to Nick, a half smirk on her face. "And you said?"

"I said that you were gorgeous." His eyes told her a lot more about his personal thoughts than he'd ever say aloud in front of Gabe and Jenna. "And that you had blue hair. And that I loved it." He shot an irritated look in his brother's direction. "And then she apparently told everyone she knows, even though she promised to keep it a secret. Fat lot of good it does being her favorite uncle," he grumbled.

"Well, there was your first mistake," Gabe announced. "Never believe them when they say you're their favorite uncle."

"You're my favorite uncle, Uncle Nick."

Nick looked down into the wide, sincere smile of the child in front of him, whose hand was now tucked inside Harper's. "Thank you, sweetheart. Do you mean that for good?"

She nodded. "Until Uncle Jaden comes home. Then he'll be my favorite."

Harper and Gabe laughed, while Jenna only continued to smile, unaware of the low blow she'd just dealt. Nick ruffled her hair, and the group entered the house through the back door. They stopped at the sound of footsteps overhead.

"Michelle came with us," Gabe said, answering the unspoken question.

"Really?"

"Mama didn't want to come," Jenna explained. "She wanted to stay and play with her friends, but Daddy wouldn't let her. He said she doesn't have a job, so there was no reason for her not to come with us."

Nick caught Harper's uncomfortable shifting, her eyes darting away from the rest of them, then he studied his brother. If Jenna's words were true, that was an interesting turn of events. In the past, Gabe would have let Michelle completely run the show. Meaning, Michelle would have stayed in California.

And suddenly she was there, right in front of them. Clothes as classy as ever, but several strands of her dark hair stuck out, making her seem unusually rumpled. She rarely looked anything but pristine.

"You lose your hair brush?" Nick asked.

Michelle shot him a laser-pointed glare. "You lose your manners?"

Nick grinned. "Never had any."

She eyed him as if he were a bull's turd dropped squarely on her designer shoes, before turning to Gabe. "Just where am I supposed to sleep? Your father and his wife took our bedroom."

During the years Gabe had run the farm, their dad had moved into an apartment in town. At that point, Gabe and Michelle had taken over the master bedroom upstairs, while Dani had kept her room on the first floor. When everyone had moved out the year before and their Dad and Gloria had come home, their dad had rightly returned to the master. And, Nick had noticed, traces of Michelle's style that had once permeated the room had since vanished.

Gabe pulled his keys from his pocket and leaned down to Jenna. "Will you get my bottle of water out of the car, sweetie? I forgot it."

"Sure, Daddy."

The second the door closed, Gabe faced Michelle. "There are four other rooms you can choose from. Pick one. It doesn't even have to be the one I'm in. But no, you will not go to a hotel instead. And while I'm on the subject, you'll also eat dinner with the family when we eat together." Gabe's eyes were as hard as his tone. "And you will *not* have a headache during any of those dinners."

Hot anger colored Michelle's face. "But there's no family here."

"Nick's here."

Nick once again grinned. He pointed to Harper. "Harper's here, too."

Harper shifted by his side.

"So she's family now?" Michelle looked the other woman up and down in an obviously rude manner.

"She's my guest." Nick quit playing games. Not only had Gabe changed, but Michelle had become downright nasty. Before, she'd simply avoided the lot of them. Now, she seemed bitter and full of rage.

Probably without realizing it, Gabe had moved so that he stood shoulder to shoulder with Nick, making a united front, and Nick decided that he'd have to text Nate to let him know of this turn of events. Their oldest brother had finally grown a pair.

Jenna came back in, and as Michelle opened her mouth to toss out what was likely to be another barb, Gabe took her by the elbow and steered her upstairs. Jenna looked momentarily forlorn, before she set the bottle of water she'd retrieved on the kitchen table and headed to the office with her doll tucked securely under her arm.

Nick would go after her soon. Make sure she was okay.

"So . . ." Harper began. "I'm just going to"—she motioned with her thumb over her shoulder—"I'm sure I have clothes to wash . . . or something." She gave a little shudder and mumbled, "Or *anything*."

"Chicken," Nick taunted.

"Not chicken. Just smart. Sorry, but this isn't my family. I don't have to do this."

"True." He kissed her, keeping it light. "Can I see you tomorrow night?" He already knew she'd be working all day. She had a contract for more stunt work.

At the sound of raised voices, she looked up—then glanced down the hallway, toward the room Jenna had disappeared into. She chewed on the corner of her lip. "You're going to check on her, right?"

"Absolutely. She'll have me playing dolls with her in no time."

"Good." Harper turned back to Nick and stared him straight in the eye. "Want to come to my house tomorrow night? We can watch a movie."

The offer had his heart thundering. "Yes. Can I bring dinner?"

"Please. Pizza. Sausage and pineapple."

Nick made a face. "That sounds like a girly pizza."

"You're coming to my house. I get to choose the pizza."

"Since I'm the one buying, seems I should get to choose."

She stepped into him, and pressed one more kiss to his lips. And she didn't keep hers as innocent as he had. "But you're still going to bring me sausage and pineapple, right?" she wheedled when she pulled away.

"Right," he whispered. Then *he* kissed her. For a *very* long time. And he fought hard to keep his thoughts from showing on his face. He liked this. He liked *her*. And he was beginning to suspect that he could do this for a good, long while. "Will you be careful tomorrow?" he asked.

"As careful as always."

He held in the sigh. It would have to be enough.

Nick stood at his bedroom door, overnight bag in hand, and closed his eyes to take in the sounds coming from other parts of the house. Just two days ago he'd thought it too quiet there, yet he'd already changed his mind. He could hear Jenna in her room on the same level as him, her childlike voice talking softly to the dolls he'd spent several hours playing with the night before, while at the same time, her mother's voice came from downstairs, complaining yet again.

Gabe and Michelle had only been there for one night, but Nick had already had enough. Maybe this had played into him staying away for so long, too. That had never occurred to him. But given that Gabe's wife had never been one to keep her unhappiness to herself, and that the personality resemblance to their mother was more than uncomfortable, it made sense that them living here would have kept him away. It would have kept anyone away, even without the mother issues.

Jenna's voice changed down the hall, it's natural rhythm becoming tighter and higher pitched, and Nick headed in her direction.

He stopped at the open door to her room, taking in the bunk beds she and Dani had picked out when they'd all still lived at the house and the pink Cinderella décor that remained. This was one room Gloria hadn't touched, and he could see why. It spoke of little girls.

"How are you doing, kiddo?"

Jenna's wide blue eyes looked up from where she sat on the floor, a Barbie in each hand. The grown-up doll had been chastising the younger one for not making her bed the right way. Jenna's immediate smile reached inside Nick's chest. "I'm good, Uncle Nick." Her gaze dropped to his bag. "Are you going somewhere?"

"I am." He was heading to Harper's house and had every finger crossed that she intended to let him spend the night. "But I could wait. I could stay and play with you for a while first."

"That's okay." The words came out too stilted for her young age. "My Daddy will play with me after he finishes arguing with Mama. He always does."

Nick's heart broke. He couldn't leave her like this. Nor could he let her stay in the house listening to the argument that continued to play out below. "Tell you what. How about you go outside with me? We'll put my bag in the truck, then we'll check on the cherry trees until your daddy comes for you."

She jumped immediately to her feet. "Can I take my Barbie with me?"

"Absolutely."

She took a minute to pick out just the right doll—then had to change its clothes before they went out—but the minute she was ready, she held her tiny hand up to his and gave him the same sweet smile she always wore, and Nick decided right then and there that he wanted to be a dad someday. In fact, he'd take this one if he could figure out how. Not to get her away from Gabe, but from her mother.

He wrapped his hand around hers, and together they headed for the stairs. But before they made it to the first floor, the bickering suddenly stopped and the back door slammed shut. Nick kept a firm grip on Jenna as her entire arm tensed, and kept marching them forward.

As they neared, Gabe eyed them from where he stood in the middle of the room, his breathing shallow, and his control still visibly shaken. "You two heading somewhere?" he asked.

"Just outside, Daddy. I'm helping Uncle Nick get to his car, and then we're going to check on the cherry trees."

Gabe glanced toward the front of the house at the sound of a vehicle flying down the driveway. "I'll come out in a minute and find you."

"Okay. And I'll tell you if the trees are ready yet or not."

That made Gabe chuckle lightly, the sound filled with both love and exhaustion. "That sounds good, baby." He gave Jenna a quick kiss on the cheek and moved past them, probably to pace the length of the room, and Nick and his niece continued outside.

After he tossed his bag into the front seat of his truck, he turned back to his niece and, hands on hips, he stared down at her. "Your Daddy loves you lots. You know that, right?"

Her head bobbed up and down. "I know. He tells me every day."

Her words comforted Nick. There'd been a time when Gabe had been almost as distant with his daughter as her mother. Not in the same way. And never because he didn't care. He'd just had no idea what to do with her, and with Dani living here with them, she'd taken up the slack without realizing it. Jenna had never gone without love, but with a mother like Michelle, he knew how it could feel that way.

He stooped, intending to give her a hug, but stopped, still on his haunches, at the sight of a vehicle heading toward them. But it wasn't Gabe's SUV barreling up the drive.

A puff of dirt trailed along behind the black sedan, and Nick put his arm around Jenna, tugging her back against him as the vehicle didn't seem to slow in speed. It careened forward until it was fifteen feet in front of them, and the second the swirling dust cleared, Nick broke into a grin.

"It's Uncle Nate!" Jenna shouted.

Yes. It was most definitely Uncle Nate.

Nate pushed open the door and climbed from the seat. He wore red flannel pushed up to his elbows, jeans that were ragged at the hem and torn across one knee, and sported a full dark beard.

"You took leave," Nick said.

Nate held his arms open as the five-year-old ran into them. "I took leave," he confirmed. When he stood, he lifted Jenna onto his hip. "Checked your schedule and decided I'd come home and see you ride this weekend." That weekend's rodeo was in Augusta.

"You staying long?"

Nate shrugged. "I'll play it by ear. Figured I'd see Gabe and Jenna for a few days, hang out until Dad gets back."

"Better stay until Dani comes home."

The back door opened before Nate confirmed one way or the other, and Gabe appeared.

"Look who came to see me, Daddy."

Gabe looked as pleased as Nick at the sight of their brother. "I see that. Did you already ask if he plans to play Barbies with you?"

Wide blue eyes turned to Nate. "Will you?"

"That's why I came home," Nate responded, and Nick and Gabe both laughed. The four of them talked for several minutes, about the weekend's rodeo and the fact that it was only a few hours away, and Jenna talked her Daddy into going without Nick having to corner him and do it for her.

"We'll even stay overnight," Gabe told her.

"In a hotel?"

"Augusta's best." Which wouldn't hold a candle to anything she'd seen since moving to Los Angeles, but Nick knew it would be a great adventure for her nonetheless.

"Is Mama gonna come?" Jenna asked.

Her excitement noticeably waned, and as Gabe answered with something noncommittal, Nate's gaze shot to Nick's. Nick could hear the words behind the look. No one had expected Gabe's wife to make the trip. And Nick hadn't gotten around to texting his twin since they'd shown up.

Nick shrugged a silent *Shocked the hell out of me, too*, and at the sound of the house phone ringing, Gabe and Jenna headed back inside. Nick was left standing in the driveway, the passenger door of his truck still open, and his brother seeming pissed.

"She's here, too?"

"I have no idea why," Nick confirmed. "Been griping since the minute she walked in the door. I'm sure she won't go to Augusta with them. I suspect Gabe will go as an escape more than anything."

"It's never going to get better for him," Nate grunted out.

"Yet it's not our call to make."

Nate's gaze landed on the bag sitting shotgun in the truck, and his brows went up. "You're heading out?" Then a knowing look appeared on Nate's face. "You're still seeing her?"

"Maybe I'm just going to the gym," Nick hedged. The bag was the right size for the gym.

"And maybe you're full of shit."

Nick's cell went off, and he ignored his brother to read the text.

Bring beer.

He smiled and punched out a quick affirmative.

"Hmpf," Nate muttered. "You actually like this one."

Nick started to deny it. He and Nate didn't "do" relationships. Yet, Harper had surpassed "just sex" whether he'd wanted to admit it or not. "I actually like this one," he confessed. "I could cancel tonight, though." He hadn't seen Nate in months. And he *would* be seeing Harper again the next day.

"Don't even think about it." Nate eyed the back door where Gabe and Jenna had disappeared. "But there's no way I'm staying here without you. The key to Dani's apartment still in the house?"

Dani had rented a small upstairs apartment when she'd returned from New York, eventually buying the entire building. She'd lived in the apartment until she and Ben had married, and had plans to turn the first floor into an office front for her marketing business.

"As far as I know," Nick answered. He nodded toward the house. "Let's find the key."

They headed inside, and while Nate rummaged through the kitchen drawers looking for the spare key, Nick called their sister. He confirmed with her that the apartment was empty, and while he was at it, he let her know that Jenna could stand to see her friend.

"We might cut our trip shorter than planned," Dani told him. "I'm not sure by how much, but we're all missing home."

"Just make Jenna priority number one when you get here, if you can. She's different."

"She okay?"

"Yes. Quieter mostly. Sadder. But strangely"—he kicked Nate to get his attention, and when he knew both brother *and* sister were listening, and their oldest sibling was somewhere upstairs, he continued—"Gabe seems different, too. Standing up to Michelle more. And she isn't taking it well. In fact, it feels like World War III is about to erupt."

"That would be another reason to come on back," Dani mused. "I'll talk to Ben."

They hung up, and Nick watched as Nate assembled a mammoth-size sandwich.

"So he's tired of her shit?" Nate asked. He shoved a fourth of the sandwich into his mouth.

"Seems to be." Nick eyed the food. "Hungry?"

"Starved. Red-eye last night. I've barely slept and had nothing but airline food all day."

Nick tried his best not to look at his watch as they stood there. He wanted to hang with his brother, but he also didn't want to miss the invite to actually *go* to Harper's house. That had been big for her.

"Go," Nate mumbled around another bite. "I'm going to finish this, then head upstairs to hand in my man card."

"Every guy needs to play with dolls now and then," Nick said dryly. "Makes you tough."

"I'm not sure about the tough part." Nate pulled a drink from the fridge. "But the kid needs a buddy. Even I know that. I'll go up and win her over like I did with Haley. Make sure I'm her favorite uncle, too."

Nick rolled his eyes. "Whatever."

Nate guzzled half the soda. "I want to ride over with you tomorrow." He wiped his mouth with the back of his hand. "That okay?"

"Sure." Nick glanced at the back door. "And it's really okay if I go?"

"Could I stop you if I wanted to?"

Nick's smile returned. Nate *could* stop him, but Nick would put up one heck of a fight before he gave in.

"I can't believe you're still seeing her," Nate said around another bite. "You going to let me get a look at her?"

"She'll be there tomorrow night."

Another bite disappeared. "And what if I don't want to wait that long?"

"Then that's too damned bad." Nick snagged the final bite of the sandwich from his brother, and grinned at Nate's shout of protest. He tossed a wave over his head as he turned for the door, shoving the food in his mouth as he went. He had a woman to get to. A woman he wanted to keep all to himself for as long as he possibly could.

And he'd already delayed too long in getting to her.

Chapter Nineteen

Jitters filled Harper as she stood at the front windows and waited for Nick. Nerves had been swirling since the evening before, when she'd extended the invitation. What was she doing? She didn't have people over to her house. Her own family rarely even visited.

Yet, the words had slipped out with little thought. She felt safe inviting Nick here.

Though still nervous.

His truck turned in at the base of the driveway, and she held her breath in anticipation. As he pulled to a stop, she stepped out onto the porch, unable to wait. And as she quickly noted, a side benefit of coming outside to greet him was the fact it allowed her to enjoy the nice scenery he presented as he climbed from his vehicle. Tonight he wore his standard jeans and cowboy boots, but he'd foregone any of his many championship buckles, as well as the hat. However, the tight black T-shirt tucked snugly into his jeans said that he was as bad as his swagger.

"Hey," he greeted her first. He stopped at the bottom of the stairs, beer in one hand, pizza in the other, and smiled up at her.

"Hey." She smiled back. It had been only twenty-four hours since she'd seen him, yet it felt like so much longer. "How's your family?" she asked.

"As crazy as ever. Nate showed up today, too."

"Your twin?"

"Yep. Right before I left." He remained at the base of the stairs, as if waiting for her to invite him up. His eyes never left hers. "He's at the house playing Barbies with Jenna."

"And you didn't need to stay home with him?"

He shook his head. "He can play Barbies without me."

Her hands began to shake. "Want to come in, then?"

"I thought you'd never ask." He took the steps two at a time, and when he reached the top, he didn't pause. He backed her to the house—his hands still full of pizza and beer—and trapped her against the stucco. Then he kissed her.

She melted into the moment.

"I missed you," he said when he released her mouth. His warm blue eyes roamed over her face as if mapping her. "How are you?"

"Good." She licked her lips. "Better now."

"Good." He kissed her once more.

When they parted that time, she laughed breathlessly and shoved at his chest. He stepped back, and she took the beer from him. "You're bad for me, Wilde."

She turned to the door.

"Wrong. I'm good for you." The tail end of his words whispered hotly over the back of her neck as he moved in closer, and goose bumps raced over her body. She paused before opening the door because she wanted to back into him. To let his hard muscles mold to hers.

She wanted that *bad*.

Forcing herself to ignore both his taunts and her wants, she pushed open the wooden door. She didn't immediately enter, instead sidestepping and motioning for Nick to go in first. And as he stepped slowly inside, she swallowed her nerves and followed him in. He stopped in the middle of the front room, and she let him take a minute to adjust. There was a view from here to the kitchen, dining room, and main living area. And all that white hitting at once was a bit much.

In fact, while she'd been here by herself the night before, she'd had the urge to do something about it. It was time to redecorate. *Again.* Only, she'd had no inspiration as to what to do. Nothing felt right.

"That's a lot of white." Nick finally spoke.

His words made her snicker. "A *lot* of white."

She moved ahead of him and led him to the kitchen. "It's kind of funny when you think about it," she said as she went. "In a sad way. I did this because I couldn't stand the thought of seeing what Thomas and I had put so much time into planning and picking out. Yet this"—she turned and spread her arms wide—"is insane."

Nick shook his head. "It strikes me as more therapeutic than crazy. You needed calmness around you to offset everything going on in your head."

"Well . . ." She took the pizza and set both food and drink on the oversize island. "It didn't work." She twisted her hands together in front of her. "I've sat here and stared at it all for months. In the same mental place the entire time. Nothing worked."

"Until me," he said.

She stood before him, unmoving, her heart pounding in her throat, until he pulled her hands free and wrapped his fingers around hers. He squeezed her hands and tugged her closer.

"Until you," she whispered. The words put a lump in her throat, but they were true. He'd pushed her out of her comfort zone, and she could no longer go back. Nor sit still.

"Show me the house?" he asked.

She nodded and he laced his fingers through hers. They roamed through the first floor together, and as they took in the additional spaces and the many rooms, she forced herself to see it through his eyes. And strangely, the impersonal nature of the spaces wasn't what stood out to her the most. It was the overabundance. What would she and Thomas have ever needed with this much square footage?

Yet he'd been insistent. They'd needed this house, this way.

Then one day he'd let it slip that it was a hundred square feet larger than his parents' home, and a chill had slid down her spine. They'd been competing with the two people who'd refused to be in their lives? She hadn't understood it at the time, yet she could see now that it had been his way of throwing their money back in their faces. Of letting them know that he didn't need them. Even though he'd desperately wanted them.

It had been his way of allowing himself to be angry with them. Kind of like the reason she'd turned everything white. Because Thomas would have hated it.

She showed Nick the guest bedroom on the main floor—also white—then led him to the other side of the house to the master suite. She'd thought about whether she wanted to bring him into this room or not, but in the end, she'd decided yes. It wasn't Thomas's room with her anymore. It hadn't been in a long time.

It was barely even her room.

They crossed the threshold, and she released his hand and stayed by the door. He went first to the lone picture sitting on top of her dresser. It was the only photograph in the house.

As he studied it, she couldn't take her eyes off him. He might want her, and want to be with her, but he'd never once shown jealousy at the fact that she sometimes needed to talk about Thomas. That she still loved him.

Maybe that was only because this thing between her and Nick was casual, but she didn't think so. She thought it was more about his nature as a man. He was respectful. Even when he'd had a much different kind of role model as a young boy. It said a lot about him as a person, to be able to overcome the way he'd been raised.

"I'm not sure if I ever really expressed my thanks for pushing me to talk about Thomas," she said now. "But thank you."

Nick looked across the room at her, the picture of her and Thomas still in his hands. "And thank you for pushing me back. I needed to forgive and forget. Holding on to anger over my childhood has provided no positives in my life, and though I'd thought I'd overcome all of that a long time ago, I'd been lying to myself. You helped me to see it."

She nodded, unable to say anything else.

Nick set the photo back on the dresser.

"That was after our first search and rescue mission," she told him. She moved to his side. "The two hikers were found safe, with practically no injuries, and though we didn't personally locate the actual rescue, our hearts were full from the fact that we'd been out there that day."

"In honor of his brother."

The lump reappeared in her throat. "It was as if Harry had been with us."

She picked up the picture. Thomas's smile was so wide. "He'd wanted so badly to save his brother. Every time we went on a search, I swear he was looking for *him*, too. As if the years hadn't gone by and his brother was still out there somewhere." She held the frame to her chest and looked at Nick. "Thomas had the helicopter equipped with lights so we could fly at night, did I tell you that? Harry wasn't found until the morning after, because they'd had to call off the search after dark. Flying at night still isn't exactly *safe*, even with the lights, but with night-vision goggles, it allows us . . . me . . . to keep searching."

She didn't comment on the fact that she no longer searched, even in the daylight.

"That must come in handy."

"Yes," she said softly. She put the picture back and moved to the connected en suite. There was more house to show him.

She pushed open the double doors to display the embarrassingly large space, and Nick walked to the middle of the room—once again, all white—and rotated in a circle. He stopped, facing the two-person shower with the multiple jets positioned both overhead and along the wall, and caught her gaze in the mirror.

"Nice," he murmured.

She blushed. That shower had seen some activity in the past.

She left the bathroom, suddenly feeling more than she was ready to feel in this room.

"Where's the other door lead?" Nick asked, and when she looked back at him, he had his hand on the handle of the unopened door.

"Don't—" She cut off her words, one hand lifted slightly in the air.

Nick didn't open the door, but he waited, hand still at the ready. And she could practically hear his thoughts. He wanted her to tell him what was running through her mind. To let him help.

She didn't want to need help.

But she nodded and lowered her hand. And Nick slowly pushed open the door. The room would have been the nursery. Nick stepped inside, and Harper crossed her arms over her chest and went in behind him. Her breathing grew heavier.

"Not white in here?" he asked.

She shook her head. The walls were a pale green.

There was no flooring, though. Only a subfloor, and a single rocking chair sat in the middle of it. She didn't open the closet and show him the small box by itself on the top shelf.

"We bought the chair two weeks before Thomas died," she said, her words barely making it out of her throat. "We'd decided to start a family, so we went shopping and picked out the chair we wanted to rock our first child in."

She turned and left the room, and Nick followed. He closed the door behind him, and when she stopped at the foot of her bed, she let herself be wrapped in his arms.

"I'm so sorry things didn't turn out as you'd planned," he whispered into her hair. His hands and warm touch comforted her.

"And I'm so sorry you had a witch for a mother," she mumbled into his chest.

Her words made him chuckle, and he pulled back and peered down at her. "You okay?" he asked. He tilted her face up so he could scrutinize it in the overhead light, and she nodded.

"It's just hard sometimes," she told him. "But yeah. I'm good."

Nick nodded. He pressed his lips to the spot between her eyes. "Want to show me the second floor now or should we stop?"

He was always so intuitive.

"Is it okay if we stop? I promise to finish the tour later. The media room is up there. It'll be perfect for watching a horror movie after we stuff ourselves on pizza."

"Horror movie?" He groaned and led them out of the room. "Why did I assume we'd be watching a chick flick of some sort?"

"I have absolutely no idea. Especially since the first time we had sex it was with a bad slasher film playing in the background."

They reached the kitchen island and she grabbed the beers while he scooped up the pizza.

"You're an odd one, Harper Stone."

She blew him a kiss and a wink. "But you like it, Nicholas Wilde."

He grinned. "That I do. A *lot*."

And strangely, neither the words nor the intense way he focused on her as he said them made her nearly as nervous as they once would have. He liked her a lot. And she was okay with that.

She led the way to the patio, and as they ate, they laughed together over mundane things, pointed out mule deer that poked their heads in and out of the woods at the back of her property, and generally acted like they were any normal couple. It was comforting.

"I talked to one of the local tour companies today," she said.

"Yeah?" Nick finished his beer and eyed another one.

She nudged another bottle over to him. "One of the things I do is custom tours, fit to customers' needs. I take them wherever and whenever they want to go. But I've been thinking that I should mix things up. Take on more everyday work."

"Finally ready to settle down and quit being so risky?"

She rolled her eyes at him. "Hardly. And quit worrying about me, will you? It's tiring."

His jaw clenched at her words, but he didn't comment. She also didn't tell him that, though they'd covered the fact that she'd been taking too many risks over the last year and a half, it didn't mean her risk-taking days were over. That was a part of who she was. And if this whole trying-to-wake-up-out-of-her-fog thing was teaching her anything, it was to not give up who she was.

At least, not all of her.

"I talked to them," she continued, "with the thought of having a steady paycheck coming in. Being more financially responsible."

Nick shot a look at the house.

"It's not my money," she explained before he could ask.

"It's not legally yours?"

"Well, yes. It is mine legally. All of it. The house, helicopter, vehicles, and a heck of a lot of green sitting in investments. But I don't want it. I never did. And I've been sitting around relying on the fact that I have money if I need it. But what I need is to get back out there. I also spent a couple of hours today looking into local charities." She shrugged. "Thought I might get involved."

Nick leaned over and kissed her cheek. "Good for you. That's who you are."

It's who she'd once been. But she was trying. Or thinking about trying.

It was better than where she'd been two weeks ago, at least.

They both grew quiet once more, and darkness began to settle around them. The candle she'd brought out before he'd arrived was burning low, flickering in the night breeze, and the pizza was demolished. They both had healthy appetites.

"You looking forward to your dad getting back Sunday?" she asked.

Nick took her hand. "You asking if I'm looking forward to leaving? Or to not having to work on the farm?"

She leaned her head back against her seat. She wasn't ready for him to leave. "Both."

"I've enjoyed being home," he said. "But I also—

The aviation radio squawked from inside the house, and Harper sat up. She kept it tuned to a station that monitored distress signals. She listened as details of a report of missing hikers was relayed, and for the first time in nearly nineteen months, she had the urge to help. It was dark. She could take her helicopter up.

This was why they'd bought it.

Two males, one female. Ages eighteen, eighteen, and sixteen.

Her heart beat harder. Harry had been only sixteen.

"You should go," Nick said.

She slowly shook her head. "I don't do that anymore." The words barely whispered out. Was she discrediting Thomas's memory by not helping? Had she hurt *him* by protecting herself?

"But you could do that," Nick said just as quietly.

She swallowed, the pizza from earlier suddenly seeming stuck in her throat. Then she looked at the darkened back door of the house. The radio had gone silent. She eyed the helicopter sitting alone in the dark. There were children missing tonight, and she had a means to save them. Her fingers began to tremble, and she felt her pulse race. She should do something.

Yet she couldn't bring herself to get out of her chair.

"Come here," Nick said, but he didn't wait for her to do as he'd suggested. He rose and lifted her up, then lowered back to his chair with her in his lap. His arms surrounded her, and she almost felt better. But there were still three kids missing in the mountains tonight.

The radio squawked again, this time with several SAR people reporting in that they were readying to join the search. The valley had purchased a light-equipped Huey within the last couple of years, so that meant someone would be going up tonight. The kids wouldn't have to wait. The knowledge released the pressure that had built behind her rib cage, and she sank back against Nick. His arms tightened, and neither said anything as another report came from one of the surrounding counties. A new team gave an ETA for arrival, and Harper relaxed a bit more. Lots of people would be helping. Those kids wouldn't be alone.

"I miss it sometimes," she finally said, admitting a truth she'd refused to even acknowledge to herself.

"Then don't give it up."

"But I don't know if I can go back."

"How about looking at it as if it's only on pause, then?"

She turned her face up to his, intrigued.

"Pause doesn't mean it's over for good," he said. "You can go back whenever you're ready."

His words hit home, only in a different way than he'd meant. "Like me? I'm on pause?"

"Like you *were*." He cupped her cheek. "But I think you're coming out of it. Maybe it's time to bring the search and rescue back out, too?"

It was all of a sudden too much. Too many questions, and not enough answers. "Can we not talk about it anymore? A search is being formed. What I do or don't do in the future doesn't matter." She climbed off his lap and held a hand down to him. "Let's go in and watch a movie."

The digital clock on the dresser clicked off another minute closer to midnight as Nick and Harper remained lying on her bed, both of them tucked under a lightweight blanket. The blanket and the TV were the only things of color in the room. Even the clock was white. But earlier,

Nick had caught a glimpse of a pale-orange strap of lace peeking out of one of the dresser drawers.

He hugged Harper tighter to him and lowered the volume as the credits began to roll. He thought she might be asleep, but he wasn't ready to move yet.

Before they'd settled in the bedroom, she'd given him a tour of the remainder of the house. As promised, there had been an impressive media room on the second floor. All red and black, with theater seating. With the top-of-the-line surround system, it was definitely a place to crank up a horror movie and scare the bejesus out of a person. But Nick much preferred the way they'd done it.

The remainder of the upstairs had been bedrooms, with one gathering area and a powder room. All had been professionally decorated— and all just as impersonal as the rest of the house.

The only room he hadn't actually seen the inside of was a single bedroom at the front of the house. Unlike when he'd started to go into the nursery, when Harper had hesitated but let him go in, the room upstairs had been a firm no.

In fact, she hadn't even looked at the door when he'd stopped beside it.

Nick suspected there was evidence of her late husband inside that room. Maybe indicators of the two of them together. That would account for the complete lack of the other man's personal possessions found throughout the house.

But all in all, even with the tense moment upstairs, the night had been terrific—though she *had* been different here. That wall of hers had inched a bit higher. It made him wonder what else might still be hiding behind it. Was there more to her story that she hadn't shared?

"Tell me how you got into bull riding," Harper said behind a yawn. "Did you ride much as a kid?"

He looked down at her in the faint glow cast from the bedside lamp. "There was that sheep I told you about when I was seven."

"Right." She wiggled on the bed, scooting up higher against him. "You didn't last the eight seconds. But what was it like? And did it make you want to try again?"

Honestly, it had made me never want to ride again.

He thought about Nate pointing out that Nick had no desire for riding as a kid, then muted the TV and rolled to his side to face her. Grabbing her hand, he brought it to his chest. "It was actually my mom's idea for me to ride that day. We had a family friend whose kid was great at the sport. The kid was my age. Shorter but stockier." He smiled wanly. "He could stay on the sheep the full eight seconds.

"Anyway, this lady was talking her kid up so my mom told her that I was better than him. That I would be a champion someday." He stared at their clasped hands as he processed what he'd just said. He'd forgotten that part of the story. His mother had planted the seed.

Sonofabitch.

He ignored the implications and ploughed on. "So the next time the youth rodeo came to town, she packed us up, and off we went. I was thrilled. My mom wanted to see me ride."

"You had her attention."

Nate had been right. "I had her attention."

He returned to his back, pulling Harper down with him.

"I got on," he said, "and then I was off. That fast. It was a short ride, for sure. But the more important thing was that I dislocated my shoulder."

"Ouch." She moved as if to raise herself up, but he kept her tight against him.

"She refused to acknowledge how bad I was hurt," he told her. His words grew tight, and he noted that the tension in Harper's body now matched his. "Told me to suck it up. She brushed it off with her friend, made up some bullshit story, then took me home and sent me to my room. That night, when I didn't go down for dinner, I used the excuse that I'd eaten too much at the rodeo. But Nate knew. He'd been there.

Plus, it was hard to miss the way the one shoulder hung lower than the other. He skipped dinner along with me. Sat on the bed, not taking his eyes off me all night long, as if the mere act of concentration could fix me. I wouldn't admit how bad it was, though. Not even to him. I sat there stoically, not moving my arm, and biting the inside of my cheek to keep from crying."

"What happened next?"

Nick closed his eyes, not wanting to see the memories, but with his eyes closed, they only became more visible. "Dani eventually came in to check on me, but I sent her away before she could get more than a foot in the door. Then Cord showed up. It was right before he went to bed. He ignored me when I told him to go away, and he figured out with one look that something bad had happened. But he was only thirteen. What could he do?"

"He could have told your dad that you'd been hurt."

"I would have denied it." He looked at Harper and pictured his brother all those years ago, angry determination covering his thirteen-year-old face. "He snapped it back into place. I was amazed. Still am. It hurt like a bitch, too. But how he knew how to do that at that age, I'll never know. The next day he told Dad that he'd hurt me while wrestling, and Dad had Dani take me to our general physician. Without that move, I probably never would've been able to ride. As it is, I wear a customized brace to keep things from popping out of place."

"Cord's a doctor now, right?"

"Yeah—not that it's a surprise. He not only fixed me up that night, but every time she hurt herself . . . the finger, the car wreck, whatever . . . Cord was the one who found her. I'm pretty sure that was intentional on her part. She was a master at fucking with us." His hand stroked down Harper's back. "Nate said something to me the other day, and at the time, I didn't give it much thought."

"What did he say?"

"He pointed out that I didn't get into riding until after high school. I'd always assumed that was due to the sheep incident. But what if it wasn't? What if"—he gulped—"what if I never really *wanted* to be a bull rider? Maybe I did it just to prove how tough I was. That I *could* be a winner."

"Prove it to your mom, you mean?"

He nodded. "To my dead mom. Pathetic, huh? She always told me I wasn't tough enough, so I had to show her."

"Not pathetic." Harper pressed a kiss to his cheek. "You were only ten when she died."

"Eighteen when I left home. When I started riding."

"But stuck at ten." She turned his face toward hers, and her gaze raked over him. "Do you think that's why you haven't gone national?"

A lock seemed to click into place. "Possibly."

She gave him a tender smile. "Well, you might not have gotten into it for the right reasons, but you can't be disappointed with the outcome, right? You're really good."

"But what if I could have been better at something else?"

He felt ripped wide open as he looked into her eyes. He didn't bring up the subject of going back to school, but he wanted to. He wanted to know what she'd think. Only, the conversation had drained him. He had nothing left tonight.

"You can be whatever you want to be, Nicholas Wilde. You know that, don't you? It's never too late to start."

He tried to return her confidence with an assured nod, but the attempt fell flat. Because he had no idea what he wanted to be. He pulled her in closer and she slid a leg over his and they lay there like that for several minutes, her hand covering his heart and her hair tickling the underside of his chin. Then he turned off the television and reached over and clicked off the lamp. Total darkness fell around them.

"Is it okay if I stay here tonight?" They remained fully dressed, but even if sex wasn't on the table, Nick didn't want to leave.

"Absolutely."

Nothing was said about them removing any articles of clothing or crawling under the covers. They simply remained where they were, tucked beneath a mint-green blanket in the middle of Harper's bed. Several minutes later, Harper began to fidget before finally rolling onto her back.

"I never did tell you about *me* riding the bull," her words floated over to him.

He smiled slightly in the darkness at the picture that formed in his mind. "Will you tell me about it now?"

"If you want to hear it."

"I would like nothing better." He captured her hand at his side and waited to hear her story.

"First of all, I didn't actually stay on for eight seconds the *first* time I rode. I might have misled you there. But I did eventually stay on one."

A rustle of movement happened at his side, and he suspected she was now facing him.

"It took me a few weeks. Thomas and I attended a bull-riding school when we lived in Texas."

Nick's brows shot up. "You considered getting into the sport?"

"Good grief, no. We just wanted to conquer it. To say we'd done it."

He was beginning to understand her. "No" wasn't in her vocabulary. Nor was "risk free."

"It was my idea to attend the school." She spoke more softly now. "I talked him into it. It was the last class, and I was determined to prove I could do it. I made it to eight seconds on my third try that day, and I was flying high. Thomas was so proud of me. And then it was his turn."

Nick immediately understood that this part of the story hadn't turned out well. "What happened?"

"He ended up in the hospital. Broken rib, punctured lung. And it was all my fault."

"Why your fault?"

"Because I made him ride."

Nick went silent to allow his words to slowly form. He didn't want to say the wrong thing, but he'd picked up on a pattern with her. The burden for whatever happened to Thomas fell upon her. But why?

"From everything you've told me about him," he finally started, "I wouldn't think him to be the type you could make *do* anything if he didn't want to. Didn't you say you two were pretty much alike?"

"I did. But at the same time, I'd asked myself on occasion if maybe we *weren't* so much alike. Did he do as much, risk as much, only because I egged him on?"

Nick turned the light back on and faced Harper. "I thought he followed in his brother's footsteps. Would Harry have wanted to ride a bull?"

"And more from what I learned about him."

"Then how do you figure any of it was your doing?"

She went totally silent and completely still. When Nick couldn't stand it anymore, he lifted a hand and brushed his thumb over her cheek. Her skin was soft and creamy, and she seemed more fragile than he'd ever seen her. But she hadn't answered his question, so he remained silent, giving her the time to get out whatever it was she needed to say.

"His parents blamed me." Her words splintered as she spoke. Her eyes were sad, the corners seeming to droop on the outer edges. "And not just for the accident, but for him living *here*. For him dying," she whispered. "Which *was* my fault, but they don't even know about that part of it. They just knew that he wouldn't have been jumping out of planes if not for me."

"Yet the army has you jump out of planes."

Her brow creased. "They do."

"And didn't you meet Thomas after you'd both enlisted?"

"I see where you're going with this, but you're off track. That was a short period of his life. Being with me was the 'after.'" Her chest rose and fell with her breaths. "While Thomas was in the hospital, his parents offered to buy me out of our marriage. If I'd only let him come home to California where he belonged, they'd give me all the money I could ever desire." The words were bitter, and Nick wanted to hold her. But not yet. She wasn't finished yet.

"But money wasn't what you wanted?" he asked.

"I had what I wanted. I had Thomas, and a good marriage. I loved my life. The only thing that could have possibly made any of it better was if they'd loved their son the way he'd loved them. He wanted their approval. Up until the day he died. He wanted them to see that him being here was an act of love. His parents hadn't handled Harry's death well, so Thomas did it for them. He showed respect for his brother by never letting him be forgotten."

Nick wrapped his arms around her. "He sounds like a good man."

"He was the best. He went to see them one final time before we tried for kids. To ask them to be in our lives." Her head moved in a negative motion. "They were so bitter. I don't get that. They had a son who died, yes, but they had another one who was alive. Thomas was the one who'd lost the most. Both brother and parents. It wasn't fair.

"I never told Thomas they tried to buy me off," she added softly, "but I did wonder if I should have taken them up on it. If I had, Thomas could have had his parents back. He shouldn't have had to choose."

"No, he shouldn't have." Nick tilted her face up to his. "But I'd take a guess that Thomas made his own choices in life. You didn't make them for him, right?"

She puffed out a short breath. "I'd like to believe I didn't."

"I'd place bets that you're right." He touched his lips to hers. "I'd also venture to guess that if Thomas had it to do over again, he would choose you every time."

The corners of Harper's lips lifted marginally, then she closed her eyes and tucked in next to him. Nick wrapped both arms around her, and when her breathing finally grew regular, he let his go there, too.

Chapter Twenty

You must be the flavor of the month."

Harper went still against the gate at the words spoken close behind her. Words that very much sounded as if they'd come from Nick. Yet, she had her eyes on Nick. He waited in the second set of chutes, one rider before him.

Therefore, these words must have come from his twin brother. Nick had mentioned Nate would be there tonight.

Slowly turning, she found herself taken aback at the similarities between the two men. She'd known they were identical—and she'd been around both of them together a few times as kids. But witnessing the grown-up specimen times two—this one also in a dusty, worn cowboy hat—was a bit shocking. The heavy beard only added to his looks.

Not letting anything show on her face, she took her time and scanned Nate up and down.

When finished, she arched her brows. "And you clearly turned out to be the less attractive twin."

Nate's entire face broke into a grin as laughter boomed out of him. And that fast, Harper remembered what a good guy Nick's brother had always been. He'd dated Chastity for a very short time.

He thrust out a hand. "Nice to see you again, Harp. Okay if I call you Harp?"

"As long as you don't call me honey."

She'd never really had a problem with that particular pet name until Nick had used it at the wrong time.

"Noted," Nate said. "How about hot ass, then?"

"Only if you want to find yourself flat in the dirt."

And once again he laughed. He moved to the gate to stand beside her and then hung his arms over the railing. The rider before Nate had finished. He'd lasted only five seconds.

"I'd heard he still had the hots for you," Nate mused. "Not that I can blame him. But I'm guessing I *can* blame *you* for me getting kicked out of his hotel room tonight."

Twenty feet away, Betsy came into view, and Harper caught Nate's eye, then very purposefully looked at Betsy. "Or maybe you can thank me. Might be that you could bunk with his favorite buckle bunny instead."

Nate eyed the other woman—as well as the men whose attentions she currently held. "I seem to be missing the big buckle for a chance at that."

"Then steal one from your brother. I guarantee that'll bring her running."

Nate's attention immediately returned to Harper, and his scrutiny unnerved her. But when Nick's name was announced, she forgot all about his brother and turned back to the arena. She stood motionless as Nick got settled on the bull. The animal was a caged ton of weight, clearly not wanting any part of being the entertainment tonight. The gate swung open, and Harper held her breath.

One . . . Two . . . Three . . .

Dang. That bull was vicious.

Four. . . Five . . .

She cringed as Nick's head whipped back. Somehow his hat stayed on.

Six . . .

"How does he not dislocate his shoulder again?" she murmured.

Seven . . .

She shot a frantic glance at the clock.

Eight. The buzzer blared, and Nick jumped free.

Harper didn't look away until the animal was steered from the arena. As the gate closed behind the bull, she heard a swoosh of air expelled from Nate, and glanced his way. "Never easy to watch, huh?"

Not that it wasn't also as sexy as hell.

But instead of replying to her question, Nate's eyes, so much like Nick's, locked onto hers. "He told you about his shoulder?"

Oh. Had she said that out loud?

"Good ride tonight, Wilde." Charlie Scott shook Nick's hand. "We'll talk more this coming week."

"Call me," Nick said.

His agent walked away, cutting through the cleanup crew, and Nick stood, hands in his pocket, watching the man go. He had a big decision to make, and the timer had started.

"What was that about?" Nate asked as he joined him.

It was Saturday night, and Nick had just earned a new championship buckle. And a potential new deal. "I got an offer," he said. He snagged a bite of funnel cake from the plate in his brother's hand.

"What for this time?"

"Ads, commercials, action figures."

Nate whistled under his breath. "I assume this offer *isn't* to stay with Montana Pro."

"You assume correctly."

"And they're willing to invest that kind of dough before you ever sit on your first bull for them?"

Nick pinned his brother with a look. "Told you I wasn't just good."

He didn't say anything else for several moments, instead letting it all sink in. He could turn down the offer and still decide to join the PBR later on. It wasn't as if this were a do-or-die situation for continuing as a bull rider. But it *was* a onetime offer. That had been made clear. They wanted him as the next face of bull riding, and they were tired of waiting.

"What are you going to do?"

Nick shook his head. "I have no idea. But I have only until next weekend to decide."

He picked up the bag that held his gear and turned from the departing crowd. Gabe and Jenna were there somewhere. But instead of finding his oldest brother, Nick's gaze landed on a truck and trailer not too far away, and his thoughts veered away from his family. Harper was in that truck.

"I like her," Nate said. Clearly he'd followed Nick's line of sight. "She's tough enough to bust your balls."

Nick smiled as he thought about all the ways she and his balls had become involved over the weeks. "She has, too. Literally. Did I tell you she's a helicopter pilot? God, she looks hot in the cockpit," he muttered, getting sidetracked for a second. He glanced at his brother. "The first time she took me up, she laid us sideways. I almost cried like a baby."

Harper saw them watching her, and when he took a deliberate chunk of funnel cake off Nate's plate and lifted it to his mouth, the grin that broke across her face had those very balls of his tightening. She didn't look at other men the way she looked at him.

"Geez, you have it bad."

"I'm afraid that I do." The truck pulled away, and Nick saw Gabe and Jenna over by the facilities.

"How did that even happen?" Nate asked as they moved in the direction of their brother.

"Beats the hell out of me. One minute I'm trying to get her to talk about her husband's death, thinking that would help her." He'd filled Nate in on the details of the accident. "And the next I'm not only having dinner with her parents but hoping I get an invite to come back."

"You think this could be something?"

At the quietly spoken question, Nick's heart squeezed. "Maybe," he admitted. He still couldn't believe the possibility of a relationship was even in his head, but over the last couple of days, the idea had played on repeat. "But to tell you the truth, she worries me sometimes. Kind of reminds me of . . ."

He couldn't even bring himself to say it.

"Who?" Nate asked.

Nick shook his head, unwilling to go there. Harper was not like their mother. Not at all. But at the same time, the same insecurities he'd dealt with his whole life kept rearing their heads when it came to her. And that made him question everything.

He realized he was walking alone and turned back to find Nate standing twelve feet behind him. "You don't mean Mom?" he asked. His features had turned hard.

"Not really *like* Mom."

"Like Michelle?" His brother's voice went cold.

"No. Of course not. Harper is a good person. You can see that."

"Then what exactly *are* you saying?"

Nick swallowed. He wished he hadn't brought it up. The very idea of one of them getting tangled up with another woman with issues similar to their mother was unconscionable. He should have kept his mouth shut and worked through his worries on his own.

"I don't know, exactly," he finally answered. He could tell Nate didn't intend to let this go without an explanation. "She's lost a lot in her life. That's hurt her. Had her pushing the edge too much." Though that part of her *had* calmed down some. When they'd gone over to Swan Valley for a hike the week before, she'd been fine taking the trail that was one step below the kill-yourself path. "She's a physical person," he told Nate. "And a huge risk-taker. And I worry." And he felt like a class-A wuss for voicing his fears. "What if she hurts herself and I can't do anything to stop it?"

The heat immediately cleared from Nate's features, and his mouth turned into a slash. "Please tell me you don't think you could have stopped Mom. Is that what this is about? You know everything she did was for attention."

"Yeah, I know. But . . ." Nick paused but then decided to throw it out there. Maybe it was time Nate knew. "I saw her cut herself that day," he said. "When we were five."

Nick held his breath as he watched Nate process the words.

Then Nate's shoulders sagged. "Christ, man. You saw her do that? You never told me."

Nick shrugged. "Didn't seem to be a need. I walked in on her, blade already buried in her finger." His voice dipped. "I *begged* her to stop. But she only wanted me to go away. To keep my mouth shut." He looked away from the too-knowing eyes that perfectly matched his own. "So I went away and kept my mouth shut."

Nate didn't say anything at first, just stared at him. Then together they began moving once again, closing the distance to Gabe and Jenna. But before reaching the others, Nate's feet stopped. "You couldn't have stopped it."

But he should have been able to. "I know."

"You also couldn't have loved her enough to keep her from doing it in the first place."

Nick didn't respond. And it was embarrassing as hell that Nate understood that about him.

"It's not just Harper's riskiness," Nick finally forced out. He wanted the conversation steered back to the present. "She keeps an emotional distance. A large one. She's the epitome of independence. And she makes it clear that she doesn't need or want my help."

"And that's a problem why? You telling me you want a needy woman now?"

Nick blew out a frustrated breath. *"No."*

But he would prefer someone who needed him at least once in a while.

"You told her about the sheep," Nate said. The words came out accusatory, and the subject change surprised Nick.

"We've been dating," he defended. "People share things when they date."

"But you shared a big thing."

Yeah, the sheep had been big. Because that had been a turning point for him. He'd suddenly known how to get his mother's attention. "So?" he questioned. He didn't see Nick's point.

"So don't push her away now."

"Who says I'm pushing?"

Nate shook his head as if disgusted with the man his twin had become. "You're looking for excuses. I know you. If you shared the sheep with her, you've shared more. Which says she means something to you. And I don't believe for a second that she's like mom. You might have actually lucked upon a good one with her, so don't be an idiot and blow it."

"What are you, her cheerleader now?"

"I'm just the guy on the outside looking in. She cares about you. And yeah, maybe she's not fully over her loss yet. Might be that she needs that emotional distance a while longer."

"But I could help her get there if she'd let me," Nick complained.

Nate smacked Nick on the side of the head. "Why would she let you? Didn't you just tell me she's the definition of independent? She needs to do this on her own. Give it time. You can't worry this one to death like you've done your whole life."

"I haven't—"

"You worry about everything," Nate interrupted. "You want to *fix* everything. To have everyone love and adore you. It's why you love riding so much, isn't it? Groupies, championships, commercials. They all come crawling to you."

Nick stared slack-jawed at his brother. Nate was right. He loved the attention. He thrived on it.

He *needed* it.

"Good God," he mumbled. "I'm just like our mother."

"Oh, for Pete's sake. You are not like her. Get over yourself, idiot."

"Kiss my ass, moron." Nick followed up his words with an elbow to Nate's gut—a move that was only half in jest.

"Now's as good a time as any." Nate held his arms out to his side. "Drop 'em. I'll plant one on you right here."

Someone cleared their throat, stopping the two of them in mid pop-up fight, and Nick and Nate both turned. Gabe and Jenna stood there, Jenna's eyes round.

"Daddy," she whispered. There was dried ice cream circling her mouth. "Uncle Nick said a bad word."

"Yes, he did, sweetheart." Gabe scowled. "You two boys about through playing?"

"You can kiss it, too," Nick said under his breath.

Jenna blinked up at the three of them, thoroughly intrigued, and Gabe took her hand and pivoted. "We'll wait in the truck."

After they walked away, Nick shot his twin a glance. And surprisingly, the fire that had flared so quickly between them was gone. What was left was a calmness Nick wasn't sure he'd ever seen with his brother.

"Don't push her away," Nate repeated. "She's good for you. Wait for her. And *then* be there when she needs you."

Chapter Twenty-One

Asoft moan drifted into the darkened room as Nick and Harper slowly moved together. He pressed lingering kisses above her ear, and without hesitation, filled her body with his.

After dinner with his family, Harper had invited Nick back to her house. He'd followed her over, then she'd taken his hand in hers and led him down the hallway and straight to the master bedroom. They'd been in there for nearly an hour now. Their lovemaking had been slow, and there had been no bells or whistles. Just him touching her and her touching him. And he knew that this was exactly where he wanted to be.

"Hurry, Nick," she whispered against his neck, and he nodded. He was getting there, too.

He brought his mouth to hers, and he showed her without words what she meant to him. She clung, with both lips and hands, as he pushed them higher, her soft whispers of noise no louder than his low grunts. And as he neared completion, she opened the door and walked through with him. With one last thrust, they both crested. It was explosive, but at the same time, like tumbling down a mountain in slow motion. They rolled and bounced, and held each other, and when they finally landed at the bottom, they were out of breath and staring in awe.

After catching his breath, Nick gave her one last peck of his lips, and rolled to his side. He brought her with him. He didn't want to let go of her yet.

They lay like that for several moments, neither saying a word, before Nick felt Harper drift off to sleep. Moving was the last thing he wanted to do, but he forced himself to get up long enough to dispose of the condom. The remaining light from the sunset was just about to fizzle out, so he left the bathroom light on and pulled the door almost closed. It provided a faint glow into the room, but not enough to disturb either one of them.

A couple of hours later, Harper stirred at his side, and Nick woke up. She turned a lazy smile up at him before pressing a quick kiss to his lips.

"You're staying tonight," she told him.

"I hadn't been planning on going anywhere."

"I just mean, you *have* to stay. Because if you go home, you'll have to deal with your family."

This made him chuckled. "I almost feel bad for making you be there tonight."

"Ohmygoodness, that was the most uncomfortable dinner I've ever been a part of." Her hand slid up his chest until one finger touched him just below the chin. Then she drew an invisible line along his skin, down to the dip in his throat. "But for the record, you didn't make me go. I rarely do anything I don't want to do."

"I know. Thank you for going."

"I'm actually glad I didn't miss it. If ever I needed a reminder to be grateful for my family, even if they *only mean well*"—she gave a fake shudder—"all I have to do is recall tonight. I do feel bad for your brother, though."

"Gabe?"

"Well, I feel bad for all of you for having Michelle as a sister-in-law. Good grief, she has a talent, and she's honed it well. Make everyone as miserable as she is." Harper stopped talking abruptly, and Nick glanced down at her. She grimaced. "But . . . does Gabe know he married your mother?"

"Right?" Nick shook his head in disbelief. "Who does that?"

"And then Nate . . ."

Nick held his breath when she brought up his twin's name. "You like him, right? Because he likes you. In fact, we talked about you after we got back last night." After returning to Birch Bay, Nick had stayed at the apartment with Nate. They'd had a good time hanging out, and Harper's name had definitely come up more than once. Nick couldn't seem to *not* talk about her.

"I do like him," Harper confirmed. "I remember him from when you two were younger, when I thought you were both essentially the same. But I see the difference now. He's a little more rough around the edges, but at the same time . . . sweet."

"He won't like you as much when I tell him you think he's sweet."

She laughed. "Yes, he will. He's a softy like you. He just doesn't know it yet."

Nick snorted at Harper's words. Nate would really not like hearing that. Yet Nick had every intention of telling him.

He shifted so he could better face Harper and took her hand in his. He kissed her palm as he thought about the offer his agent had presented to him. And not only about the offer, but about his dad being back in town. It was time to go home. Get back to his own life. But he didn't want to leave Harper.

Which meant, it was time to talk about the future.

"I think this could be something," he said the words quietly, and then waited for her eyes to find his. "I *want* it to be something," he added.

"But we're . . ." She shook her head and a wrinkle of confusion crossed her brow. "We're good like we are, Nick. We're fun. Why change that?"

"I'm supposed to go home this week." He pictured his small apartment, with the only personal contribution he'd added in the seven years he'd been there a few pictures of his two nieces. He didn't want to go home. He didn't want that life anymore.

"Butte's not that far away," Harper pointed out. "If you want to continue this, I can come see you once in a while. In fact—"

"I want marriage."

Her mouth snapped shut.

"I want a family, Harper. I didn't know that before, but things have changed for me since I came home. I want more than riding bulls." That was not happiness he saw in her eyes. "And you think you want that with me?"

"I think I might. You're special to me. You're the only woman who's ever made me think about kids. About growing old with someone." He kissed the tips of her fingers and ignored the fact that her shoulders had gone tight and that she'd already pulled a couple of inches away. "I'd like to see where we can go."

She looked away from him then. In the tight quarters of lying together, there wasn't much space to avoid each other, but she did an excellent job of it nonetheless. Her gaze locked somewhere above his head, and sadness filled her face. Nick's heart began to break before she ever opened her mouth.

"It *can't* go anywhere, Nick." She swallowed. "My chance for happily ever after was with Thomas. *He* was my love." She closed her eyes. "And I don't want kids."

Though her bluntness about Thomas burned, Nick held on to hope. She was just scared. He had to make her see that Thomas didn't have to be her one and only.

"People get second chances, Harper. And I don't believe for a second that you don't want kids. You have a room you'd intended to be a nursery. You're amazing with children. Jenna fell in love with you on the spot."

Her eyes opened and she stared at his chest. But even more telling, she pulled her hand from his. "I did want children. Once. But that part of me died with Thomas."

Fear bloomed inside him. *Damn.*

He shouldn't have said anything. Not yet. She wasn't ready.

"It's not something to be answered today." His words sounded weak. And it pissed him off. But he couldn't simply give up. "We can stay as we are for now. But I just wanted you to know that things have shifted for me. I see a future for us. It's only fair that you know that."

Her eyes finally came back to his. "Then in good conscience, I can't let this go any further. Because I'm not going to change. That isn't what I want."

And he finally got it. *He* wasn't what she wanted.

He wasn't enough.

He had never been more than a good time for her.

Pain sliced deep. How could he have been so mistaken? But he could see the conviction in her face. She didn't want him. Not the way he wanted her. He should have known. Hadn't his mother taught him that he couldn't make someone love him?

Without another word, he nodded. He stood from her bed and began dressing. When she remained silent, the hurt only intensified. There would be no second-guessing her decision.

As he yanked on his boots, she finally moved, standing from the bed and disappearing into her closet. She came out wearing a robe, and he put up a hand.

"Don't bother. I can see myself out." When he got to the bedroom door, he paused but didn't let himself look back. She said nothing, nor did he hear movement. "Good luck with your life, Harper. It's been nice."

Silence was the only thing that followed him out of the room.

At the sound of the front door closing, Harper remained where she was. Shock coursed through her, but mostly she felt nothing. Why had Nick said all that? Why had he even felt it? He wasn't supposed to want more.

His truck started up outside, and she pictured him driving away. She'd hurt him. But she hadn't meant to.

But what else could she have done? She couldn't let him go on thinking this could be something. She'd done the right thing.

The silence in the house suddenly seemed to ring loud in her ears, and she began wandering through the downstairs rooms. She hated the white so much. It taunted her tonight. Pointing out how ridiculous she'd been to change everything. The taunting was so bad that she found herself heading upstairs to get away from it. Maybe she'd watch a movie.

Only, she ended up outside of Thomas's room.

She put a hand to the door, then leaned into it and closed her eyes. Resting her forehead against the cool wood, anger began to build. How could Nick ask for more? Had he listened to nothing she'd told him all this time? She'd *killed* her own husband.

She couldn't go on from that. People didn't get second chances after that.

And *then* she'd let her baby die.

She shook her head back and forth against the door, denying all the words that had come out of Nick's mouth. He didn't see them going anywhere. They weren't anything. Just sex. Just passing the time. She couldn't have more. Because she was the one who should have died.

She stopped shaking her head, her chest now rising with each breath, and put both hands flat on the door. It wasn't fair. None of it was fair. She and Thomas were supposed to be a team.

Turning, she slid to the floor and closed her eyes.

She didn't want any of this anymore. Not the feelings, the pain. Not this house.

She didn't want to live in a house that didn't fit her. With money that didn't belong to her. And spend every single waking moment of every single day thinking about what she no longer had.

But if she moved, she'd have to remove Thomas. She'd have to go into this room.

There were people she could hire to handle it. They could pack up his things, and even send it all to charity. Or to his parents. She hadn't talked to them since the funeral, but they might want his stuff. She'd tried to make Thomas proud during those first few weeks. He'd never stopped loving his parents, so she'd called and left messages. She'd wanted to check in on them. But they'd never returned her calls.

In a fit of misery months later, she'd tried once more. That time, their house phone had been disconnected. If she could have grieved with them—with people who'd once loved Thomas—that might have made things better.

The radio on the first floor burst to life, and she went still as she listened. The missing hikers had been found. Hurt, but all safe. The sixteen-year-old was in critical condition, and was being transported to the hospital. "I'm sorry, Thomas." She rolled her head back and forth again, seeing nothing but pain. She and Thomas would have been out there tonight. "I didn't mean to mess everything up."

Standing on trembling legs, she took a moment to steady herself before returning downstairs. But instead of heading down the hall, back to her white dungeon, she turned before she could think about what she was doing and opened the door. Stale air hit first. Next was the sight of the cardboard boxes stacked one on top of the other. They lined the far wall, holding all the knickknacks, pictures, and random paraphernalia that had once been her husband's. Spread out in the room around her was ski equipment, hiking gear, a mountain bike, and weight-lifting machines. Anything and everything he'd ever loved taking part in. The room was full of Thomas.

Yet Thomas wasn't here.

She moved through the carnage until she reached the closet and opened the doors. After her mother had brought all of his things back inside the house, Harper had moved the totes up here and had spent one painstakingly long afternoon rehanging each and every article of clothing.

It was all still there. Waiting. For nothing.

Without making a sound, she cleared a small spot beneath his T-shirt collection, accumulated from their travels, and lowered herself to the plush carpet. Where she curled up in the fetal position and fell asleep.

Chapter Twenty-Two

Warm drops of rain danced on Nick's head and the back of his neck as he came out of the electronics store. He hunched his shoulders and picked up speed, hurrying through the parking lot, and the second he reached his truck door, his cell began to ring. In one fluid move, he slid onto the driver's seat, tossing the box beside him, and pulled out his phone.

His momentary letdown over not seeing Harper's name pop up on the screen was quickly overshadowed by the fact that his sister was FaceTiming him. He swiped the droplets of water from his hair and connected the call—only to find two gorgeous five-year-olds giggling at him.

"Hi, Uncle Nick!" They both shouted at the same time.

He relaxed into the seat. "Hi, girls. How are you? What are you doing together?"

"Haley camed home," Jenna squealed. "I'm at her house right now, and we've been playing and then we're going to help Aunt Dani make cookies and then go outside and eat them while we have a picnic with our other friend Leslie."

Nick sucked in a breath as if he'd been the one to rattle out all those words. "That sounds like a very fun time to me. I wish I could have a picnic with you."

Dani's face appeared behind the girls. "Hey, Nick, how are you?"

"Good."

"The girls couldn't wait to call you. Haley brought you something that she wanted to show you, and Jenna said she needed to make sure you weren't sad anymore." Dani blinked at the camera. "Are you okay, Nick?"

The way she asked the question, he knew she had a specific meaning. Was he okay over breaking up with Harper? "Never better," he replied.

Who'd ratted him out to his sister?

A white object appeared in front of the screen, too close to be in focus. "Look what I brought for you," Haley said.

"Pull it back, honey, so he can see it better," Dani said in the background, then the white was pulled away and Nick could make out a small doll-size igloo in Haley's hands.

He grinned wide.

The child giggled again. "I found you an igloo like you wanted!"

"I see that you did. Is it big enough for me to sleep in?"

"No, silly. But I'll let you play with one of my babies if you want to. She can sleep in it."

"That sounds perfect to me. Will you keep it at your house for me, and when I come to visit we can both play with it?"

"Yes. I *will* do that."

"Can I play, too?" Jenna asked. "I'm going to be here *all weekend*. Daddy said I could. He and Mama had some talking to do."

"You absolutely can play with us, too." He was glad to hear she wouldn't be around her parents this weekend if they planned to "talk," because their talking was rarely at a volume that excluded others. "But I won't be back this weekend," he told her. He'd only been gone for three days, and he certainly wasn't ready to return.

"Then I'll play with it the next time I'm here." Jenna's round face suddenly leaned in closer to the screen. "Are you still sad, Uncle Nick?" she whispered.

Broken was more like it. It pained him to realize that Jenna had picked up on his mood. "I'm really good, sweetheart. Not sad at all. Don't worry about me, okay? You just play with Haley and have lots of fun."

"Okay. I can do that."

After a few more minutes of chatting with the girls, they said their good-byes and ran off. Then Dani was back on the screen. She sat at her kitchen table, and Nick could see the worry in her eyes.

"Stop it," he said.

"I can't. You brought a woman to the house, Nick. You've never done that before. Is it serious?"

"Come on. You know I don't do serious."

"But Gabe said—"

"Gabe makes things up," he cut in. Which wasn't true. "Don't believe anything he says, he's just trying to shift the attention off of him. It was nothing. A fling while I was at home." He reached for the new laptop box and began picking at one of its corners. "It's over."

And he wished it had never begun.

"Oh, Nick."

He gave a bored look at her weepy-sad tone. "One more word about it and I hang up. You can either tell me about your trip, you can let *me* tell you about my new plans, or you can give me one more long puppy-dog face and this conversation is done. You choose."

Her puppy-dog face cleared before he'd finished speaking. "What new plans?"

"I suspected that would get you." He turned the camera to the laptop box. "I plan to take over the books for the farm."

What he didn't tell her was that he also planned to use the new computer for his fall college courses. He'd registered that morning.

"Why?" she asked. She sounded at a loss as to why he'd want to be a part of things.

"It's time I helped out." He brought the camera back to him. "I took a look at the financials while I was at home, and I could tell Dad needed some help. Probably it would have been nice if it'd crossed my mind to be useful long before now, but it didn't. And I'm sorry about that. I'm sure you could've stood to delegate a task or two to me over the years, too."

"I was fine," she assured him. "You were busy with your career."

"Yeah." He shrugged. "But still. Better late than never, huh? I haven't told him yet, though. Save that for me. I'll call him later tonight, and then I'll be back in town in two weeks for the local rodeo. I'll transfer everything over to my computer then."

If he weren't mistaken, pride washed over his sister's face. "I'm sure he'll appreciate the help."

They talked for a few more minutes, and just before they hung up, he said, "One more thing."

"What's that?"

"Let's start a regular family dinner. I know not everyone is home very often, but I'll be back in two weeks, and I think Gabe still plans to be there. I have no idea about Nate"—Nate had been gone before Nick returned from Harper's—"but maybe we can talk Cord into a weekend trip home. Possibly it could grow into everyone being in the same place a few times a year."

Love shone from his sister's eyes. "That sounds really good."

"You want to talk to Gloria about it? It should be at the farm, don't you think?"

Dani nodded, and Nick could see that the idea appealed to her as much as it did to him. They'd come a long way since the previous summer. "I'll talk to her," she said. "And I'll call Cord. And Jaden, too. With it being so close to harvest and both of them planning to come in for that, it's possible neither can fit in another trip home. But I'll ask. I might even beg."

"Thanks." The world somehow felt better in that moment than it had in a while. "I'll see you in two weeks. Let me know what I can bring for the dinner."

They hung up, and he looked down at the computer. He'd already made several big moves today. College, the farm's books, suggesting a family dinner. Might as well make one more.

He pulled up his agent's number and placed a call.

The pain in Nick's thigh wasn't the worst he'd ever had, but he certainly could have gone through the rest of the weekend without it.

He cringed as he lowered to a seat on the bleachers, an unopened beer in his hand. He'd be skipping his second round that night but had been cleared for the following evening. After getting tossed, he'd barely had time to roll out of the way before taking a kick to his femur. A split second slower and the bone could have snapped instead of leaving him with a deep bruise.

"You good?" Nate asked. He waited beside Nick, letting him get settled with his bad leg stretched out on the riser before him like some kind of invalid.

"Feel like a hundred bucks," Nick grumbled. He'd been stupid tonight. Let his mind wander when he should have been focused.

And it had wandered to the woman who didn't want him. Who'd sent her youngest sister in her place this weekend instead of having the guts to show up herself. Five days, and there'd been no word.

Big shocker.

As if he'd thought she might realize she'd been wrong. But no. The idea of them developing into something had only been in Nick's pathetic head.

Nate offered his plate of funnel cake.

"I hate the stuff," Nick growled.

His brother rolled his eyes. "Whatever. Your attitude could use some work."

"And I didn't ask you to show up and point that out to me all day."

"Then it's a good thing I'm the type who does things without being asked."

Even though he complained, Nick had actually been glad to see his brother. Given that Nate had been silent all week, Nick had assumed he'd made it halfway around the world already. Yet when Nick had checked into the hotel that afternoon, there his twin had been, sitting in the lobby.

Nick ignored him now and watched the action in the arena. Female barrel racing was up, and there were some top-notch riders at this event. The two brothers watched in silence for several minutes. After Nick had been seen by the medic, they'd made their way to the far end of the stands. It wasn't a sold-out crowd, so they had the area to themselves.

When Jeb Mauley passed in front of them, the green fringe on his chaps flapping around his calves, he tossed Nick a nod. "You okay?"

"I will be soon enough."

"Good deal. Let me know if you need anything. Hope to see you out there tomorrow."

"Thanks, man."

Jeb had put in a near-perfect ride earlier, and if he stayed on track for the weekend, he'd take home the pot. After he moved on, Nate set his now-empty plate to the side and unscrewed the top off his beer. He leaned back, his elbows on the seat behind him.

"That kid's got some skill," Nate noted, indicating Jeb. "Watched him ride earlier."

"He has a lot of skill. That's why I put in a good word for him with Charlie."

This brought Nate back upright. "You made a decision."

"PBR isn't for me," Nick confirmed.

"Good for you. You're going to school, then?"

"Full-time. I already registered." Nick finally gave up trying to focus on barrel racing and decided to put it all out there. See how his brother took it. "I'm also moving back to Birch Bay."

"No kidding?"

"Not to the farm, but in town," he clarified. "And I think you should come home, too."

That wiped the superior look from Nate's face. "I think you should be careful not to let any more bulls ring your bells."

"I'm just saying that Dani changed. She was wrong about what she wanted out of her life. Gabe moved to LA, so clearly he wasn't happy with his choices, either. I'm moving back to town. Maybe we've all been wrong."

"Gabe moved because if he didn't, he would've had to get a divorce from the witch of the west."

"Regardless, if he'd really wanted to run the farm, wouldn't he have fought harder to stay?" Nick had thought about that a lot over the months. Yes, Gabe and Michelle's marriage was rocky. Hell, it was flat-out fractured right down the middle. It had been for years. Yet he'd left the farm. And it had almost seemed to Nick as if he'd been glad to go. "He spent years managing the place," Nick pointed out. "However, he had no issue packing up and heading out. Staying wasn't what he wanted."

Nick continued. "Jaden split. Cord not only left home, but he bought a permanent place in Billings. Not that I expect him to fill it with a wife and babies, but he made it clear he has no intention of coming back. And then there's you. You roamed the country for years before ending up about as far away as you can get, and you still spend months at a time on a fishing boat, drifting far away from civilization. We all ran. We all hid. I'm saying that maybe it's time we stop."

Nate had turned away about halfway through Nick's spiel, and though his eyes were trained on the action in front of them, Nick suspected he saw nothing but the past.

He finally faced Nick. "We all had to leave, didn't we? To get away from her."

"But she's gone now. The house isn't the shrine to her that it used to be, and we're no longer pretending our childhoods were anything more than what they were. What if what we're doing isn't what we should be doing?"

Nate shook his head in denial. "Love has made you stupid. You're moving back to Birch Bay for a piece of—"

He cut his own words off before saying something that he had to know would piss Nick off, and at the same time, Nick didn't bother filling him in on the fact that he and Harper were done. Nor did he dispute Nate's words of love.

Nick did love Harper. For all the good it had done him.

He still couldn't believe he'd fallen in love with a woman who didn't want him. When would he learn? When would he stop hoping someone would care?

"Sorry," Nate mumbled. "You know I like her."

"The thing is, I'm not moving back for her. I *want* to be there. I knew that the minute I went home."

Nate shook his head again. "I'm in a good place where I am. Don't mix me into your crap."

"You're in a worse place than I've ever come close to being."

"Drop it." Nate's jaw went hard. "I can't come home, and you know why."

"You weren't the one who messed up."

"I *won't* come home. End of story."

Instead of fighting it out, both of them went silent. They finished watching the barrel racing and sat through a comedy routine from the bullfighters that the kids in the audience ate up. They were just settling in for cattle roping when Jewel and Patti sat down on a set of bleachers not far away. Nate looked at Nick.

"I assumed Jewel didn't have any bulls here this weekend since I hadn't seen Harp. Who's that with her?"

"Patti. Their youngest sister."

"Harper okay? I thought she was helping for another week?"

Nick didn't look at his brother. He shrugged. "Patience was never my strong suit, okay?"

It took a second, but Nate got it. "You dumb fuck. You ruined things with her?"

"Yep."

"What did you do?"

Nick didn't answer, and for the first time in weeks, he found himself glad to see Betsy strolling toward him. Her presence shut Nate up, especially when she stopped in her tracks and looked them both over. Nate had shaved at some point during the week, and if the two of them had been wearing the same clothes tonight, it would be difficult to tell them apart.

"Well, what have we here. My favorite cowboy times two." Betsy climbed the bleachers, and deposited herself between the two men, wiggling her hips against their thighs until she fit between them. "My day has just been made, boys."

Nate met Nick's eyes over Betsy's head, and all Nick could do was shrug. Yep. This was his life.

Betsy was a small thing, her head barely coming up past their shoulders, and as she looked from one brother to the other, the woman actually licked her lips. As if presented with a fat, juicy steak. Or two.

"I sure have missed you." Her green eyes lingered on Nick's. "And I haven't seen your army girl here tonight. You two over?"

Nick didn't answer.

Betsy's lips curled. "Either way, doesn't matter to me. I've moved on." She put a hand on Nate's thigh and turned to him. "How about buying us a motel room, good-looking?"

Nate had just tipped back his beer, and ale spewed at Betsy's words. Her laughter trilled out, and Nick noted that her hand inched higher on Nate's thigh.

Playing the part of annoying brother, Nick interrupted before Nate could find any words. "Not that I don't think my brother appreciates your offer, Bets, but you might want to reconsider tonight. Nate, there, is on some scary-ass medicine, and he can't get it up right now."

More beer spewed out.

"Awwww." Betsy turned back to Nate. "Poor baby." Her eyes dropped to his lap. "That really is sad to hear." She then patted Nate right smack on the dick, her hand gripping more than patting, and stood to leave. "Maybe next time."

She sauntered off, the perfect amount of sway going on in her shorts, and Nick heard Nate curse under his breath. "No wonder Harper looked like she wanted to stick that woman on a skewer and roast her last weekend."

Nick eyed his brother. "What are you talking about?"

"She had eagle eyes on that one. Big, green, jealous eagle eyes."

It thrilled him to know Betsy still riled Harper. Or, at least, she had the previous weekend. By tonight, Harper had probably forgotten he existed. He finally opened his own beer and took a long pull.

"You do know you're an idiot, right?" Nate said as his eyes continued to follow Betsy's progression until she disappeared in the crowd. "You're the one of us who stands a chance to get it right, and you lose the one woman who might have been willing to put up with your ass."

"You miss the point," Nick ground out. "She *wasn't* willing to put up with me." At least, not in the way his brother meant. Because he'd never been more than sex to Harper.

He threw down his beer, the liquid spilling onto the rocks beneath the bleachers, and stood. The pain in his leg roared, but he ignored it. Same as he ignored the pain in his heart. "I'm done here. If you want a ride back to the hotel, either get in my truck or get left."

When he reached the ground, with Nate two feet behind him and holding the bottle he'd picked up off the ground, Nick jabbed a finger in his brother's direction. "And if you *do* get in my truck, no more talk of Harper again. *Ever.*"

Chapter Twenty-Three

Harper returned to her living room, stopping midstride as the sight of all the new additions filling the space struck her as odd. Not that it wasn't anything she hadn't witnessed every time she'd walked into the room over the last few days, but it finally hit her how very different it was. There was color everywhere.

The white was still there, underneath it all, but on every available surface lay something of color. Random swatches of material and paint were scattered throughout the room, in among stacks of food, vibrant bags of primary colors waiting to be filled with the food, bolts of brightly colored fabrics, and a box stuffed with wrapping paper. It was possible she'd gone a bit overboard in her projects, but since she'd woken in Thomas's closet four days before, the ideas had been churning.

First of all, she had to get rid of the white. She'd called a designer who'd come right out—then had almost run when she'd encountered the situation at hand. But in the end, the woman had walked the rooms and taken notes. She'd then shown up two days later with samples and ideas.

Harper had spread out all of them for consideration.

Meanwhile, she'd signed up for a handful of charities. The local Meals on Wheels program had not only needed monetary and food donations but a temporary delivery person, as well. Harper had raised her hand. The local Girl Scouts had been seeking help with a project to clothe area children in need. Again, Harper's hand had shot up. She'd ordered hundreds of yards of material and had even bought a top-of-the-line sewing machine. She had a lesson lined up for tomorrow to learn how to sew.

But her favorite was the Christmas in July idea she'd come up with herself. There was a children's home a few hours from Birch Bay, and she just knew that the kids there would be thrilled to receive festively wrapped presents for no reason at all. She couldn't wait to get started on that one.

It had been too long since she'd taken on any projects for others, and with every click of the button to order needed items online, it was as if her soul was reawakening.

Her cell rang, and she looked around at the sound. She had no idea where she'd left her phone. Most of the week she hadn't had it with her. It tended to mock her because Nick wasn't calling. Not that he should call. But that hadn't kept her from wanting him to.

Such as now. As she hurried out of the room to follow the sound, she couldn't stop the heavy thump of anticipation at the thought that it could be Nick on the other end.

It stopped ringing before she found it, and her shoulders sagged when she saw it had only been Jewel. She punched Jewel's number to return the call. It was night one of this weekend's rodeo, and though Harper had talked Patti into going in her place, Harper hadn't stopped worrying about her pregnant sister. Harper had been the one to sign up to be Jewel's keeper. She should have gone with her tonight—even though it might have turned uncomfortable had she run into Nick.

"He misses you," Jewel said in greeting, and once again, anticipation thumped inside Harper.

"Did he tell you that?"

"No. I actually haven't talked to him. But he's going to lose this weekend. In fact, he's pretty much already lost. He's not on his game." Jewel paused for just a second before adding, "And he got hurt."

Harper quit breathing. "But he's okay?"

"Probably sporting a hella bruise, but he walked away from it. And I checked, he'll ride tomorrow night. But he's looking for you, Harp. It's obvious. What happened between you two, anyway? You never really said. And though it shouldn't surprise me given the size of his crush all those years ago, I think he might really care."

Jewel sounded as shocked as Harper had when Nick declared that he wanted marriage.

She started to deny her sister's words but decided to go with honesty. "Maybe he does, but he's better off without me."

"You might be right about that. You're a mess of a person. But are *you* better off without *him*? I've watched you these last weeks, and he's good for you. And even more surprising to me, I think you might care for him, too."

"I . . ."

She couldn't bring herself to say that she *didn't* care. Because she did. She liked Nick. He was a great guy. Wasn't that why she'd ended it? She didn't want to hurt him any more than she already had.

"Trust me on this," she said. She made a spot on her couch and dropped to the cushions. "He *is* better off without me. What I may or may not need is unimportant."

"Harp."

"Don't. It's not worth arguing over." She looked around the room, suddenly in no mood for any of her causes, and grabbed the remote from the side table. "I need to go, hon. I'm busy right now. I signed up for some charities, and they're depending on me."

She hung up and slumped into the corner of her couch, and tried not to rehear Jewel telling her that Nick might be good for her. That he missed her.

None of it mattered.

She turned on the TV and began to flip. She was busy paying her dues. Nick, her wants, her needs . . . they all came second. She'd messed up. She'd had her chance, and now Nick would go on to find the right woman for him. Because she wasn't it.

As if she'd known it would be there, her fingers stopped pushing the button at the exact moment Nick's latest commercial appeared on the screen. She increased the volume, and didn't take her eyes off the screen for the next forty-five seconds. The first time she'd seen this, she'd been in bed with Nick. Instead of rewinding the commercial and letting herself watch it again, she turned off the TV and curled up on the couch. And she admitted something to herself for the very first time.

If not for Thomas, she could have totally fallen in love with Nick Wilde.

Doors slammed in the driveway, and Harper put down the roller and hurried to the front of the house. She was testing out the paint samples her designer had brought over—as well as a few more she'd picked out herself—and there were no fewer than four colors on the walls in each of the main rooms.

She opened the door as her parents reached the top step, and motioned them in. "Thanks for coming over."

Her parents entered behind her, but their footfalls immediately fell silent. Harper glanced back over her shoulder.

"You painted," her dad said.

"I'm trying to decide on the right color. That's what I need your help with. You sell real estate—see a lot of houses—so I thought you might be able to help me decide on the right neutral."

"You're selling the house?"

Harper studied the sandy-gray color she'd tried out by the front door, but couldn't remember its name. She thought Thomas would have liked that color. "Maybe," she answered vaguely. At this point, she wasn't sure, but the idea did keep gnawing at her. "But either way, I can't handle the white anymore. I thought a nice neutral would be the way to go."

"Sounds like a good plan." Her dad leaned to the side to see farther into the next room, where more colors lined the walls. "I'll walk through and see what you're thinking."

He sounded as perplexed as the house probably looked.

"Thanks, Dad."

When he'd left the room, her mother asked, "And you needed my help for?"

Harper could see that her mother was already keying in on why she'd been asked to come. The charity situation was out of hand. As far as the eye could see, there was food, bags, gifts, wrapping paper, material, a new sewing machine, two large folding tables in the middle of all of it, and stacks of empty boxes for packing everything up.

Possibly, she'd overcompensated. Which, granted, hadn't been the best way to make up for lost time. But it wasn't as if she could back out of her commitments now.

She grinned at her mother, going for an I'm-sweet-and-you-must-help-me look. "I thought you might want to help me wrap a few gifts? And bag some food."

Her mother simply stared at her.

"I know it seems like a lot," Harper began, "but I realized I haven't been volunteering in a while. And if you'll remember, that was one of my passions." She turned toward the pile of gifts. "I like to do things. To help."

"Participating in search and rescue missions is what you should be doing." Her mom moved to her side. She put an arm around Harper's waist. "That's your passion."

Harper shook her head. She kept her eyes locked on the baby doll dressed in purple at the very top of the pile. "I don't have time for that now. I have all these other things to take care of. I'm helping people again, Mom. It's a good thing."

"Are you flying at all?"

"Mom," Harper's voice cracked, and she quit trying to talk. She was breathing too hard to speak. She glanced at her mother, who wore "the look" Harper had grown so tired of seeing over the months. Only, the look seemed to be joined with another this time. It wasn't merely concern and pity shadowing her mother's face but determination, as well. As if she were finished letting Harper hide from the facts.

Her dad returned to the room and stood with her mom.

"It's okay to move on," her mom said.

Harper's rib cage felt as if it were going to split open. "I just need help wrapping these presents," she croaked out.

"Glen." Her mother nodded toward the front door. "Go outside. Give us a minute."

Without saying a word, her dad kissed her on the cheek and stepped to the porch, but he didn't go far. He remained right outside the door, as if to let Harper know he was there if she needed him. Yet he was far enough away to give her the space she and her mom required.

"You and Dad are great parents," Harper said. She had the thought that if she started the conversation, then she could control it.

"We've always tried."

"I'm so lucky." She thought about Nick's family and how their mother had been. Then of Thomas's. "Thomas's parents loved him, too. Like you and Dad love us. But in the end, they hurt him. They weren't good parents after all." She gave her mom a tremulous smile. "So thank you for being there for me. I love you both."

"And we love you, baby." Her mom hugged her. "We'd do anything for you."

"I know," Harper whispered. She wrapped her arms around herself and crossed to stand in front of the doll with the purple dress. "Thank you, also, for giving me time. I needed it." She pulled in a breath deep enough to get her through her next words. It was time to talk. "Because Thomas's death was my fault."

Her mother didn't immediately deny Harper's words or ask why she might say that, she simply let Harper tell her story. And as the words poured out, Harper recognized that she'd needed to share this with her mother. Her mom consoled when Harper needed it and listened when she didn't. And as Harper ran out of words, she looked at her mother.

"And if all of that wasn't bad enough," she added in a thready voice, "I was pregnant when he died. I didn't know for certain until that day, and I miscarried five weeks later."

Her mom nodded, sadness settling on her face. "I'd wondered if that might have been the stain on the nursery room floor."

Harper had finally accepted her pregnancy when her period the following month hadn't shown, either. She'd gotten a home test, and as she'd waited on the results, she'd prayed that it would be positive.

When two lines appeared, a new purpose had settled over her, and for the first time in a month she'd felt as if she could go on. She would bring her and Thomas's baby into the world, and she would provide as much love for that one child as two parents could have ever given it. She'd spent a week in a cloud of happiness, shopping for healthy food and planning what furniture she'd buy. She'd bought only one item of clothing up to that point, and that had been an "I love Daddy" bib. That bib was currently in the box at the top of the nursery closet.

"I'd just found out that I inherited everything of Thomas's," she explained. "There had been a lot of paperwork to deal with, and waiting to find out if his parents would fight the claim, but his lawyer called and said it was iron proof. All Thomas had was now mine. It overwhelmed me. I didn't want any of it; I just wanted Thomas. But I did have our baby. So I slept on the nursery floor that night. I fell asleep talking to the baby, explaining that we'd be okay. That I wouldn't let anything happen to either one of us." Her voice trembled and she pulled away when her mom tried to reach for her. "I woke up in a pool of blood. Again, I'd failed my husband. I couldn't even bring his baby—*our baby*—into the world. He left me with that gift, and I let that gift die."

She lowered her head in shame.

"It's hard," her mom said. Her words were quiet. "You blame yourself. I get that. It's the nature of motherhood."

"But I caused it."

Her mother's eyes narrowed. "What did you do to cause it?"

"I wished it away," she whispered. "When the doctor first told me I was pregnant in the hospital, I didn't want it." She blinked, her eyes dry. "I wanted my baby gone."

"Oh, honey." Her mom reached for her that time, and pulled Harper into her arms. "You know better than that. You can't wish a miscarriage upon yourself. You were hurting. You'd just lost Thomas and you couldn't imagine a world without him in it. You were angry."

"I was furious." Her words were muffled against her mother's shoulder. "He was supposed to be here with me forever."

"I know, sweetie. And I wish he were here with you. You didn't deserve all this. You were my toughest kid, but also my most tender." She pulled back and peered into Harper's eyes. "You were the one who saved yourself for the right man."

Shock widened Harper's eyes. "How do you know that?"

"Sweetie. Moms know these things. Whereas my other girls . . ."

"Oh, Mom." Harper pushed out of her mother's arms. "Stop it. You aren't supposed to know anything about your kids' sex lives. And even if you do, you certainly aren't supposed to talk about it."

"You'll know these things one day, too." Her mother nodded. "When you *do* have kids."

"But I don't think I ever will."

"Why not?"

Harper lifted her shoulders. "Because I don't deserve them."

"Baby." Her mother took Harper's hand and pulled her down to the couch. "If anyone in this world deserves to mother a child, it's you. You have so much love to give."

"But I—"

"Thomas wouldn't want you to mourn him forever."

"I know that, Mom. But he died *because* of me. How can I move on after that?"

"No, baby. He died doing what he loved."

"But I talked him into too much stuff. He wouldn't have done half of it if not for me."

Her mother scowled. "That's a load of bull, and you know it."

Harper chuckled dryly at her mother's words, but explained, "You don't understand. His brother was the adventurous one."

"And maybe his brother's accident *did* lead Thomas into taking more risks than he would have. Didn't you tell me he'd always looked up to his brother? That he was already following in his footsteps, even before Harry died?"

"He was. He'd talk Harry into taking him on the difficult slopes with him. Or climbing the experienced trails. They did lots of things together. But he quit all that after Harry's death."

"Why?"

"Partially because his parents wouldn't allow him to do it." At least, that's what he'd told her. "But he said he didn't want to, anyway."

"Yet when he no longer needed their permission," her mom said, "didn't he start up again?"

Harper nodded.

Her mother looked directly into Harper's face and said, "He lived his life the way he wanted, baby. He didn't do anything that he didn't want to do. Don't you see that? He loved his life with you, being with you. He loved taking care of you. In fact, your father and he had a long talk before you got married. Thomas was good for you, Harper. You two fit. He would have died for you."

"He did die for me."

"And do you think he could have lived with himself if he'd lived without saving you?"

Harper lowered her eyes, because she knew the answer. "I think that might have destroyed him."

Yet that didn't mean her not being able to save him hadn't also destroyed a piece of her.

"I know it would have." Her mom squeezed Harper's hands. "Ever thought that maybe he's the one who sent you Nick to be in your life?"

Harper's gaze shot to her mom's. "We're not even talking about Nick."

"Aren't we?"

She shook her head, but her mouth didn't get the message to stay shut. "I hurt him, Mom." She sucked in a breath. "He told me he could see us long term. But we're not long term."

"I don't know," her mom mused. "I could see it. You two are good together."

"Why do you say that?"

"Sweetie." She cupped Harper's cheeks in both her hands. "He looked at you the same way Thomas did. How did you not see that? He cares about you."

"But what if I . . ." She didn't finish the sentence. Was she really afraid her actions would end up killing Nick as they had Thomas? Nick was high-octane long before he met her. He was also the kind of man who did what he wanted.

Yet, the fear was real.

"I wouldn't want to hurt him, too," she whispered before once again dropping her gaze. "Or for me to hurt *because* of him."

Her mom pulled her in for another hug and spoke with her mouth near Harper's ear. "You already know you're not going to hurt him. He can take care of himself. But life isn't without risks, and you know that, too. You may be my tender one, but you were born walking the edge. It's who you are."

"But I'm tired of hurting."

She pulled back. "So you'd rather not live at all? Thomas died protecting you, Harper. Why would you stop living now? He would hate that." She stood and moved to the door and asked Harper's father to come in. "Tell your daughter that love isn't always easy," she instructed. "That people deserve second chances."

"What are you talking about?" Harper asked.

Her dad looked at her then, and a feeling of trepidation come over Harper. "Did your mom ever tell you that I was married before?" he asked. "That I married *her* best friend?"

Harper stood. "What?"

"I fell in love with her best friend," her dad said matter-of-factly. "Before I ever had eyes for your mother. We ran off and eloped. It was wild and passionate. Oh . . ." He let out a sigh. "We were crazy about each other."

"Mom . . ."

Her mother put an arm around her dad. "What can I say? He liked her better than me."

"You didn't even like me then." Her dad pulled a face. "You thought she could do better."

"It's true. I did."

"But you're both so happy." Harper looked from one to the other. "I thought you were made for each other."

"We are happy," her dad explained. "And we always have been. But Annie was taken from us both. She died of cancer only a year after she and I married. Your mom and I both hurt from that. Tremendously. But because of *her*, *we* came together. And we've never regretted that."

Shock kept Harper where she was. "I had no idea. How have you kept that from us all this time?"

Her mother gave a soft smile. "It was a special thing between us. There was no need to share it. Until today. Things happen for a reason, baby, and we'll never be able to understand why. But without Annie's death, I wouldn't have any of you. And without Thomas . . ."

Harper gulped at the implication. She shook her head back and forth as she tried to sort through her thoughts. They were all too jumbled. "I just don't know. And anyway, I hurt Nick. I told him no. That Thomas was my one and only."

"He's a bright boy," her dad said. He kissed her mother's cheek and gave her a wink before adding, "You might consider giving him a second chance. Sometimes they pay off."

"Maybe," Harper muttered. Could she really do that, though? Have a second-chance love? She still found that hard to believe. "The thing is, he might not be willing to give *me* a second chance?"

"There's only one way to find out."

It all seemed too improbable. "I'll think about it. But I'm not making any promises."

Her dad crossed to her then and took her hands. The warmth of his grip comforted her, and strangely, made her feel as if Thomas were there in the room with them. "You're a smart girl, too, Harp. You'll make the right decisions. And Thomas will be cheering you on every step of the way."

"Thanks, Dad." She just wished she had a clue what the right decision was.

She hugged her father, grateful to have him in her life, and let her head rest on his shoulder an extra amount of time. Before she stepped away, she opened her eyes and saw a new light now shining in her mother's eyes. One she hadn't seen directed toward her in months. Hope.

And for the first time, Harper wanted to have hope.

Her dad stepped back, and in true Margaret Jackson fashion, her mother lifted her brows and pinned Harper with a look. "You're also smart enough to know that you're not about to rope me into this mess of yours all by myself." She eyed the pile of presents and the mounds of food. "But I'll tell you what I will do. I'll get my women's club to help us. I'll line up a group and we'll get this mess out of here within days."

Harper breathed a sigh of relief. "Thank you, Mom."

"But on one condition."

She waited, instinctively knowing that her mother was about to push.

"Before you volunteer for anything else, you have to promise to have a long, serious conversation with yourself about going back to search and rescue. That's who you are, baby. It's horrible that Thomas will never again be in the helicopter with you. I hate that for you and him both. But you've wanted that since you first learned that people *could* get stranded or lost. You've found people. You've saved them. You've made a difference, sweetheart, and before you never take that flight again, you make sure you're quitting because it's the right decision for *you*."

They left after that, and Harper watched them drive away. And it surprised her that the thought that showed up in her head next wasn't of Thomas, but of Nick. Could her parents be right about him? About them?

Did she really deserve a second chance?

She honestly wasn't sure how she felt about anything they'd said, so she decided to wait and ponder everything later that night. Right now, she wanted to return to her painting. And she wanted to paint the living room the color by the door. She had only a sample at the house, but she quickly went out and purchased several gallons. And as she painted long into the night, she surprised herself by carrying on a one-sided conversation with her late husband. They'd once picked out everything for these rooms, and she suddenly wanted to do that with him again.

She didn't need a designer. She just needed to channel Thomas.

Several days later, all the downstairs rooms were repainted and all the charitable donations had been packed up and delivered. And as she stood in the middle of her newly colored spaces, Harper began to smile again. Because another question had been answered over those days of painting, as well. She would sell the house. And the proceeds would start a foundation in Harry's name.

Which also meant she'd have to remove Thomas's belongings from the house. It was time. And she would do that job herself. No hiring it out to impersonal movers. Thomas deserved to have her in his life for the last time, and instead of dread, she'd begun to look forward to the task.

Sore and exhausted from the painting, she could have easily gone to bed, but instead, she headed up the stairs. As she opened Thomas's door, an explosion of color burst over the lake in the distance, and she moved to the window. She hadn't even realized what day it was. Independence Day. That must be why her family had all been trying to get in touch with her. They usually got together as a group and grilled out on the Fourth.

But she'd ignored all calls that had come in that day, texting that she was busy. And she was fine with that. They could be over there watching it together. Because Thomas had loved fireworks, too, and it seemed appropriate that she and he watch them together this one last time.

She spread open the drapes and picked out a spot on the guest bed so she could both sort through boxes and watch out the window at the same time. But she didn't open a single box. Instead, she grabbed a pillow and stretched out to watch the show through the bedroom window. And she began to talk to her husband.

"I love you, Thomas. You know that. And I always will. And I'm so very sorry that I panicked, but at the same time, thank you for saving me. Mom was right. That's the kind of man you were, and you wouldn't have had it any other way. And I knew that. As angry as I was, I knew that all along.

"I guess I should apologize for being angry, too, but you always did love my passion, didn't you? So I can't really say that I'm sorry for having strong feelings about losing you. I am sorry I lost our baby, though. Maybe it wasn't my fault. I don't know. Or maybe it was. Possibly my grief caused too much stress. I'll never know."

A burst of red, white, and blue showered down in the distance.

"It's beautiful, Thomas. I wish you could see it with me."

Another round went off, and she opened the window so she could hear the booms. She sat down in front of the glass and leaned against the windowsill.

"I shouldn't have gotten out of SAR work, though." She said those words as much to herself as to Thomas. "I know that probably hurt you the most, but I just couldn't do it. I was too mad. And yes, I'll admit that partially I wanted to hurt you. Because I couldn't figure out how I was supposed to live after you left me. But you know what I figured out this week?" She looked at the closet, as if her husband were just behind the doors. "You may have left me, but you went to be with your brother. And Harry probably needed you more than me. So that's okay. Tell him I said hi."

She closed her eyes as the booms echoed in the background, and she thought about all the things that her life was supposed to have been. And then she thought about Nick. She missed him so much. It had been over two weeks, and she wanted to see him now as badly as she'd wanted to go after him the night he'd walked away.

"I didn't want to help anyone for a while," she whispered, "because there was no way anyone could help me. But I do now. My anger is fading. I may not be able to save you or our baby, but I can help others. So I *will* do that. I make that promise to you now. I'll never stop being what we were again."

More booms sounded, and she opened her eyes. She could practically see Thomas smiling back at her, and she nodded. "I wish I had you back in my life, but I'm ready to let go."

Orange and green rained down on the lake, and tears began to fall over Harper's cheeks.

"I love him, Thomas. I'm not sure how or why or when. And I know it hasn't even been two years without you yet, but I love him. And I think he could learn to love me. If I haven't already run him off."

She wiped at her cheeks, but more tears immediately replaced the ones now on her fingers.

"I don't want to be sad the rest of my life." Her voice shook. "And I know you don't want that for me. So will you make me one last promise? Will you and our baby watch over me as I try to move forward? Maybe send me the strength to attempt this thing with Nick? Because I need him, Thomas. I never imagined I'd get a second chance, but he's as good as you. I promise. And I know you would have loved him, too."

A burst of fireworks so loud and so big stopped Harper's words, and she watched silently until every last color faded away. Then she stood and got busy sorting through Thomas's things. It was time to do something other than sit still.

Chapter Twenty-Four

Nick perched on the bottom rung of the gate, adrenaline zapping through his body, as he waited for his turn. He was back in Birch Bay for a one-night event, and the ride he was about to take would be it for him. He was hanging up his rope.

He'd had a good run, earned plenty of money, and had only broken a handful of bones. It had been a fantastic career. And though he'd gotten into it for all the wrong reasons, he didn't regret his decision one bit. Bull riding was a part of him now. But he was ready to move on. There was more waiting out there for him.

He caught sight of Jewel and Bobby watching from the corner, and he mentally patted himself on the back for not looking around for Harper. Seemed she was in his past, too. Though he had considered texting to let her know he'd be making his final ride here tonight. They might not be a couple, but they had been friends. He would've liked to have seen her here for him.

The speaker in the middle of the arena fired to life. "Next up is a local boy, folks, and with this ride comes a huge announcement. Two-time Montana Pro champ Nick Wilde is taking his final ride tonight."

The crowd gasped with shock, followed by groans and the beginning of clapping.

"He wanted to take that ride here with us, so let's get behind him and make this one count."

The speakers went quiet, and Nick rose up to the next rung. He waved his hat at the cheering crowd, taking in the moment. He did love this attention. And he'd miss it. But he also knew he'd made the right decision. There were bigger things waiting for him, and this time he planned to live his life for himself, not for anyone else.

The crowd died down as he and his spotter got into position, and then Nick slung his leg over the gate. His focus was strong tonight. Legs set, rope tight, back straight. He said his prayer and gave the nod.

The gate flew open, and he and bull went out as one. The bull gave it everything he had, but there was no way Nick wasn't staying on for this ride. The buzzer sounded, and a grin arrived before he'd even hit the ground. That had to be darned close to the best ride he'd ever taken.

As a score of ninety flashed, contentment settled over him. Life was finally heading in the right direction. The fans showed their gratitude with a minute-long standing ovation. Cameras flashed, and he even caught a couple of faces wet with tears. His friends and family glowed with pride. This was the way to go out.

Forcing himself to turn away from it all, he gave one last wave and exited through the gate. Jeb's was the first face he saw.

"Hell of a way to end it," the younger man said. "Congrats, man. Terrific ride. And thanks for putting in that word with your agent."

Nick shook Jeb's hand. "Charlie's a good guy. I hope you two can work something out."

"I think we can."

"Make him a rich man, will you? I went back on my promise for that."

They parted, and as the next rider climbed into the chute, Nick moved away from the gates. Normally he'd stick around and watch everyone else, but he had no interest in that tonight. He didn't even care to stick around to take the prize. He was mentally and physically done, and the adrenaline in his system now pumped for a different reason. He had a new life to figure out. Maybe that wouldn't include the woman he wanted, but he'd still make it a life worth having. And he could thank her for giving him that much, anyway. He no longer had any intention of just going through the motions. He intended to live.

As he came out of the rider area, eleven wide smiles greeted him. His entire family had come home for this. Not only had they had their first official Wilde family dinner the night before, but they were all here supporting him tonight. Even Jaden's girlfriend, Megan, had shown up.

Jenna and Haley each sat on their dad's shoulders, and both were shaking pink pom-poms over their heads. "You did so good, Uncle Nick," Jenna squealed. "I loved watching you ride."

"You were the best!" Haley added.

Everyone else began talking at the same time, too, and Nick reveled in the moment. After years of running away, it was good to be home. Good to know this *was* his home.

As he talked to his sister, getting the scoop on her business and the receptionist she'd recently hired, Haley began tapping him on the top of the head. He looked up, and fell in love with the little girl even more when she grinned, and her blue-stained teeth flashed at him. The remains of her cotton candy were in her dad's hand.

"What can I do for you, Haley?"

She pointed behind him. "The woman with the blue hair is looking at you."

Her words caused his heart to clench. Harper was here? He glanced at Nate, who was now looking behind Nick, as well, and Nate shot him an I-told-you-so look. Maybe it wasn't over with Harper just yet. But Nick wasn't about to get his hopes up.

He turned, and sure enough, Harper stood watching him. And good Lord, did she look good.

"Did you still like her, Uncle Nick?" Haley chirped from atop her Daddy's shoulders.

Nick didn't answer, waiting instead for Ben to instruct his daughter not to ask such personal questions, but Ben didn't utter a sound. Nick glanced at him to find that not only had Ben remained silent, but he also seemed to be awaiting an answer. As was everyone else.

But an answer wouldn't be coming. Not in this crowd.

"I wanna be a 'copter pilot when I grow up," Haley announced.

"Me, too," Jenna added. "Dad says Miss Harper flies all over the place, and she could even fly to Disneyland if she wanted to."

"That's where I'll fly my 'copter." The girls' chatter continued in the background as Harper slowly edged his way. She got stopped a couple of times, either by someone blocking her path, or another who wanted to talk to her. And as she moved, Nick stayed where he was. He really didn't want to hope that she was there for any reason other than to congratulate him on his retirement, but his wants and his reality had mixed in a heated battle.

"I'm going to have blue hair, too," Haley said, the words filtering though Nick's head. "And I might make my lips blue. I get to wear makeup when I get older."

"I'm going to have pink hair and lips."

Nick couldn't help but chuckle at the girls. He wanted that in his life.

And he wanted it with the woman now only ten feet away from him.

"Come on, girls." That came from Gabe. "Let's go find ice cream."

"I think we all could use some ice cream," Gloria interjected. "Pops is buying."

The crowd of them headed off, taking all the noise and madness with them, and all that was left was Nick looking at Harper. She made it to his side, her thoughts unreadable, but her hesitant smile good to see.

"Hi, Nick." She chewed on the corner of her lip. "Can we talk for a minute?"

"Sure."

They moved beyond the building that housed the concession stands, but there were still people around. A couple of guys walked alongside their horses, and the flag girl who'd kicked off the evening stood to the side of the walkway, allowing kids to greet both her and her horse. She wore sparkles from head to toe and couldn't be much older than sixteen.

Not wanting to risk interruption or being overheard, Nick kept going. They got beyond the perimeter of the buildings, and they were suddenly alone. He forced his legs to quit moving, and, turning, he tucked his hands into his pockets. Then he waited.

Harper licked her lips. "So you're quitting?"

He gave a small nod. "As of tonight."

"For good?"

Surely this wasn't what she wanted to talk about. He tried not to let his disappointment show. "It was never what I wanted long term. You know that."

"I know. And I'm glad you figured out what you want." Her words seemed to dry up. Nick could see her thinking, but having no idea what else she had to say, he couldn't begin to help her out.

So he stood there, and he refused to let his joy at seeing her show on his face.

Finally, she drew in a deep breath and lay both hands flat on her stomach. "I didn't tell you my entire story before," she said. "In fact, there was a small white lie in what I did share. I *was* pregnant when Thomas died."

Nick's gaze dropped to her stomach, and his heart stopped.

"That's what made me panic the day we jumped. I hadn't taken a pregnancy test so I didn't know for sure. And I was just one day late. But deep down . . ." She nodded, and he swore tears began to pool in her eyes. "I knew," she whispered. "And all I could think when my chute didn't open was that I was going to kill my baby. That I would die without ever telling my husband that we'd made a child together."

She took another breath, seeming to gather herself. "We both survived the crash—the baby and I—but I miscarried five weeks later. I'd finally accepted that I was pregnant, and I wanted the baby. Desperately. It was suddenly all I could focus on. But then . . ." She paused long enough to touch her nose and mouth with her fingers. "Then I lost it, *too*," she finished on a shaky whisper.

"Harper," he said. But he had no idea what else to add. He had no idea why she was here, why she was pouring her heart out like this. But he ached for her because of it. He wanted to take her in his arms, yet she'd pulled her own up and around herself.

"It wasn't fair," she continued, and all he could do was stand there and listen. "And I hated the entire world for it."

"Of course you did. Anyone would."

The words didn't slow. "So not only have I been carrying around guilt for Thomas's death for over a year, but guilt for our baby's death as well. I was all my baby had to rely on. And I failed."

"Harper—"

"I know." She held up a hand to stop him. "These things happen," she said by rote. "It was likely not viable. Yes. Logic. I get that. I even got it at the time to some extent. But the heart doesn't have to make sense, right?"

His heart broke for her. "I'm so very sorry you had to go through that."

"It ripped me in two, Nick." Her eyes never looked away from his. "Both husband *and* child? I didn't ever want to be fixed. I wanted to hurt. I wanted to die." Her voice broke on the last sentence, and he reached out a hand, but she shuffled a tiny step away. "But then you came into my life," she whispered. "And against my will, you began to fix me. And for that, I'll never be able to thank you enough. For waking me up to living again."

He swallowed. Her pain echoed deep inside him. "I didn't do enough. I wish I'd known. I wish I'd . . ." He trailed off. He didn't know what he would have done, but it destroyed him to know that she'd experienced more hurts within the span of five weeks than anyone should ever have to suffer.

"You said that night that I was special to you," she told him. "But, Nick, you're the special one. Your mother might never have been able to see it—and that's her loss. None of that was on you. But I'd be willing to bet that everyone else in your life is aware of it. You make a difference to the people you meet. So I wanted to come tonight because of that. To thank you for being in my life."

She suddenly seemed to run out of words, and they were both left standing there, staring at each other, and one question rang loud in Nick's head. Was that the only reason she'd come? Had she just needed to speak the words to someone?

He wasn't sure what to do or say next, but a ticking clock seemed to start inside him.

She gave one last broken smile and took another tiny step away. "That's really all I needed to say," she finished. "So I guess I should go now."

When she turned to leave, it was do or die. And if he didn't get this woman back in his life, he thought he might die.

"I love you."

Harper froze at the words. Had she heard Nick right?

Her heart was pounding so hard, she could have imagined the words. Wanted them too badly. He might not have said anything at all. She'd only taken a couple of steps, so she slowly turned back. He stared at her with purpose, making her believe that he'd actually spoken.

"What did you say?" she whispered.

"I should have made that clear that night, but I was shocked to discover it myself. I don't just see us going somewhere, Harper. I see us going all the way." He kept his hands in his pockets. "But my feelings aside, your future is up to you. You do what you need to. For *you*."

She hadn't expected that. Any of it. She'd hoped when she came tonight that he could get there. Love her someday. That maybe he hadn't given up on her yet. But after seeing him, she'd shut down all hope. He was too distant. He remained that way now, too, even though he'd said he loved her. He seemed shut down.

"I've already moved back to Birch Bay," he added when she continued staring at him. "I'm living in town. And I've been accepted to UM. I start in the fall."

Harper's jaw unhinged. He really was figuring his life out. "That's good." She nodded. She hadn't realized he'd been thinking about going back to school.

"I haven't decided where I'll live when school starts. I might rent a place in Missoula. Or I could drive from here. But I think I might be an accountant."

A broken chuckle slipped out of her, and she put a hand to her mouth. "An accountant?" Tears showed up again. She'd been crying for days. Over everything. She'd never cried so much in her life. "That's a far cry from bull riding, isn't it?"

"It is." The lines on his face softened the longer he looked at her, and a smile finally began to form. "But I've always liked numbers. And if accounting isn't what I want, then I'll find something else. Something 'normal.' I want to be that guy. No commercials, no screaming crowds."

"No buckle bunnies?" she asked, trying to come across as teasing.

"You know I gave them up the day you came into my life." Nick's smile faded, and he was Mr. Serious again.

"I know," she said softly. And she did. Because *she* was special to him. And he was special to her. "But if you decide you want to keep something a bit higher octane in your life, as well, let me know."

Confusion clouded his eyes.

"I'm rejoining the SAR team," she explained. "I could use a good man beside me. If that's something you might be interested in."

"You're going back?"

"I shouldn't have quit."

She recognized the pride in his eyes. "You just paused," he said.

She stared at him, wanting him to touch her but afraid to ask. He still hadn't moved any closer to her. "I've also started a foundation in Harry's name. It'll support a number of causes, most of which will be search and rescue."

"You're doing good. I'm glad to hear it."

She nodded. "I am doing good. I'm trying. It's been a long couple of weeks. I talked to my Mom."

She didn't say more, wondering if he'd understand what she'd just shared with him. She'd finally opened up with the people in her life who'd been there for her forever. Who'd supported her the most. That had been the final shove she'd needed to begin to see a new life for herself. And she had no doubt she wouldn't have been ready to accept that shove without Nick.

"That's really great to hear." Though he hadn't moved, it suddenly felt as if he'd wrapped her in his arms. "And I meant what I said."

Oxygen quit making its way to her brain. "That you love me?" she squeaked out.

He nodded.

Nerves kept Nick rooted firmly in place. She'd said she'd come to thank him, but his hope had become unmanageable. There had to be more to it. He'd seen the flare in her eyes with his words, but he couldn't make her feel things she didn't want to feel. And if she refused to go there, then he would walk away from her again.

But this—*she*—was worth one more try. It was worth putting his heart on the line.

"I know you loved Thomas," he told her. "But do you think it could be possible to have two loves in your lifetime?"

Legit tears streamed over her cheeks, and she sniffled. "It's possible," she choked out.

Nick almost reached for her, but he forced himself to wait. She had to be sure. And he had to hear it.

With both hands, she scrubbed at her eyes, but it did no good. More tears waited in line. "I had a long talk with Thomas." She hiccuped on a breath. "I told him about you. About us." She dipped her chin. "He gives his blessing," she whispered.

Nick lifted her chin then, but he didn't say a word. Instead, he showed her with his eyes everything he felt.

"I love you, too," she wailed.

His arms closed around her, and he silently swore that he would never let her go.

"Would it help to know that I'm scared, too?" He kissed the top of her head. "I wasn't supposed to fall in love at all," he told her. "You get it twice, but I didn't even want it once. I don't do vulnerable. Not after my mother."

She sniffed, and he could feel the dampness of her tears soaking through his shirt. She'd somehow cried behind his leather vest.

"I want this to last, Harper." He kissed her hair again and then brushed it back from her face. He pressed his lips to her red eyes. She was salty, and he made a mental note to replace that taste with powdered sugar later tonight. He'd pick up a funnel cake on their way out. "We're real," he told her. "This thing we feel. I want it to last."

"I do, too. And yes, it's real. I know that. I still can't believe I'm lucky enough to get a second chance, but I'm not so stupid that I won't take it. I ache without you, Nick."

"Then don't be without me."

She held his face between her hands, and he stared down at her. He loved this woman.

"Will you love me forever?" she asked nervously. "Can it last that long?"

"That's already a done deal."

She nodded, and he could see the love shining in her eyes, as well as something else. Something . . . mischievous. It made him wonder what had run through her head. When she opened her mouth, her words were the last thing he expected to hear. "You love me for my big balls, don't you?"

Nick dropped his forehead to hers. "Babe." He chuckled with the word. "You're one of a kind." Pulling back, he once again turned serious. "Don't you know it's that particular trait of yours that won't let you give up on life. On love? Yes," he whispered, his tone now urgent. "That's *exactly* what I love about you. You're tough and strong. And I want to be strong with you."

She nodded, blinking against her tears. Her lashes had turned spiky, and black smears outlined her eyes. "Then I have to tell you that I might need to be held up occasionally. I've discovered that I'm not quite as tough as I once thought myself to be."

"You're more tough than you ever realized." He kissed her, relishing the fact that he had the right to do that. "But as I've always told you, I've got broad shoulders. And I think they may have been made solely to hold you."

Epilogue

Be honest. What do you think?"

Nick stood on the other side of the room from the wall he'd just painted, and waited for Harper's response. While waiting, he formed his own opinion. And that was that he was no painter.

"Uh . . ."

"I know," he said. "I see it." Somehow he'd left roller marks along the entire wall.

He put down the roller, propping the head on the edge of the paint tray, and moved in to inspect the damage. They were in the house they'd moved into only the Friday before, and they had a houseful of guests showing up in thirty minutes for a Labor Day cookout. And he'd just destroyed their guest room.

Thankfully, only family would be coming today, so the room didn't actually have to house an overnight guest. He'd just wanted to show off the new color, so he'd pulled out the paint.

"I think you better keep searching," Harper muttered. She remained three feet from the wall, her head tilted to one side, and studying his mess. "Painting is *not* your passion."

"I never said it was my passion," he grumbled. But he'd expected to be better at it than this.

Since July, they'd continued to date and had worked together to redecorate Harper's house and put it on the market, and last week Nick had started classes at the University of Montana. Harper had not only rejoined search and rescue but had been hired on full time, as well. And now they had a new house to take care of. Their lives were mapping out even better than Nick could have ever imagined.

"You'd better get cleaned up," Harper said. She took another long look at the wall, patted him on the chest as if in sympathy, then headed out of the room. "I'll get the grill going," she called back.

As it always was between them, she thought she was the tougher one.

"*I'll* get the grill going," he stressed. He headed down the hallway after her but drew up short when he found her standing in the middle of their spacious kitchen, staring silently out the back windows. The view was beautiful from here. They'd picked a home in her parents' neighborhood, and though the house wasn't on the lake, it sat on a slight hill, and they caught glistening glimpses of blue from this spot any time the sun shone bright.

Nick eased up next to her and slid an arm around her, and when she immediately molded herself against him, he thought of how far they'd come.

"I love you," he told her. He kissed the top of her head, and she tilted her face up to his.

"And I love you." She glanced back at the view. "I love this, too."

"It's not nearly as big as what you had before." Nick had worried he'd come up lacking.

"I had too much before. That was more about Thomas and his parents than anything." She'd tried once again to contact her late husband's parents after she'd gotten the Harry Stone Memorial Foundation set up, but they'd never returned her query.

"You don't miss having a helipad in the backyard?" Nick asked. They had a walking path at the perimeter of their property and a view of the community playground, instead.

"I will admit that I miss looking out the back and seeing my baby every day. But she's not far away." Since Harper now worked full time for SAR, the helicopter remained parked at the station.

He shifted to position her in front of him and wrapped both arms around her as they watched a boat bob far off on the lake. In the foreground, neighborhood children squealed on the playground. Nick touched his lips to the side of Harper's neck. "We could call our families and cancel," he murmured. They'd been so busy moving in and unpacking, they had yet to properly christen the house. "Just you and me, enjoying our view together." He pulled a groan from her as he tugged her back against his erection. "We could start by checking out the view in the shower together."

"Not on your life, Wilde." She arched her neck to allow him better access, and her words came out soft. "Everyone is anxious to see the house. And I want to show it off."

"Then we'll just have to kick them out early." His hands closed over her breasts.

"I wouldn't argue with that." Gorgeous eyes met his as she tilted her head back to look up at him, and Nick knew without a doubt that he'd found where he belonged.

"Marry me," he said. They hadn't talked about it in weeks, but his desire had never been secret. "Put me out of my misery."

She nodded, and tears appeared in her eyes. "But you have to promise me babies."

His life was complete. "I'll promise you anything." He kissed her gently. "I promise you *everything*."

Acknowledgments

As usual, this book wasn't written by my imagination alone. Which is a good thing, because I probably would have gotten way too much of it wrong. But thankfully, I have great friends and terrific readers, and they always hook me up with excellent sources of knowledge. I'd like to thank Darynda Jones for always seeming to "know someone," and for reaching out to her brother-in-law in my time of need. David Scott, you were a great wealth of helicopter and SAR information, and just a really cool guy to chat with. Thank you so much for answering my random questions, and not for making me feel like a moron for all the things I didn't know. I suspect I probably got some things wrong in the book, but I promise I tried hard not to. And rest assured that without your help, I would have gotten much more incorrect!

And Montana McDade and Rhonda Ziglar. Thank you, Rhonda, for sharing your daughter with me, and thank you, Montana, for (like David) answering an eclectic selection of questions. Your and your husband's knowledge of all things rodeo, bull riding, and bull raising astounds me, and because of you, I had a blast putting my own stock contractor in this book. She is not you. I swear. But her occupation did totally come about because of you. I think a girl raising bulls is the coolest thing ever!

And then, there's Google. Probably all authors should always thank Google. Without it, there would be a lot of question mark placeholders in every single book I write.

About the Author

As a child, award-winning author Kim Law cultivated a love of chocolate, anything purple, and creative writing. She penned her debut work, "The Gigantic Talking Raisin," in sixth grade and got hooked on the delights of creating stories. Before settling into the writing life, however, she earned a college degree in mathematics and worked for years as a computer programmer. Now she's living out her lifelong dream of writing romance novels. She's won the Romance Writers of America's Golden Heart Award, has been a finalist for the prestigious RWA RITA Award, and has held various positions with her local RWA chapter. A native of Kentucky, Kim lives with her husband and an assortment of animals in Middle Tennessee.

Made in the USA
Las Vegas, NV
19 January 2021

16214054R10173